DARK SHAMAN

ETERNAL HOPE

THE CHILDREN OF THE GODS
BOOK ONE HUNDRED

I. T. LUCAS

Dark Shaman: Eternal Hope is a work of fiction! Names, characters, places, and incidents are products of the author's imagination or are used fictitiously and are not to be construed as real. Any similarity to actual persons, organizations, and/or events is purely coincidental.

Published by Evening Star Press, LLC.

EveningStarPress.com

ISBN: 978-1-962067-96-6

1

TAMIRA

As Tamira trekked through aisles of uninspired, practical clothing, searching for something to catch her eye, the lights flickered, went off, and then came back on. Since power generation had been impacted during the rebellion that had torn through the island just two days ago, the lights had been going out quite frequently. Still, they'd all gotten so used to the outages that she hardly noticed them anymore.

The island's clothing store seemed untouched, though, miraculously escaping the destruction that had leveled entire buildings in other areas of the island.

Perhaps the rebels hadn't targeted this section because it served the humans, whom they deemed irrelevant. After all, they were nothing more than indentured servants, slaves to the immortals who ruled this Fates-forsaken place.

The irony was that the lives of most of the immortals here were not much better; they were also regarded as property of Lord Navuh, and that included Tamira and her fellow harem ladies.

Some would argue that their status was elevated because they lived in luxury and didn't suffer the hardships others who lived here were subjected to, but the truth was that the harem was much more restrictive. At least the humans and immortals could routinely enjoy large open spaces, including access to the island's beaches and the ocean. The harem inhabitants had only been allowed out in recent days because their home had been flooded, and they had to be evacuated.

"Why do they use such cheap fabrics?" Raviki ran her fingers along a rack of sundresses, ignoring the flickering. "Is this what humans are wearing these days?"

"This store sells clothing to the service personnel," Sarah said. "That's why it's all simple and cheap."

"What about the visitors?" Raviki asked. "Passion Island is an exclusive location, and only the rich and influential can afford a vacation here." She turned to Tamira. "Can anyone with enough money book a vacation, or is it by invitation only?"

Tamira shrugged. "How should I know? I assume that the right people find out about the island from others like themselves, who have already been here. But we all know why people come here, and it's not something that would attract female visitors. Very few women, if any, come. It's mostly men, and they can shop for fancy things in the hotel store."

"I wish they had quality clothing for women in the hotel." Beulah pulled out one of the dresses and crinkled her nose while draping it over her front. "I have a new appreciation for whoever got us dresses from this store. They chose the best it had to offer."

Areana wasn't looking at the meager selection. Instead, she gazed out the front window at the buildings across the street. "We are lucky that it's the monsoon season. Imagine trying to explain the revolt to a bunch of tourists. I doubt it would have been possible to thrall all of them to forget the explosions. Trauma is not easy to erase."

Tamira narrowed her eyes at Areana. "The types who come to this island to enjoy the deviant pleasures it offers would have deserved to be haunted by the sounds of explosions in their dreams for years."

"Not all of them are deviant," Areana said. "Many just want to be with young, beautiful women who are eager to please them. That doesn't make them monsters. Just weak."

Did Areana truly believe in what she'd said?

She couldn't be that naive.

She'd probably spoken for the benefit of the people working in the store and the cadre of guards that were trailing her and the other ladies to keep them safe.

Tamira had heard the horror stories from the maids who'd been sent to work in the harem. No longer young and pretty enough for the brothel, they'd been thralled to forget most of what they'd endured; but, after years of service, that wasn't really possible, and they still had nightmares about their time there.

"It feels strange, doesn't it?" Areana held a blue one-piece swimsuit up against her slim body. "I've never shopped in an actual store. Back home, I had seamstresses who created my dresses, my maids shopped for everyday things, and merchants delivered goods for me to choose from. It wasn't much different in the harem."

Tamira's memories were similar, even though her family had not been royal or noble. They had been simple immortals but wealthy enough to lead a privileged lifestyle.

"I haven't either." She walked over to the display and chose a modest one-piece in black with white stripes.

There were no other customers in the store, and Tamira had a feeling that was intentional. Other than the ladies and their cadre of guards, there was only the shopkeeper, a nervous-looking human woman who kept glancing at the door as if expecting trouble, and her assistant, who was doing most of the work.

"This one would look lovely on you." Areana held up a deep purple suit with elegant cutouts along the sides.

It was nicer than the one Tamira had chosen, but it was too revealing for an outing on the beach with numerous guards watching. "Perhaps Raviki would like it." She walked over to the men's clothing section. "I need to get swim trunks for Elias."

Lord Navuh had generously allowed the men to join their beach excursion, probably because he was in such a great mood following his victory.

Half the island lay in ruins, and all the planes and boats had been destroyed, and yet Tamira had never seen Navuh so upbeat.

It was more terrifying than his usual cold austerity because it was such a significant deviation from what Tamira had been used to seeing during the five thousand years she'd known the lord. Surely he wasn't that happy about the destruction or even about winning. He must have discovered something that would advance his ultimate goal of global domination.

"We have more men's swimwear in the back," the shopkeeper's assistant said, pulling her out of her thoughts and bringing her attention back to the task of finding a nice pair of swim shorts for Eluheed.

As Tamira followed the woman, she tried to guess what size would fit him. He was such a handsome man, lean and muscular like a runner or a swimmer.

Not a man, she corrected herself—*an immortal.*

It had only been a few days since he had revealed his true identity to her and confessed his love for her. Knowing that she wasn't going to lose him to mortality, which had been her greatest concern, and that they could be together forever, had her soaring on a happy cloud. The problem was that if they didn't find a way to escape the island and

Eluheed's immortality was discovered, their happiness would be short-lived.

For now, she had to remember to call him Elias unless they were alone and to keep his immortality and his alien identity a secret.

Stifling a sigh, she selected a simple pair of black swim shorts that matched the swimsuit she'd chosen for herself but then grabbed a second pair in navy blue just in case he didn't like black.

"Should we get cover-ups?" Tula asked, eyeing a display of light fabric wraps.

"Definitely," Areana said. "It's not like swimming in our private pool in the harem, where we have privacy. Here, we are being watched constantly, and we need to be mindful of that."

Tamira glanced at the guards who were keeping some distance so as not to crowd them, but they could still hear every word they were saying.

These males believed Mortdh's teachings, or the bastardized version of them that Navuh was passing off as his father's words. They thought that women were created for the sole purpose of serving men, and even wearing a tent wouldn't deter them. She knew that they wouldn't dare to touch Lord Navuh's possessions, but just knowing what they were thinking was enough to make Tamira's skin crawl.

Not all of them, she reminded herself. Some must be able to think for themselves and not believe the hateful teachings.

She hoped her son was one of the enlightened ones. Navuh would have claimed him as his own, so he was probably a commander by now, a general even. Provided that he was still alive.

What if he had been one of the enhanced ones?

No, that couldn't be.

Surely, Navuh would not experiment on his sons, certainly not those who were his by blood and hopefully not even those he had merely claimed as his.

"How are we going to pay?" Tula asked when they'd exhausted what the store had to offer. "We don't have any money."

Areana laughed, and as always, the sound of her laugh raised goosebumps on Tamira's arms. Its unearthly beauty was one of the few things that identified her as a goddess.

Tula cleared her throat to remind Areana that she shouldn't laugh in front of the guards.

Tamira doubted any of them could recognize a goddess's laugh, but they might notice the different quality of it and wonder.

No one was supposed to know that Areana was more than an immortal and that she wasn't like the rest of the harem ladies. The secret of her existence had been kept for over five thousand years, and Navuh would do anything to keep it that way. If any of those guards were to suspect anything, they would be put to death immediately.

"I'm sorry." Areana put a hand over her mouth. "It's just that I find it funny none of you thought about money until we were ready to go. Naturally, Lord Navuh will pay for everything." She turned to the shopkeeper. "Prepare the invoice for me to sign. You can forward it to Lord Navuh's purser."

"Yes, my lady." The woman bowed.

As the shopkeeper's assistant folded their purchases into bags, Tamira looked out through the store windows, her gaze drifting to the mountain that separated this part of the island from the part that housed the underground barracks and other Brotherhood facilities.

The answers to the question that had been haunting her for over a century were somewhere out there, so close, and yet so far.

She moved to stand next to Areana. "You know, this could be an opportunity to find out what happened to our sons," she whispered.

Areana's face went pale, then flushed with what might have been anger or fear. "Don't even think that."

"The harem is nearly restored, and once we are back there, we will be completely isolated again. When will we have another chance like this?"

Areana shook her head. "Even if we could find out anything, which I assure you we can't, abusing our hard-won, limited freedoms will only backfire. We should enjoy them while they last."

"But—" Tamira started.

"No." Areana's tone brooked no argument. "Lord Navuh is being generous, allowing us this outing, and even permitting Tony and Elias to join us at the beach. Don't ruin it for the rest of us by being foolish."

Tamira wanted to argue, but she recognized the fear beneath Areana's stern words. The lady had also lost her sons to Navuh's system. Perhaps not knowing their fates was better than confirming their worst fears. Then again, Areana might not be kept in the dark like the rest of them. Navuh loved her, so he might have taken mercy on her and told her the fate of their sons. No doubt they were high-ranking generals in the Brotherhood, and he whispered their praises to their mother at night.

"You're right." Tamira averted her gaze so Areana couldn't see the anger burning in her eyes and walked away, pretending to find the hat display fascinating. "We should all get hats," she said. "The sun is going to be scorching at the beach."

"We are immortal," Tula said. "Our skin doesn't burn in the sun. Not even Areana's, and hers is almost entirely devoid of pigment."

The discussion continued while the others chose large hats to provide some shade in the sun, and after a few moments, Tamira's ire subsided. Perhaps Areana was just as clueless as the rest of them. Maybe she didn't know what happened to her boys.

"Thank you for your assistance," Areana told the shopkeeper once all the purchases were tallied and recorded.

As they left the air-conditioned interior they were met by heat and humidity, but the salt breeze from the ocean made it bearable.

"Navuh's sons are treated well," Tula suddenly said, and Tamira realized she'd been listening to her exchange with Areana. "They all became high-ranking officers in the Brotherhood. He values them greatly."

"He does," Areana agreed.

"I wish that were also true for the women in the Dormant enclosure," Tamira couldn't help adding. "We don't know how they're treated."

They were Dormant but kept human so they could have one child after another. The poor women were probably treated as nothing more than breeding stock and kept perpetually pregnant.

"There is nothing we can do for them," Areana said. "So, there's no point dwelling on it. I did my best to advocate for them so that at least their living conditions would be adequate. The rest cannot be avoided."

"And then there's the brothel," Tula murmured, and all three of them shivered despite the heat.

Young, beautiful girls were trafficked from all over the world, given drugs so they would be compliant and addicted, and put in the brothel to service the warriors and visitors. When they outlived their usefulness as sex providers, they were moved to different jobs, primarily as maids, and some of them had ended up working in the harem, which was how Areana and the ladies had discovered what the island was known for in certain need-to-know-only circles.

"Let's not think about such unpleasant things today," Areana said. "We're going to the beach, and we're going to swim in the ocean for the first time in forever."

Living on an island surrounded by water and never being allowed to dip their toes in it had been its own sort of torture. Now, they were finally going to visit the beach.

As they were driven back to the mansion, they passed by buildings that showed various degrees of damage from the rebellion. Numerous building crews were working to restore the area to its previous state, clearing rubble, replacing windows, and rebuilding walls.

Tamira wondered where they had all come from. It didn't make sense for the small island to have so many construction crews or building materials on hand. Navuh must have activated his network outside the island, and they'd delivered the men and materials.

"It's remarkable how quickly they're restoring everything," Tula murmured.

Areana followed her gaze. "Lord Navuh wants all traces of the rebellion erased as quickly as possible."

It had to be done, not only because the tourists would begin to arrive on the island soon, but also because the lord didn't want to see signs of the uprising. Not that it was possible to erase it from the memories of those who'd been affected by it, especially those who had cowered in the basement while enhanced soldiers tried to get to them.

Nor could it be erased from the mind of Lord Navuh. He would never forget how close he had come to losing everything.

2

ELUHEED

Eluheed's feet burned against the hot sand, making him quicken his pace toward the waterline, where the damp surface cooled his steps. With a sigh of relief, he turned back to study the cluster of showers and changing rooms.

Tamira emerged a few moments later, wearing a black and white striped swimsuit, and looking beautiful, excited, and carefree. After everything they'd been through, seeing her like this, relaxed and happy, felt like a miracle.

Perhaps it was the jubilation of survival.

They'd escaped the flood that had destroyed the harem, and then they'd lived through the rebellion that had nearly torn the island apart and ended Navuh's empire.

She caught him looking at her and smiled, but it was the careful smile reserved for public performance.

They both knew the rules.

A dozen guards surrounded their small group, rifles slung over their shoulders, their eyes scanning for threats but also scrutinizing the ladies and their companions.

"The water looks inviting," Tony said beside him, somehow having managed to put on a pair of red swim trunks without Eluheed noticing. Had he changed in the car?

"It does," Eluheed agreed. "It's warm."

"Could be fun to go for a swim," Tony said. "When was the last time you went swimming? And I mean other than the pool in the harem. That doesn't count."

Eluheed thought back to his homeland, where the sea was at the bottom of the rugged Elucian mountains, but no one had ever thought about voluntarily taking a swim because the water was freezing. There had been that lake in Russia, over a century ago, and that water had been cold as well, but not nearly as bad as the Elucian sea. After that, he had swum in the Mediterranean, which had been a treat. But he hadn't allowed himself to indulge often. His endless quest to recover the treasures buried beneath Mount Ararat hadn't left him much time for recreation.

"It has been a long time," he admitted. "Perhaps later." He sat down on the cool sand. "I just want to enjoy the view for a little while."

"Right." Tony chuckled but sat down next to him. "The view is magnificent." Neither of them was looking at the waves.

The ladies had claimed a spot near the water's edge, where the guards were spreading out towels. Evidently, the ladies didn't want to take advantage of the beach loungers and the umbrellas that provided shade. They wanted to be close to the water where the breeze cooled the air.

Areana sat gracefully on a white towel, her blue swimsuit contrasting with the paleness of her skin. Next to her sat Tamira and Beulah, while Sarah and Liliat headed for the water where the others were already splashing around.

"Come on!" Raviki called her friends. "The water's perfect!"

Tamira rose to her feet and glanced at Eluheed before joining them, and he had to force himself not to follow. He had to pretend that she was just another of Lord Navuh's ladies, and he was merely one of their escorts, a shaman who was entertaining enough to be included in their outing.

At night, they could enjoy their basement sanctuary where they could be together in every way, but here, under the blazing sun and watchful eyes, they had to keep their distance.

"Tula looks so happy," Tony murmured. "After everything we've been through, it's good to see her like this."

Tony hadn't been with them in the basement during the attack on Navuh's mansion, so he hadn't seen Tula helping the servants and keeping calm under pressure.

"She did great," Eluheed said. "Tula is made from strong stuff."

"I know." Tony grinned. "She's something else."

Tamira hadn't fared as well. As explosions had shaken the mansion above, she'd trembled against Eluheed, not because she'd been afraid of the ceiling collapsing on top of them but because she'd been terrified of the enhanced soldiers winning. She'd even asked him to kill her rather than let her fall into their hands.

The knife she'd pressed into his hand still haunted his dreams.

"They've been waiting for a shore excursion for a long time." Eluheed watched Tamira wade into the water, her face lighting up as the waves lapped at her legs.

"I don't know why Navuh didn't allow it before." Tony leaned back on his forearms. "What could he possibly be afraid of? The ladies swimming away to freedom?"

Eluheed glanced at the nearest guard, but the man seemed uninterested in their conversation, or maybe he couldn't hear them over the noise of the waves crashing to shore. Nevertheless, it was dangerous to speak so freely about their captor.

"The lord has been generous," Eluheed said carefully, the words tasting like ash in his mouth. "We should be thankful."

Tony snorted, but he was wise enough to shut up and not continue in the same vein. They both knew that this outing was a reward that could be withdrawn at any moment.

All the ladies were in the water now, laughing as waves knocked them about. Tamira was splashing Raviki, who shrieked and retaliated, and for a moment, Eluheed allowed himself to imagine Tamira with him, free and away from this place.

What would she be like in a world where she could make her own choices?

"Want to swim?" Tony stood and brushed sand from his legs.

Eluheed rose as well, pulling off his shirt. The sun immediately attacked his pale skin, but he knew he wouldn't burn, and not just because of the copious amounts of sunscreen he'd slathered all over himself to hide the fact that he didn't burn in the sun.

His immortal body wouldn't allow that to happen.

They waded into the water, and Eluheed had to suppress a groan of pleasure as the cool ocean embraced him. For a moment, he could forget his failures, his centuries of fruitless searching, the oaths that bound him to an impossible mission, and his predicament of being captive on this island and needing to find a way out for himself and Tamira, and possibly the other ladies and Tony as well, because Tamira wouldn't agree to leave without them.

"Race you to that rock." Tony pointed to an outcropping about fifty meters out.

"You're on."

They dove forward, but Eluheed held back. His body was stronger and faster than that of a human, and definitely more capable than Tony's. He matched the other man's pace, letting Tony pull slightly ahead as they neared the rock.

"I win!" Tony slapped the stone triumphantly.

"Well done." Eluheed treaded water easily while Tony panted from the exertion.

"You let me win," Tony accused, but he was grinning.

"I paced myself because I'm careful, but you are a stronger swimmer."

From the shore, they heard the sound of clapping. The ladies had been watching, and Tula waved at Tony with a big, proud smile on her face. Tamira was clapping too, her eyes finding Eluheed's across the water, and in that look was everything they couldn't say aloud—pride, love, and understanding.

He and Tony swam back leisurely, reaching the shallows just as servants appeared as if by magic and started setting up refreshments under one of the large umbrellas.

"Lord Navuh thinks of everything," Areana said as they gathered under the shade.

It had been more likely the head butler's initiative, but Eluheed kept that to himself. If she wanted to believe that her mate was that considerate, who was he to shatter that illusion?

He took a cold bottle of water and drank deeply while watching Tamira dry her hair with a towel. Water droplets still clung to her skin, catching the sunlight like tiny diamonds. He wanted to trace each one with his fingers, to taste the salt on her lips, to hold her against him and feel her heartbeat match his own, but those were dangerous thoughts to have while wearing swim trunks.

He sat on the sand at what would be considered a respectful distance but was meant to give him a moment to get a grip.

"Here." Tony handed him a wrapped sandwich. "These are really good." He sat down beside him.

"Thank you." Eluheed unwrapped the offering and bit into it, not really tasting anything.

"This is wonderful." Liliat stretched out on her towel. "I'd forgotten what it felt like to simply be in the sun."

"We should do this more often," Sarah said. "I don't know why we had to wait so long to enjoy the beach when we live on a tropical island. It makes no sense."

In Eluheed's experience, searching for sense in the world was as futile an endeavor as searching for fairness, and that was true not only for Earth. His home had been no different.

"I intend to speak with Lord Navuh about this," Areana said. "Perhaps we could have regular beach visits even after we return to the harem."

"Do you think he'd allow it?" Raviki asked hopefully.

"I don't know," Areana admitted. "But perhaps now that he has seen that the sky didn't fall because we were allowed into his house, traveled daily between the harem grounds and the mansion, and have even been shopping, he might be more amenable to the request."

"I can't think about being locked up in the harem again," Liliat said. "I mean, I don't mind living there. I actually like it, but it would be nice to be allowed out now and again. It would be wonderful if we could have beach excursions once or twice a week."

Tula laughed. "Are you out of your mind? It took Lady Areana weeks to arrange this one beach visit for us. Do you really think the lord would allow us to come here twice a week?"

"Not when the tourists are back," Areana said. "That's for sure. And frankly, I don't want to be out here when they are on the island."

Everyone went quiet after that.

"Maybe there are other beaches?" Sarah suggested hopefully. "It doesn't have to be a nice one like this, but if there is a piece of sand somewhere secluded, maybe we could have it to ourselves."

"I'll ask," Areana said, but she didn't sound hopeful.

The mention of a secluded beach evoked in Eluheed's mind the image of Navuh's secret submarine pen. Somewhere between the mansion and the harem was a hidden tunnel leading to an escape route, and he was determined to find it.

Navuh's secret had been revealed in a vision, but Eluheed had no reason to doubt its existence. It was true that visions could sometimes speak in hints and allegories and could not always be taken literally, but he knew the difference, and the submarine was real.

Perhaps the universe would take mercy on him and reveal more details in subsequent visions, such as the location of the tunnel's entrance and the means to access it without being discovered.

"We should swim again before we have to leave." Tula rose to her feet and walked over to Tony, offering him a hand up. "Who knows when we'll have another opportunity?"

As the others rushed into the water, Eluheed remained seated, and he wasn't alone. Areana and Tamira didn't join the others either.

"The rebellion was traumatic for everyone," Areana said quietly. "Surviving it has given us all a new appreciation for life's simple pleasures." She rose gracefully, brushing sand from her cover-up. "I'm going to join the others. You should, too, Tamira. The water is wonderful, and we don't know when we will get to enjoy it again."

Eluheed stood, walked over to Tamira, and offered her a hand up. "Lady Areana is right. We should take advantage of every moment we are allowed out here."

3

TAMIRA

Tamira stood at the water's edge, letting the waves lap at her toes, trying to memorize every sensation—the warmth of the sand, the salt breeze on her skin, the sound of the other ladies' laughter behind her. The sun was beginning its descent toward the horizon, and soon they would have to return to the mansion, then to the harem. Moments like this would become memories to sustain her through the endless monotony of captivity.

Eluheed and Tony were competing again, and she and the other ladies were cheering them on. She knew that Eluheed was holding back on purpose and letting Tony win, but she clapped and cheered him anyway.

"My lady?"

She turned to find one of the guards standing at a respectful distance, holding a towel.

Tamira smiled at him. "I don't need a towel, but thank you for thinking to bring it."

"Forgive me, my lady." He glanced around nervously, checking the positions of the other guards, most of whom were focused on the ladies still playing in the water or on the men competing in the distance. "I need to tell you something." He extended his hand with the towel despite what she had told him.

It dawned on her that the towel was an excuse, and she took it from him. "Thank you." She patted her eyes as if salt had gotten into them. "What is it?"

"I knew your son. I served under him. He looks so much like you that I know for sure you are his mother."

The world tilted.

Tamira's legs suddenly felt as though they could no longer support her, and she had to lock her knees to keep from swaying. "My son?"

"The resemblance is unmistakable. You have the same eyes, the same unusual deep shade of blue, and the same way of tilting your head when thinking." The guard's voice dropped even lower.

"What's his name?" she whispered.

"Darien, my lady."

Tamira was barely able to remain standing. Her knees were trembling, and she was holding on to the towel like a lifeline.

Navuh hadn't ordered that the name be changed.

"Darien," she breathed, the name feeling simultaneously foreign and familiar on her lips. Precious. "His name is still Darien?"

The guard nodded, but something passed over his eyes that gave her pause. Suddenly, the other things he had said registered. "I knew your son," he'd said, using the past tense.

She felt like throwing up. "Where is he?" The words came out strangled, desperate. "Where is my son?"

The guard shifted uncomfortably, glancing around again. Two of his fellow guards had moved closer, not quite within earshot but close enough to notice their continuing conversation.

He swallowed, then reached for her towel, as if he was collecting it. When she handed it to him, he whispered, "Officially, he died in World War II—killed in action in Japan—the nuclear bombs. But the rumors claim that the entire unit defected. They were never found and never confirmed dead."

Hope and confusion warred in her chest. "That's impossible. They couldn't have. The compulsion—"

"Another of Lord Navuh's sons led them," the guard said in a barely audible voice and turned around with the towel. "Commander Kalugal. He had a reputation for being different." He walked away, leaving her stunned and angry.

Kalugal.

She knew that name, and it hit her like a slap. Kalugal was Navuh and Areana's younger son, taken from her as a little boy just like all the other boys born in the harem.

Did Areana know that he had defected? That he had taken Tamira's son with him?

There was no way Navuh hadn't told her, and if she thought that Kalugal was dead, she would have been crying her eyes out for decades. But there had been no crying, no mourning, which meant that she knew he had defected, which meant that Navuh knew that as well.

What else did Areana know that she hadn't told anyone?

But it didn't matter. The important thing was that Darien was alive and free.

Somewhere in the world, Darien was living a life she could never have given him. The joy of that possibility was overwhelming, but a profound sense of betrayal tainted it.

Areana should have told her.

If she knew that Kalugal had taken Darien, she should have told her.

"Tamira?" Eluheed walked up to her. "What's wrong? You look like you've seen a ghost."

She couldn't speak at first, couldn't find the words to explain the storm of emotions tearing through her. Instead, she grabbed his hand and pulled him further down the beach, away from the others, away from the guards, even though she shouldn't be alone with him or show that he meant anything to her.

After a moment, she dropped his hand. "The guard who brought me the towel said that he knew my son. He served under him."

Eluheed's eyes widened. "How did he know that he was your son?"

"He said the resemblance was unmistakable. And..." She had to stop, take a breath, force the words out. "He said his name was still Darien. The name I gave him. Navuh never changed it."

"Tamira, that's wonderful—"

"Supposedly, he's dead." The words came out flat, emotionless, because if she let herself feel them, she would shatter. "Officially killed in World War II. But the guard said there are rumors that Darien's entire unit defected, led by another of Navuh's sons." She met Eluheed's eyes. "Areana's younger son, Kalugal."

Understanding dawned on his face. "You think Areana knew?"

"How could she not know?" The betrayal burned in Tamara's chest like acid. "You think Navuh wouldn't have told her that their son had defected with his entire unit?"

"Maybe he told her that they were dead."

Tamira shook her head. "I would have seen Areana grieve. She didn't. She must have known. And if she knew about

Kalugal's fate, she must have known about Darien's too. Navuh would have told her."

"Tamira—"

"I trusted her!" The words exploded out of her. "She's been like a sister to me. How could she keep this from me?"

"Maybe she wanted to protect you," he said. "Think about it. If she told you that your son had defected, that he was possibly alive and free, what would you have done?"

"I would have—" She stopped. What would she have done? Tried to escape? Demanded answers from Navuh?

"Maybe Areana thought it was kinder to let you believe he was just serving in Navuh's army like all the other adopted sons. You couldn't have done anything, anyway, so why cause you heartache?"

Tamira wanted to argue, to hold on to her anger, because it was easier than facing the complex tangle of hope, loss, and uncertainty. But Areana was wise and cautious, and she must have weighed her options and decided that it was better to say nothing.

"You are right." She let out a breath.

"Are you okay?" Eluheed dipped his head to look into her eyes.

She nodded. "We should go back. The guards trailing behind us are burning holes in my back."

He chuckled. "You feel it too?"

As they returned to the others, Areana regarded her with worried eyes.

"Is everything all right?" she asked, her blue eyes full of worry.

For a moment, Tamira couldn't speak. Had this goddess, who had been her anchor for millennia, been lying to her for years?

"I'm fine," Tamira managed, though her voice sounded strange even to her own ears.

Areana studied her face, and Tamira saw the moment she realized something had changed between them. The lady's expression shifted, becoming neutral, as the mask she wore when navigating dangerous waters slid into place.

"We should head back soon," Areana said. "The sun is setting, and Lord Navuh is expecting us for dinner."

"Of course." Tamira couldn't meet her eyes. "I'll gather my things."

"You have to talk to her," Eluheed murmured as soon as they had gotten a few feet away. "Not now, but soon. Otherwise, this will eat away at you."

He was right, of course. But how could she confront someone she'd trusted absolutely and discovered that she had lied to her?

On the drive back, Tamira sat between Sarah and Liliat, half-listening to their conversation about the restorative properties of seawater while her mind churned through everything she'd learned.

"You're very quiet," Sarah observed. "Did the sun tire you out?"

"A little," Tamira lied. "It's been a long day."

"It was the best day in forever," Liliat said with a satisfied sigh. "I feel more alive than I have in years."

Alive.

That was part of what Tamira felt as well. The possibility that her son lived, even if she could never see him, never know him, changed everything. He'd found freedom.

But Areana's betrayal tainted Tamira's joy.

How could she have remained silent about something so monumental?

4

NAVUH

Navuh stood before the reinforced glass and metal bars, studying the sand-filled enclosure in the basement with satisfaction.

Fifty tons of carefully leveled sand had been delivered to complete the climate-controlled environment needed to maintain perfect conditions. This was his insurance policy, though no one else knew what lay beneath the sand and what it insured against.

Out of all his possessions, this was probably the most valuable one, even though he might never trade it, but that was the nature of insurance policies.

The construction had been completed just before the rebellion, and he'd been concerned that the enhanced soldiers might discover it during their rampage, but if they had managed to get into the basement, he would have bigger problems to worry about than his insurance policy expiring.

Thankfully, that disaster had been averted, but the problem was far from solved. He still needed to deal with the enhanced soldiers, both those imprisoned on the island and those who were still at large, scattered around the world where he had dispatched them.

There were those who remained active in Iran, embedded within the Revolutionary Guard, while others were positioned near key government officials in Egypt, and still others were scattered across major cities in the United States.

Or rather, there had been that many. The clan had significantly reduced their numbers.

Turning around, Navuh headed back to his office, and as he climbed the stairs, his mind churned.

How had Annani's cursed offspring found his soldiers and eliminated them?

Was there an informant in his organization?

He had suspected Lokan, but he'd kept Lokan in the dark about the whole program, so he couldn't have been the snitch, and Navuh had no other suspects.

How had they known?

Sitting behind his desk, he drummed his fingers on its glossy surface, the rhythm matching his agitation. The placement of the enhanced soldiers had been known only to him and a select few commanders, whom he had no reason to mistrust.

The only explanation that made sense was that the clan had a seer. Someone like Elias, who could glimpse possible futures but with more precision. They had known precisely where to find the different cells and had not only taken them out simultaneously but had also been prepared to deal with the enhanced ones.

What kind of a seer could do that?

If the planned attacks had been successfully executed, it would have triggered World War III, and in the aftermath, humanity would have been so weakened that it would have been ripe for the taking. The damn clan had prevented a global catastrophe without the world even knowing it had been threatened.

No matter. This was the nature of things. Not every plan came to fruition, and out of those, only a small fraction turned out the way he had envisioned them.

Plans always needed to be adjusted.

As his phone buzzed, and the display identified the caller as Losham, Navuh picked up the receiver. "Losham. What have you learned?"

"Good morning, my lord." Losham's voice was smooth, cultured.

Unlike Navuh's other adopted sons who were all military men, Losham was a strategist, a thinker. He managed the Brotherhood's interests in the drug trade and human trafficking, distasteful to him but necessary under the circumstances. The Brotherhood needed sources of income, and the traditional methods of earning it had been scarce as of late.

There was no shortage of conflicts in the world, but they were mostly localized, disorganized, and with no money to spare. The days of well-paid mercenary armies were gone, probably never to return.

"I have done as you have instructed," Losham said. "I've probed the cells of enhanced soldiers to see if they were aware of what transpired on the island, but they seem ignorant of recent events."

Navuh had ordered a communication blackout to test his hypothesis that the enhanced ones were communicating telepathically with each other.

"Or perhaps they're simply hiding their knowledge of it," Navuh said. "During the rebellion, they coordinated perfectly despite not using any communication channels we could detect. Zhao said something about hand signals, but that's nonsense. They couldn't have coordinated their attacks that way."

Losham was quiet for a moment. "Most telepaths can't project or receive thoughts over distances. They have to be close to each other. Perhaps that's the case with the enhanced ones as well. They can't project their thoughts to those who are outside the island."

"That's possible." Navuh leaned back in his chair. "Several of the enhanced soldiers used the term transcendence, implying that they achieved a higher level of cognition. Zhao said that he was altering their brain chemistry, and he might have triggered something he hadn't intended. He broke something in their brains, and the side effect of that malfunction was opening their receiving channel to more information than nature designed."

Once again, Losham took a moment before replying. "Our brains limit what we can perceive, what we can access. It's a survival mechanism. If we were aware of every electromagnetic wave, every quantum fluctuation, and every thought from every person around us, we'd go insane from the overload. We wouldn't be able to function. If that limiting factor is artificially stretched out, all kinds of things can get through that otherwise would have been filtered out."

"Precisely." Navuh swiveled his chair to face the window.

He could always count on Losham for fast thinking that was not confined to or limited by conventions. It was humbling to realize that this adopted son, who a human had fathered, was smarter than Navuh's own progeny.

Lokan and Kalugal were no fools, but they couldn't hold a candle to Losham.

"The enhanced soldiers' consciousness expanded beyond normal limitations," Losham continued. "They might have developed a shared awareness, a collective consciousness of sorts."

"That's what I'm thinking. It's like swimming in a sea of consciousness. Most of us wear consciousness-proof diving suits that keep us separate, and the only way we can communicate with others in the ocean is with the aid of technology. But the enhanced soldiers' suits stopped working properly, and they got immersed in that ocean, no longer separate."

By that logic, Navuh's own compulsion ability was a malfunction. He'd never thought of it that way, but the fact that his father had been a powerful compeller and also insane added credence to the hypothesis.

His entire bloodline carried that seed of insanity along with varying degrees of compulsion ability.

Many cultures revered the insane as touched by gods. Perhaps they were onto something, and madness was just a different way of interfacing with reality.

But this was not the time for philosophy. This was the time for planning.

"The question is if we can replicate the positive effect without the negative side effects." Navuh turned his chair back. "An army of enhanced soldiers that doesn't require communication devices and can be instructed telepathically would be the next step in the evolution of warfare."

"The challenge would be control," Losham cautioned.

"I know. But now that we know what pitfalls to look out for, we can design a better product. Have you been able to locate a replacement for Zhao?"

"I have a few candidates," Losham said. "But none is as brilliant as Zhao, and all will be difficult to extract."

"Then assemble a team. Several brains to replace the one. A biochemist, a neurologist, a psychologist, a psychiatrist, and any other 'ist' you can think of. This is the future, Losham. I feel it in my gut."

"Yes, my lord. I shall get right on it. Have you given any thought to how the clan found out about our planned operations in Los Angeles? Someone knew where those soldiers were stationed, meaning that someone leaked that information."

"I think they have a seer."

"A seer, my lord?" Losham sounded incredulous. "Seers are never good enough to pinpoint locations. It must have been a leak or a betrayal."

Judging by how vague Elias's predictions were, Losham was right, but then some of them had been eerily accurate.

"Maybe they have someone who can tap into the shared consciousness of the enhanced soldiers," Navuh suggested. "They were in the same city, not on the other side of the world, so that's possible. And if that's true, we shouldn't have any enhanced ones anywhere near the clan."

"How can we know if it's true, my lord?"

"We can't." Navuh leaned forward. "But I'd rather err on the side of caution and move those cells out of California. I don't think the clan has any presence in New York, and we should move the cells there and plan something big. I'm curious to see if they will be able to sniff this one out as easily as the ones in their own backyard."

"That's an excellent plan, my lord."

Of course, Losham would say that. He never contradicted Navuh, and not just because he was an accomplished politician who knew how to manipulate others, but because he had learned to trust Navuh's instincts.

After ending the call, Navuh stood and walked over to the window, looking out at the island that was slowly being rebuilt. Somewhere in the detention facility, thirty-nine enhanced soldiers sat in isolation, possibly still connected to each other despite the physical separation.

The rebellion had been a setback, but it had also been educational. He'd learned that consciousness might be more fluid than he'd imagined and that his soldiers could evolve beyond his control.

The enhanced ones had transcended most of their limitations, but they still failed because they'd tried to escape the fundamental truth of existence that all power came with a price.

They thought they could shortcut that process and achieve godhood through Zhao's drugs. But gods weren't made in laboratories. They were forged in the crucible of time, madness, and will.

5

KIAN

The knock on Kian's office door came precisely at nine, which surprised him. Shuttling between the keep in downtown Los Angeles and the village wasn't easy, especially during high traffic times, and it was the second time in a row that Carol had been on time. Was it China's influence on her, or just the business environment she'd operated in while posing as a fashion entrepreneur?

"Come in," he called, setting aside the report on the power requirements for the new exoskeletons.

Carol walked in looking as fresh and energetic as always but then dropped into the chair across from his with a sigh.

"Long week?" he asked, pouring her a cup of coffee from the carafe Shai had brought earlier.

The coffeemaker that his assistant had gotten for him a few days ago had been moved to Shai's office, where it should have been placed from the start, and now he was showing up every couple of hours with a fresh carafe.

"You could say that." Carol accepted the cup gratefully. "Between the paranormals and the recruiting for the new female spy corps, I've been putting more miles on my car than a traveling salesman."

"Let's start with the spy program." Kian leaned back in his chair. "Who are your final candidates?"

Carol's expression brightened. "That's actually pretty good news. Five agreed to begin training. Marlene, Teresa, and Grace are enthusiastic about the opportunity. Regina is nervous but committed, and Greta is reluctant because of what's involved, but she's patriotic and wants to contribute. I think that her experience from World War II will be invaluable, even if she'd rather leave that part of her past buried."

"Did you bring me a list of what you need?"

Carol was a force of nature, but she wasn't the best at keeping things organized, and Kian had been reminding her that he needed an itemized list of things and not generalizations.

She pulled out her tablet. "I didn't forward it to you before because new items keep popping up. Can we agree that the list is fluid?"

"That's fine. You can update it every few days."

She clicked on her tablet, and a moment later, his phone pinged with an incoming email.

"The fake identities will cost a bundle," Carol said. "William promised to provide us with all the miniature spyware, so I don't know if I should include it in my budget or let him include it in his." She pouted, looking like a little girl and not the centuries-old immortal she was. "See how difficult it is? What do I put down for makeup and wigs when Eva is the one providing those? I asked how much those would be, but she refused to tell me. Claimed she was contributing them to the effort. So, what do I need to put down? Wigs for zero dollars?"

Kian smiled. "You asked and answered. List all the items you are receiving for free so you and I know that those are taken care of, and if anything changes and you have to order them elsewhere, just change the cost from zero to what you need to pay for them."

"Wow." She looked at him with rounded eyes as if he had just revealed the secrets of the universe. "That sounds so simple when you say it."

"It is simple. Have you thought about taking a course in management? It could help you with stuff like that. Now that you are heading two projects, you need to get better organized."

She laughed. "Now I don't have time for that."

"True. So, when do you start the training?"

"Monday. I've invited the candidates to the penthouse. With only five, I can do most of my training there. At least until we are done with the paranormal project."

"What's the status with that?"

He hadn't heard of any transitioning paranormals, and if they hadn't after over two weeks, it wasn't going to happen.

"That's less encouraging." Carol set down her coffee cup with a soft clink and met his eyes directly, the way she always did when delivering news, whether disappointing or encouraging. "None of the males Lokan induced have transitioned. It's been over two weeks, and Jeremy, Spencer, and Dylan are still disappointingly human." She sighed. "Lokan is taking it hard. He thinks that there is something wrong with his venom, but that's ridiculous. As a three-quarter god, his venom should be among the most potent. Only Toven could deliver anything better."

Kian frowned. "It can't be about the venom quality. Perhaps he's not injecting enough of it. It's a delicate balance between injecting too little or too much. But the more likely possibility is that these males simply aren't Dormants."

Carol nodded, looking relieved that he'd said it first. "That's what I've been thinking. We've always known this was a long shot. Just because someone has paranormal abilities doesn't mean they carry the Dormant gene."

"How are the men handling the situation?"

"They're frustrated," Carol admitted. "They're obviously comfortable at the keep, but they have nothing to do. Jeremy keeps asking if we can try again. Naomi is growing increasingly anxious and is trying to convince him to give up, get thralled to forget the entire thing, and start their normal life."

"We can't keep them in limbo indefinitely," Kian said. "It's not fair to them."

"I agree." Carol tucked a curl behind her ear. "Lokan says we need to try again."

A loud knock on the door was followed by it bursting open, but Kian wasn't startled or surprised since he knew who was coming and recognized Anandur's style of entry. The brothers were supposed to escort him to his meeting in town later.

"Carol! I didn't know you were here." Anandur grinned. "How have you been? Enjoying the penthouse life?"

"I am, but I don't have time to enjoy the good life. I've been running around between the keep and the village, trying to head two programs that are supposed to eventually merge into one."

"I've heard." Anandur pulled out a chair and sat down. "Anything I can do to help?"

Her eyes brightened. "In fact, there is." She shifted her gaze to Brundar, who remained standing by the door. "Would you like to join us? I might need your help as well."

Brundar didn't move. "We are supposed to escort Kian to a meeting in town."

"That's okay." Kian glanced at his watch. "We have time. Sit down, Brundar."

Carol waited until the Guardian relented and pulled out a chair on the other side of the conference table. "Lokan failed to induce any of the three males he injected with his venom, and we want to give them another try before we give up. The two of you could do the second round. I doubt your venom will do any better than Lokan's, but it wouldn't hurt to try."

Anandur chuckled. "Yeah, it would. Those poor men will hurt a lot, but hey, immortality is worth a little ouchie. Even if it's just a remote chance." He glanced at his brother, who gave one of his characteristic single nods, condensing an entire conversation into a single gesture.

"When do you want us to do it?" Anandur asked.

"We have a meeting in the city." Kian opened his daily planner. "But I don't have anything scheduled after that. We can stop by the keep, and each of you will induce a guy."

Carol shook her head. "They need to prepare mentally for another round. They've been through the process once already—the fighting, the biting, the waiting. I should talk to them first, make sure they're even willing to try again."

"Fine." Anandur shrugged. "Just tell us when and we will do our best to be available."

"Perfect." Carol gave him one of her charming smiles. "You two are the best."

"What about the others?" Anandur asked. "There are more paranormals in the group. Perhaps we should start with them."

"We have five men and four women," Carol confirmed. "But we decided to induce the men first and see if they transition because all the ladies are in committed relationships with the men in the program. If the men prove not to be Dormants, the women will have to decide if they are willing to have sex with immortal males to attempt transition."

Anandur turned to Kian. "What will you do with them if they are not Dormants?"

"Send them home. They are under compulsion not to reveal us. Naturally, we will need to keep in touch with them and reinforce the compulsion from time to time."

"Naturally," Anandur repeated while rubbing the back of his neck. "Can they be useful to us in other ways?"

"Some of them might still work with us in other capacities," Carol said.

"Such as?" Anandur asked.

"Well, Jeremy's remote viewing could be invaluable for intelligence gathering. James's telepathy is limited, so I'm not sure about him. Abigail's energy healing works on humans, so she might be more useful out in the human world." She shifted her gaze to Kian. "Maybe you can incorporate all of them into Project Titan. After all, you intend to hire human soldiers, and they will need medics and healers. That way, they can continue to get paid and stay in a controlled environment where we can reinforce the compulsion when needed. It's a win-win for both sides."

On the face of things, Carol was right, and this was a great idea. But on the flip side, it meant moving the paranormals once again. They needed a permanent place that they could call home.

Kian rubbed his temples, feeling the beginnings of a headache. "Let's take this one step at a time. As soon as the men are ready, Anandur and Brundar will attempt to induce them again. If that fails, we'll have another discussion about offering them a place in Project Titan."

"Fair enough." Carol glanced at her watch. "I should head back."

"What about the Echelon program?" Anandur said. "Any new leads there?"

Kian had had high hopes for the government's massive spying program. After all, it had helped identify the candidates for the paranormal program. They were still receiving lists of names that the computer was flagging from billions of conversations it was listening to, but so far, it had proven to be a huge waste of resources because none of the people they had investigated had shown real promise. The best had been the fortune teller and the gambler, who had initially looked promising, but upon further investigation they had been found to be fraudsters rather than genuine psychics.

Kian shook his head. "I'm pulling the plug on that. All the leads we followed turned out to be duds. It's a waste of time and resources."

Anandur nodded with a sage expression on his face. "It is up to the Fates who we find and when. We should stop searching for ways to identify Dormants."

"I don't agree." Kian pushed to his feet. "We need to keep trying new things. Eventually, something will work."

6

AREANA

Areana held her breath as she gently separated two pages of a leather-bound volume, the paper making a soft whisper of protest before yielding.

No tearing, thank the merciful Fates. A small victory, many more to go. Books and moisture didn't coexist in peace, and even though the library hadn't been flooded, the moisture that had traveled through the walls of their underground palace and permeated the air had done plenty of damage, especially to the older books, which naturally were more valuable and often irreplaceable.

Every recovered book felt like a triumph.

"This one's salvageable," she announced quietly, setting it in the growing pile of books that could be restored.

Sarah looked up from her own work, using a soft brush to clean mold from a gilt-edged tome. "We're making good progress."

"Better than I expected." Beulah lifted her head from her work. "It's just that there are so many. We will never be done."

Liliat snorted. "Don't say never when you have forever to do it. We have nothing but time on our hands."

Areana surveyed their restoration area with pride. They'd started the project in the tent on the harem grounds, drying what they could, and then moved it inside, but Beulah was right about there being so many. She hadn't realized that until they had returned to the library and saw that only a fraction of the books had been carted out by the staff. Most were still on the shelves, still needing careful restoration.

Since returning to the harem, they had fallen into a rhythm. Sarah handled the most damaged texts, deciding what could be saved and what was beyond salvage, and Beulah sorted them into piles according to what needed to be done to them. The others did the actual cleaning and drying.

The work was meditative, almost healing after the chaos of recent weeks.

"Pass me that cloth, would you?" Liliat asked Raviki, who was working beside her. "This binding is so beautiful, but it's falling apart." She turned to Areana. "We need better equipment for restoration and materials. I could get into handmade book binding, embossing, and whatever else goes into making a beautiful new book. It would be fun."

Areana nodded. "I wish we had access to computers. I don't even know the names of the tools and materials needed for that. But perhaps we can order a book on the craft."

Raviki handed the soft fabric over to Liliat, then returned to her own task. "Remember when we first started collecting these books? Lord Navuh would bring them as gifts, and we'd argue about who got to read them first and then where to shelve them."

"You wanted them organized by color," Sarah reminded her with a small smile. "You said it would be more aesthetically pleasing."

"It would have been!" Raviki defended. "But you insisted on being practical and organizing them by subject and author."

Sarah chuckled and waved at the enormous library. "Imagine what a nightmare it would have been finding anything if the books were organized by size and color like you wanted. It's difficult enough to find anything in here as it is. We need to create a catalogue and mark the shelves so we can notate the location. I think this is a perfect opportunity to do that since we are taking all the books down anyway."

The gentle teasing felt like slipping into a comfortable old garment. Here in their library, surrounded by the accumulated knowledge of centuries, they could pretend that nothing had changed and almost forget the explosions that had rocked the mansion, the terror of their stay in the basement during the battle, the brief taste of different freedoms.

"Some of these will definitely need professional rebinding," Sarah said, examining a volume whose spine had partially separated. "The water damage weakened the glue."

"Put it over there." Areana waved her hand at the table where other books in similar condition were starting to form a pile. "If we can't get the proper equipment to rebind the books ourselves, we can ask Lord Navuh to send them off the island to be professionally restored."

The lights flickered and sputtered out, but before the emergency lighting could come online, the power returned.

"I prefer to get the tools and do it ourselves," Liliat said, ignoring the brief outage.

There were so many of them throughout the day that people barely noticed them anymore.

Tamira wiped the sweat off her forehead with the back of her hand. "The humidity is still too high in here. These books will develop mold if we don't address it."

The climate control was back online, but it was struggling to control the humidity. The entire island was still in a state of disrepair, but not for lack of effort. Areana knew that Navuh was doing everything to speed up the repairs.

"Lord Navuh ordered an additional dehumidifier." She smiled at Tamira, who had been strangely distant since their return to the harem. "The equipment will be delivered within the week."

"That's good," Tamira said, and though the words were neutral, something in her tone made Areana look at her more closely.

Tamira was troubled by something, and Areana resolved to catch her alone and ask if she could help in any way.

Beside her, Tula stood and stretched. "I need to go on a walk. My back is protesting all this hunching over books, and frankly, I'm bored and tired."

"Why don't we take a break in the indoor garden?" Areana suggested. "I'll come with you. We can check on Tony and Elias's progress."

The indoor garden hadn't suffered a lot of damage, but it had been enough to need some tender loving care from someone who knew his way around plants.

They left the others to their work, taking the stairs to the second level instead of the elevator, even though it was safe to do so. Something about getting inside the small box was still frightening, but Areana knew she had to get over it sooner rather than later. It was okay to use the stairs while moving between the first three floors of the underground pyramid, but she needed to visit the servants on the lower levels, and she had delayed doing so for too long already.

When they reached the second floor and walked through the familiar corridors, Areana couldn't shake the feeling that the harem felt different now. The walls were the same, the paintings hanging on them perfectly restored, but something indefinable had shifted.

Perhaps it was they who had changed, not the place.

The indoor garden occupied a large atrium on the second level, with the ladies' quarters surrounding it on all four sides. Each section had a set of doors leading outside, and as they stepped out through them, the sound of soil being turned and quiet masculine conversation drifted from a far corner.

"These should go here," Tony was saying. "These peace lilies will look good with the ferns and dracaena."

"I'm impressed," Elias said. "You remembered their names."

"I wrote them down." Tony patted his back pocket.

Both men were covered in dirt, their shirts abandoned in the heat of their work, soil streaking their arms and faces. The garden showed signs of their efforts, with pieces of broken irrigation lines and cracked planters tossed into a large pile, and new plants carefully positioned to replace those that didn't look good after the trauma.

"You've made a lot of progress," Areana announced their presence.

Both men looked up, and Tony's face immediately brightened at the sight of Tula. The emotion was so naked, so obvious, that Areana felt a pang of pity for the man.

Tula didn't love him back. She liked him, enjoyed his company, but she didn't love him. It was smart on her part, but sad for him.

"Lady Areana." Elias straightened, brushing soil from his hands. "Most of the plants are recovering, and the root systems are largely undamaged."

"Some of the irrigation lines broke during the earthquakes," Tony added, his eyes still on Tula. "We fixed most of them, and we are adding new plants to fill in the gaps."

Areana walked further into the garden, impressed by the change their work had produced. "It looks better than before. What are these?" She gestured to a collection of flowering plants she didn't recognize.

"Kalanchoe," Elias said. "They're succulents, very hardy. They'll bloom for months with minimal care, and they do well indoors under artificial lighting."

"The colors are lovely." Tula got closer to examine the small clusters of flowers in pink, orange, and yellow.

"We thought bright colors would help." Tony looked at Tula with smiling eyes. "Make the space more cheerful."

"It's so pretty." Tula's gaze was still on the flowers.

"Like you," Tony said.

"Like us," Tula murmured. "I mean, this garden is like us. Nice to look at, but more hardy than it seems. It held up much better than we'd expected."

An uncomfortable silence settled over the group. They all knew what she meant.

"Well," Areana said briskly, breaking the moment. "The garden will be beautiful again. Thank you both for your hard work." She turned to Tula. "Shall we check on the servants? I want to see how they're settling back in."

Tula nodded, though Areana caught the look she cast at Tony as they left.

Perhaps she was wrong, and Tula loved Tony but was only pretending not to because she saw falling for a human as a failing.

As they entered the elevator, Areana felt her chest constrict. "Are you also afraid of getting into this little box?" she asked Tula.

"No." Tula looked up at the camera that hadn't been there before the flood, smiled, and waved. "Our fishbowl has gotten another viewing port. I wonder why? Additional cameras are not going to safeguard us from earthquakes and water breaches."

"Not the natural kind, that's for sure." Areana pressed the button for level seven. "But if the breach was sabotage, cameras in the elevators and the emergency stairs might have caught the perpetrators."

Tula rolled her eyes. "That sounds paranoid even for our lord."

Areana lifted a finger to her lips. "Watch what you are saying. Besides, after the rebellion, security was tightened all over the island. Not just here."

When they exited the elevator on the seventh level, it was bustling with activity. The familiar sounds of daily life filled the corridors, conversations, laughter, the clatter of dishes, and even the occasional shriek of a child.

Something loosened inside Areana at the sounds. Despite them being deep underground, this was what real life sounded like.

They found a group of maids in the common area, folding linens and chatting. The women rose when they saw Areana and Tula, but Areana waved them back down.

"Please, don't let us interrupt. We just wanted to see how everyone was settling back in."

Marta, an elderly maid who had served in the harem for decades, smiled warmly. "It's good to be home, my lady. The hotel was nice, and the beds were comfortable, but it didn't feel like home. Here, everyone knows their role, their place. No one judges us or looks down on us."

Elda, who was in her late thirties, nodded enthusiastically. "It's funny, but I feel freer here than I felt outside. I don't need to pretend. I can be myself, and no one is giving me the evil eye."

Marta slapped her arm playfully. "No one was giving you the evil eye, Elda. You have a wild imagination."

"Yes, they were!" Elda insisted.

"Freedom is relative," Areana murmured. "Sometimes the cage we know feels safer than the world outside."

Tula's hand moved to her stomach before she caught herself. The gesture was subtle, but Areana had been watching her more closely lately. The other ladies gossiped about Tula being potentially pregnant, and perhaps she was, but until Tula told her, she wasn't going to ask.

Until today, Tula had managed to avoid pregnancy, and if she was expecting now, she wasn't happy about it.

None of them wanted the heartache that they knew was coming, but Navuh expected them to produce sons for him, and although he was patient, his patience would eventually run out.

Each one of them had given him a son, and now it was Tula's turn, whether she liked it or not.

"We should let them return to their work," Areana said before turning to the maids with a smile. "Have a wonderful rest of your day, ladies."

They toured the kitchen, visited the laundry room, and when they were done, they returned to the elevator.

"Are you alright?" Areana asked when they were alone, but with the camera overhead, that was an illusion.

"I'm fine." Tula leaned against the mirrored wall. "I'm just thinking about what you said, that freedom is relative."

"It's a complex thing, freedom," Areana agreed. "Sometimes I wonder if it truly exists or if we all just choose different cages."

They returned to find the library abandoned.

"Is it lunchtime already?" Tula asked.

"It must be." Areana turned around and started toward the emergency stairs.

They climbed to the second floor and indeed found the other ladies in the dining room.

"How's the garden?" Sarah asked as they took their seats.

"Recovering well," Areana reported. "Tony and Elias are working hard. Did you tell them to come for lunch?"

"I did," Tamira said. "They are cleaning up, and then they will join us."

"They're good males," Beulah said, then caught herself. "I mean, for humans."

The qualification had them all feeling awkward. They all knew what she meant—Tony and Elias were temporary, mortal, would age and die, while the ladies remained unchanged. It was the fundamental tragedy of any attachment to humans.

"The servants seem happy to be back," Tula offered, changing the subject.

"Of course they are," Raviki said. "This is their home."

"Is it though?" Tamira unfurled her napkin. "Or have they just been here so long they've forgotten anywhere else existed?"

"That's rather harsh," Liliat said. "But true. Being out of here reminded me that there was a world out there, but it's not a nice one. I'd rather be here in our hiding place where no one can get to us."

"The beach outing was nice," Raviki said, probably to salvage the mood. "Perhaps we could arrange them monthly?"

"That would be lovely," Beulah agreed. "Something to look forward to."

"Lord Navuh seemed amenable when I mentioned it," Areana added.

"Once a month," Liliat mused. "Twelve beach visits a year. After five thousand years, that's progress, I suppose."

There was a bitter humor in her voice that Areana didn't like. The brief taste of different freedoms had awakened something in all of them. Small things like shopping in a store, traveling between locations, and living aboveground.

She was a goddess, and her kind loved underground structures. Her home back in the old country had been built mostly underground, as were the abodes of the other gods. Her eyes were sensitive to the sun, and she had to wear filtering sunglasses, but back then, she hadn't been a prisoner in her underground rooms, and that made a difference.

Even here, she could come up to the surface whenever she wished and sit in the sun if she wanted, or in the shade of the gazebo, but it was still different somehow.

"We could also ask about other outings," Sarah suggested. "Perhaps stay a night or two in the lord's mansion."

"Did you like it there?" Tamira sounded incredulous.

"No, not really," Sarah admitted. "I would have enjoyed our stay more if the staff had been replaced with the harem servants so we could be ourselves. Perhaps that can be arranged. The mansion servants won't complain if they get a couple of days off once a month."

Tamira shook her head. "I prefer this prison to that one. The chains are prettier here."

Several of the ladies flinched.

"That's enough," Areana said firmly. "We all process our situation differently. If some find contentment here, that's their right. If others struggle, that's valid too. But we support each other. That's how we've survived this long."

7

TAMIRA

Ever since finding out about Darien's escape, Tamira had been doing her best to avoid Areana, sitting at the far end of the library while they were working on saving the books and on the other side of the table during meals, but she couldn't pretend anymore.

It festered inside of her, making her bitter and even affecting her relationship with Eluheed, who had nothing to do with any of it. It was between her and Areana, but the sense of betrayal permeated everything. It was eating away at her like acid.

It was time to air out her grievance before it destroyed her.

She found Areana exactly where she'd expected, sitting on the carved stone bench beside the fountain in the interior garden.

How many conversations had they shared on that bench?

How many secrets whispered, tears shed, small rebellions planned?

Areana looked up as Tamira approached, and something in her expression suggested she'd been expecting this. Perhaps even waiting for it.

"May I?" Tamira gestured to the space beside her.

"Of course." Areana shifted slightly, making room. "I'm surprised that you are actually seeking me out. You've been avoiding me for the past few days."

There was no accusation in the words, just a statement of fact.

Tamira sat down, the familiar stone cool through the thin fabric of her dress. For a moment, neither spoke. The fountain's gentle splash filled the silence, a sound that had once been soothing but now seemed to mock the turmoil in Tamira's stomach.

"The beach was lovely," she finally said, her voice carefully neutral. "The water was warmer than I expected. I hope we get to experience that again soon."

Areana tilted her head with a frown. "It was indeed lovely, but it seems a little random to bring it up now."

"A guard brought me a towel." Tamira kept her eyes on the water, watching the ripples spread and fade. "I told him I didn't need one, but he insisted."

Areana nodded. "I remember wondering what was going on."

"He wanted to tell me something." Tamira's hands clenched in her lap, fingers twisting the fabric of her dress. "The towel was an excuse."

The air between them seemed to thicken. Areana had gone very still, the kind of stillness that came from five thousand years of learning to control every reaction.

"He told me that he knew my son." The words came out flat, emotionless, because if Tamira let herself feel them, she might shatter. "My son, Darien. The guard served under him."

She turned then, watching Areana's face with the intensity of someone who had learned to read the smallest tells. There it was, the flash of recognition, quick as lightning. Then came the calculation, the rapid assessment of what to say, what to admit. And finally, what seemed like a decision to stop pretending.

"You knew." Tamira's voice was barely above a whisper, but it carried the gravitas of centuries of trust. "You knew Kalugal took him when he defected."

Areana closed her eyes briefly, and when she opened them, they held a weariness that seemed infinite. "I didn't know that Darien served with Kalugal."

"But you knew Kalugal defected. You knew he took others with him."

"Yes." The single word fell between them like a stone into still water.

Tamira felt something crack inside her chest. "How long have you known?"

"Since it happened." Areana's voice was steady, but her hands trembled slightly before she clasped them together. "Navuh told me. Not everything, he never tells me everything, but he gave me morsels of news about our sons. Occasional fragments. It's not like I got daily accounts."

"Morsels." The word tasted bitter in Tamira's mouth. "And you never thought to share these morsels with the rest of us?"

"What was I supposed to say?" Areana turned to face her fully now, and there was pain in those ancient blue eyes. "That I occasionally received news while the rest of you heard nothing? That my mate's love, twisted as it is, granted me privileges you were denied?"

"You could have told me about Kalugal. You must have known there was a chance—"

"I didn't know." Areana's interruption was sharp. "Navuh told me Kalugal staged his death in Japan during the nuclear attack. He had no proof, but he said it didn't make sense. Kalugal and his men had no reason to be anywhere near the epicenter, or even in the outer zones."

Tamira studied her face, searching for deception. "But you suspected that they survived."

"Navuh believes they did. Whether he told me that to spare me grief or because he genuinely believed it, I don't know." Areana's composure cracked. "Navuh is not kind, but he's not needlessly cruel to me either. It's complicated."

"Complicated." Tamira stood abruptly, unable to sit still any longer. She paced to the fountain's edge, staring into the cascading water. "This is simple. My son might be alive and free, and you knew there was a possibility, and you said nothing."

"I didn't know that Darien served under Kalugal," Areana repeated. "Navuh prefers to keep his sons away from one another so they won't collude and plot against him, so I didn't have a reason to even suspect that. I didn't even know that he was allowed to keep the name you gave him. Most of them have their names changed when they're taken from us."

There was something in her voice, a note of genuine surprise about the name that rang true. But Tamira could sense layers beneath, secrets within secrets.

"What else do you know?" She turned back to Areana, her gaze boring into her friend's eyes. Could she still call her a friend? "What else are you hiding?"

"I don't know anything else about Darien."

"You're lying." The accusation came out flat, certain. "Maybe not about Darien, but I know that you are not telling me everything. I've known you for five thousand years, Areana. I know when you're holding back."

Areana's mask slipped for just a moment, revealing something raw and desperate underneath. "There are things I cannot say. Things that would endanger everyone if spoken aloud."

"Cannot or will not?"

"Both." Areana stood as well, moving closer but not touching. They faced each other like adversaries, though they'd never been that before. "There are secrets that aren't mine to share, Tamira. Burdens I carry that I cannot divulge, not even to you."

"Tell me this at least—if you learn anything more about Darien, will you tell me?"

"Yes," Areana said immediately.

But she averted her eyes as she said it, a tell so obvious that Tamira almost laughed. Areana rarely let her true emotions show through the mask of tranquility she usually wore.

"You won't." It wasn't a question. "You'll weigh the information, calculate the risks, decide what's best for everyone, and you'll keep it to yourself if you think that's safer."

Areana's silence was answer enough.

They stood there, two females who had survived together through thousands of years, and Tamira felt the foundation of their relationship shifting beneath her feet. Not breaking—it was too strong for that, forged in too much shared pain and small joys—but changing into something a little colder.

"I would have probably done the same," Tamira admitted suddenly, surprising herself. "In your position, with your privileges and your burdens, I probably would have made the same choice."

"Tamira—"

"But that doesn't make it hurt less." She moved past Areana toward the bench, sinking onto it with a weariness that seemed to pull her bones toward the earth. "It erodes my trust in you."

Areana sat beside her, careful to leave space between them. "I never lied to you, and the information I withheld had nothing to do with you. I never knew the names of the soldiers Kalugal had taken with him. Navuh had no reason to tell me."

Tamira nodded. "What else did he tell you about their escape? Now that I know Darien's fate is entangled with Kalugal's, everything you find out about your son might shed light on mine."

"I don't think Navuh knows where Kalugal is or what he's doing. And just because he occasionally tells me things doesn't mean I know my sons. Lokan—" She stopped abruptly, pressing her lips together.

"Lokan, what?" Tamira pounced on the slip.

Areana was silent for a long moment, clearly warring with herself. Finally, she spoke, her voice barely audible. "He thinks that Lokan was captured. He's alive, and..." She trailed off, shaking her head. "I shouldn't be telling you this."

"Who captured him?"

Areana shook her head. "I've already said too much." Areana rubbed her face with both hands, a gesture so uncharacteristically uncontrolled that it startled Tamira. "I'm tired of carrying all these secrets."

The fountain continued its eternal cascade, indifferent to the small drama playing out beside it.

"What kind of man did Kalugal become before he defected?" Tamira asked.

Areana's expression softened. "Brilliant, learned. He was never meant for military life, but he excelled at it anyway. Navuh said he had a talent for strategy but hated the application of it. He would have made a great leader. He is a leader. I have to believe that he still leads the group of soldiers who defected with him. Including your son."

"He gathered others like him," Tamira mused. "Others who hated wars. They were all so brave to escape."

"Or desperate," Areana countered. "We don't know what drove them to take such a risk. What pushed them to do it?"

"Does it matter? They got out. He got them out." Tamira felt tears prick her eyes. "My son might be free, Areana. Actually free. Not serving in Navuh's army, but free to make his own choices."

"If he survived," Areana said gently. "We don't know that for sure."

"Don't." Tamira's voice turned sharp. "Don't take this hope from me. It's all I have."

"I'm not trying to take anything from you. I'm trying to protect you from disappointment."

Tamira laughed, but there was no humor in it. "What could possibly hurt more than not knowing? More than wondering if my baby is alive, if he remembers my face, if he ever thinks of me?"

"The certainty that he doesn't," Areana said quietly. "That's what could hurt more."

The words hung between them like a blade. Tamira wanted to argue, but she knew Areana was right. The not knowing was agony, but it also allowed for hope. It allowed her to imagine Darien happy somewhere, perhaps with a family of his own, perhaps sometimes wondering about his birth mother, who had held him for nine precious months before he was taken away. But he could've forgotten her and believed that the Dormant who had raised him in the Dormants' enclave was his real mother.

"I still want to know," she said. "Whatever the truth is, I want to know."

"I understand." Areana reached out tentatively, her hand hovering near Tamira's. "May I?"

She looked at the offered hand for a long moment before taking it. Areana's fingers were cool, familiar, and, despite everything, comforting.

"This changes things between us," Tamira said, not a question, but a statement of fact.

"I know."

"I still don't trust you the same way I did before. I can't."

"I know that."

"But I still love you." The admission surprised Tamira, but it was true. "You're still my sister in everything but blood. That will never change."

Areana's grip tightened. "I love you too. And I'm sorry. Not for the choices I made because I still believe they were right, but for your pain."

Tamira squeezed back before releasing Areana's hand and standing. "I need time to process all of this."

"Of course." Areana remained seated, looking up at her with those ancient blue eyes that held so many secrets.

"Thank you," Tamira said before walking away.

Their altered relationship shifted her reality. They would continue as they had for millennia—supporting each other and maintaining the delicate balance that kept them all sane. But underneath, everything had changed.

The trust that had been absolute was now conditional. The secrets that had been invisible were now known to exist, even if their content remained hidden.

But to know that Darien might be free, might be living a life she could never give him, burned in her chest like a small, precious flame that kept her hope alive.

8

ELUHEED

The large Boston fern was heftier than Eluheed had expected, its fronds brushing against his face as he maneuvered through the harem's corridors. The pot alone had to weigh thirty pounds, and with the soil and root system, he was carrying at least sixty pounds of an excuse. But it was a good excuse—one that would get him exactly where he needed to go.

"Lady Areana requested this for her private sitting room," he told the guard stationed at the entrance to the first level's private quarters. The man, one of the regulars who'd seen Eluheed tend the gardens countless times, barely glanced up from his post.

"She's in the library with the others," the guard said, which Eluheed already knew. He'd waited specifically for this time, when the ladies would be occupied with their book restoration project.

"I've just been there and showed her the plant, and she asked me to place it in her bedroom." Eluheed shifted the pot in his arms, pretending it was heavier for him than it was. "Do you need me to go back and get a note from her?"

He wasn't lying. Areana had actually asked him to put the plant in her apartment, but only after he'd suggested it, explaining how crucial greenery was to a sense of well-being.

"No need." The guard waved him on. "Don't take too long."

"Of course not."

The private quarters were through a set of ornate double doors that opened into a beautiful anteroom, which thankfully wasn't decorated in Navuh's preferred palette of black, white, and splashes of deep red. This was Areana's domain, and everything was soft, tasteful, and inviting.

The ceilings were higher than in the rest of the harem, probably four meters tall if not more, with crown molding that appeared to be hand carved. Everything spoke of wealth and soft indulgence.

Eluheed crossed the anteroom into the seating area, his footsteps muffled by thick Persian rugs. He couldn't see cameras, but he was sure they were tracking his movements. Hopefully, there were none in the bedroom.

He had to believe that Navuh drew the line at surveilling his and Areana's bedchamber. He also suspected that was where the entrance to the secret tunnel was located.

The bedroom was massive, dominated by a four-poster bed that could have comfortably accommodated six. The walls were adorned with pale silk wallpaper featuring a subtle pattern of vines and leaves. Eluheed set the fern down carefully on the floor, then straightened, rubbing his lower back as if the weight had strained it, just in case there were cameras in the bedroom as well.

This gave him the perfect excuse to walk around the room, stretching and examining the space from different angles. "Where would you like to live?" he murmured to the plant, playing his role even though no one was watching. "Perhaps in that corner where I can put you under a daylight lamp?"

As he circled the room, he paid careful attention to the walls. The silk wallpaper was perfectly applied everywhere.

Except—*there.*

Along the north wall, near what appeared to be a built-in bookshelf, the pattern didn't quite align. It was subtle, the kind of thing that could easily be explained by moisture warping from the recent floods. The seam where two pieces of wallpaper met showed a gap of perhaps two millimeters, and the molding at the base had a similar discontinuity.

Eluheed got closer, pretending to examine whether the corner was a good location for the large plant. The bookshelf was built into the wall, its shelves filled with leather-bound volumes that looked purely decorative. The proportions were off. The bookshelf was shallower than it should be, given the wall's thickness.

His fingers itched to press along the seam, to search for whatever mechanism might open what he was increasingly certain was a hidden door. But the fear of alarms kept him still. Navuh might not have cameras in his bedroom, but that didn't mean there weren't other security measures. Pressure sensors, infrared beams, and who knew what else?

"I think you'll be happiest over there," he told the fern, carrying it back to its original position. "If Lady Areana doesn't like it, I can move you later."

He spent another few minutes adjusting the plant's position and picking off a few dead fronds. He still needed to bring the daylight lamp, which would give him another excuse to come up here. But the problem of the potential alarm remained, and he didn't know how to solve it.

As he headed out, an idea struck him. Hassan, the engineer overseeing all the restoration work, would have the architectural plans of the harem. He had to have them in order to supervise the restoration work. The question was whether he would be willing to show them to Eluheed.

The excuse came to him fully formed, so perfect he almost smiled. The indoor garden's irrigation system had been damaged in the earthquake, and he needed to understand the drainage patterns to prevent future flooding of the plant beds.

Nodding to the guard on his way out, he even received a grunt of acknowledgment. The man had no idea he'd just allowed someone to scout what might be the only escape route from this underground prison.

Hassan's office was on the sixth level, and it was now the command center for the restoration efforts that were still going on despite the residents moving back in.

Eluheed found the engineer bent over a tablet, comparing something on the screen to a physical blueprint spread before him.

"Hassan," he called from the doorway. "Do you have a moment?"

The engineer looked up, his weathered face showing the fatigue of weeks of non-stop work.

"Elias." Hassan straightened, stretching his back much as Eluheed had pretended to do earlier. "What can I do for you?"

"I'm concerned about the irrigation system in the indoor garden on the second level." Eluheed stepped into the cluttered office. "The earthquake damaged some of the drainage pipes, and while Tony and I repaired what we could, I want to make sure we're not creating future problems."

Hassan nodded. "Water damage is insidious. It can take months or even years to show up. What specifically concerns you?"

"I need to understand how the water flows through the structure." Eluheed moved closer to the blueprint on the table. "If we're overwatering or if there's inadequate drainage, we could cause problems for the levels below."

"Smart thinking." Hassan pulled out a roll of blueprints from a tube beside his desk. "You can find the complete plumbing and drainage systems in these."

"Great." Eluheed lifted the tube and walked over to one of the tables that wasn't overly cluttered. "Do you mind if I take a look over here? I don't want to take your time."

Hassan waved a hand. "Go ahead. Just put them back in the tube when you are done. The moisture level in the structure is still too high, and I don't want the blueprint pages to stick to each other. We only have two sets of those."

So, there was another set. That was good to know.

Eluheed spread the blueprints out and started leafing through them one by one, then going back to look at them again. "I'm trying to understand what I'm looking at," he murmured to excuse his interest in pages that had nothing to do with drainage. Especially the structural plan of the first level.

The area he'd identified in the bedroom was marked as "structural support," but it was far too large for a simple load-bearing column. It was rectangular, about three feet by seven feet—the size of a doorway and a small landing.

"Why are you looking at the plans for the first level?" Hassan asked.

"I want to make sure we're not creating problems for the lord and lady's quarters."

"Water usually doesn't climb." Hassan chuckled. "But I can't really say that after what happened here. The water definitely climbed." He walked over to a pile of tubes and pulled out another blueprint.

"The first level is actually the most protected," Hassan explained, spreading out the new blueprint. "See this reinforcement here? And here? The whole level could withstand significant water pressure without failing."

Eluheed studied the plans intently, no longer needing to feign interest. The "structural support" was clearly marked, and now he could see it connected to something labeled simply as "infrastructure access." The tunnel. It had to be.

"This support column seems massive," he commented, pointing to the area.

Hassan glanced at it and shrugged. "Original construction. Probably over-engineered. The whole structure is built like a bunker. Lord Navuh values his ladies' safety."

"Understandably," Eluheed murmured, continuing to trace the water pipes with his finger while memorizing every detail of that hidden space.

They spent another twenty minutes going over the blueprints, Hassan warming to his subject as he explained flow rates and pressure calculations. Eluheed asked enough intelligent questions to keep him talking, all while building a mental model of the escape tunnel's structure.

"You know, most people don't care enough to understand these systems." Hassan rolled up the blueprints. "They just want things to work." He rubbed his eyes. "Half my problems come from people who don't understand that buildings are living systems. Everything affects everything else."

"Like bodies," Eluheed suggested. "A problem in one area can cause symptoms somewhere else."

"Exactly!" Hassan's face lit up. "You understand. Buildings breathe, they settle, they respond to changes in temperature and humidity. Ignore that, and you get disasters like the flooding we just experienced."

Eluheed kept the chitchat going for a few minutes longer, talking about the repairs and building rapport with the engineer.

He still might need his help.

Hassan was a good man, competent and dedicated. Under different circumstances, they might have been friends.

When Eluheed returned to his room on the second level, he sat down at his desk, pulled out a notepad, and sketched what he'd memorized, translating the mental images to paper before the details could fade. The first level's layout, the location of the suspicious wall section, and the dimensions of the "structural support" that was too large to be what it claimed to be.

He drew it from multiple angles, adding measurements Hassan had inadvertently provided. The tunnel entrance was definitely hidden behind that bookshelf in Navuh and

Areana's bedroom. The question now was how to access it without triggering whatever security measures protected it. The only one who could answer that question for him was Areana, but he couldn't just ask her if the door in her bedroom was rigged with an alarm.

The door to his room opened without warning, and Tony walked in. Didn't the guy ever knock?

Eluheed quickly covered his sketches with a book about medicinal herbs that he kept on his desk.

"Working on the garden plans?" Tony flopped onto the couch.

"Something like that." Eluheed casually closed the herb book to further hide the sketches. "What do you need, Tony?"

"A friend." Tony stared at the ceiling. "Tula barely looked at me during lunch. Sometimes I wonder if she's pulling away. She told me right from the start that she had no plans of getting attached to a human, but I thought it would change over time, and that she wouldn't be able to resist falling in love with me."

"She might be protecting herself from heartache, or she might be still in the mode of pretending you two are not together even though it is no longer necessary in the harem."

Eluheed still caught himself being cautious with displays of affection for Tamira. They'd been forced to act distant while residing in Navuh's mansion, not because of Navuh, who encouraged their relationship because he wanted them to produce a son he could claim as his own, but because of the servants and the need to maintain the fiction that Navuh was active with all of his concubines, and all the children born to them were fathered by him.

"I don't know." Tony sat up, running his hands through his hair. "But logic doesn't help when you're in love." He turned to look at Eluheed. "You are lucky. Tamira loves you despite you being human. How did you do that?"

Eluheed wasn't human, but Tamira had fallen in love with him before she had known that. Still, it wasn't something he could reveal to Tony. "Each person has a set of rules they live by. Tula might just be more pragmatic than Tamira."

"I suppose." Tony sighed. "I'm not giving up yet. I can't give up. What will happen to me if Tula says she doesn't want me anymore? Unless one of the others takes me on as her lover, I will be demoted to the servants' quarters on the lower levels."

That was an odd thing to be concerned about. If Tamira told Eluheed that she was done with him, his first thought wouldn't have been about his accommodations or about one of the others taking him on as a lover.

Did Tony really love Tula?

Or did he love the comfortable living conditions that came with being her lover?

9

CAROL

The mocktail was perfect—fresh mint, lime, and just enough sweetness to make Carol forget it lacked the rum that would have completed it. She stood on the penthouse terrace and checked her watch. In ten minutes, five women would arrive at the penthouse for a lesson in the art of seduction for information and influence.

It wasn't the same as seducing a guy in a bar and taking him to bed. That was simple. Making high-ranking men fall desperately in love or in lust with them required a different set of skills.

From inside, she could hear Lokan's deep voice carrying through the open sliding door. He was heading toward the office, phone pressed to his ear, and his voice was getting more distant until he closed the door behind him.

The brothers had a complicated relationship—united in their escape from their father's tyranny but divided by centuries of different experiences and perspectives.

Kalugal was a baby in immortal terms, but his phenomenal success and strong compulsion ability made Lokan feel outclassed.

It couldn't be easy for her guy to have a much younger brother who was so much more successful than he was.

Carol didn't have any siblings, and although she had many friends, none of them were particularly close. Perhaps people still held her past against her, frowning on her wild courtesan years and her decades of abusing drugs and booze. But hadn't she proven herself above and beyond?

Who else could have pulled off an operation like infiltrating Navuh's harem to rescue Areana?

Regrettably, Areana hadn't wanted to be rescued, so Carol had returned empty-handed, but she'd succeeded in establishing communications between Annani and Areana, and that in itself was a monumental achievement.

At least Kian appreciated her, she knew that. He wouldn't have entrusted her with two projects if he didn't.

When the penthouse doorbell rang, Carol walked back inside, closed the sliding door behind her, and set her drink down on the kitchen counter.

When she opened the door, she was surprised to see that all five women had arrived together.

"Good afternoon, ladies." She motioned for them to come in.

"Good afternoon," Marlene said. "We carpooled. That's how I made sure that we all made it on time."

Marlene was dressed to the nines, her emerald dress hugging her curves, her hair perfectly styled, and her makeup flawlessly applied. She looked like she was attending a cocktail party, not a training session.

"Good thinking." Carol ushered them into the living room, letting them absorb the view and the decor while using the time to observe them.

In contrast to Marlene, Teresa wore jeans and a simple t-shirt, her dark hair pulled back in a practical ponytail. Grace surprised her. She wore a short skirt that showed off her legs, a fitted blouse that was professional but subtly sexy, and fake glasses that transformed her face. She was already in character—the eager intern or assistant to someone powerful. It showed initiative but might indicate a problem. Some people felt more relaxed behind a disguise because they were uncomfortable in their own skin.

Regina had chosen a safe outfit of a nice pair of slacks and a blazer, her hand repeatedly moving to touch her earring before catching herself and lowering it.

Greta wore a long-suffering expression, along with a severe gray pantsuit that had gone out of style decades ago. Everything about her screamed reluctance, from her rigid posture to the way her jaw was clenched.

Why was she even there if she dreaded it so much?

"Please, make yourselves comfortable." Carol waved her hand at the couches. "Can I get anyone a drink? I can offer mocktails, cocktails, wine, or soda." She smiled. "What other course would offer you alcohol in your first class?"

"Wine would be lovely," Marlene said.

"Water's fine," Greta murmured, as if accepting anything more would be a capitulation.

"Let's move to the dining room," Carol said once everyone had their drinks. "I've set it up as our makeshift classroom and conference room."

The dining table had been cleared of its usual decorations, replaced with notebooks, pens, and a small camera on a tripod in the corner. The women noticed it immediately.

"We're being recorded?" Teresa asked.

"Everything we do here will be recorded," Carol confirmed, taking her seat at the head of the table. "You need to get comfortable being watched, analyzed, and having your every gesture studied. Your future targets will be doing exactly that, whether consciously or not."

She let them settle, watching how they chose their seats. Marlene took the chair directly opposite her—a position of power. Grace sat to Marlene's right, seeking alliance with perceived strength. Teresa chose the middle, noncommittal. Regina sat closest to the door—an escape route. Greta took the furthest corner, distancing herself from everyone.

Carol sat at the head of the table and put down her glass. "Before we begin, I need to reiterate what you're signing up for so there will be no misunderstandings." She paused, meeting each woman's eyes in turn, letting the weight of the moment settle. "This isn't about simple seduction, though it will be one of the tools you'll be using. Your objective is not to score a one-night stand with a powerful man and get him to reveal some secrets or peek into his head. You will learn to identify who your target's dream girl is and become her. The real you will be tucked away in a hidden corner of your mind so deep that she won't surface even when you're drunk or otherwise compromised—though I strongly advise against ever allowing yourself to be in such a state."

Marlene's confident smile faltered slightly. Grace stopped fidgeting with her fake glasses.

"You'll get close to targets who may be good people—though that's rarely the case with politicians—and you'll still deceive and manipulate them without hesitation. You'll be betraying people who trust you, who might even fall in love with you, and you'll be okay with that."

The room had gone completely silent.

"You'll smile at men whose politics disgust you. You'll laugh at jokes that make your skin crawl. You'll share beds with people you find repulsive, and you'll make them believe that you adore them and want nothing more than to be there. You'll gather information that might destroy lives and end careers but could also shift the balance of power and save countless people. Remembering why you're doing this is important. It's not about money or prestige; it's about saving the world."

Regina's hand moved to her earring again, but then she caught herself and lowered it, clasping both hands in her lap.

"It will be hard," Carol continued, her voice softer now but no less intense. "Especially when your targets are not monsters. Sometimes they'll be decent people caught up in bad systems, trying to do their best with impossible choices, but you'll have to deceive them and potentially destroy them because your mission requires it."

"Fates," Teresa muttered, then caught herself. "Sorry, I just—"

"Don't apologize for honest reactions," Carol said. "This is the time for them. Once you leave this room after saying yes, honest reactions become a thing of the past."

Marlene straightened in her chair, the socialite mask slipping to reveal something harder underneath. "I've attended countless socialite parties and seduced every type of man. How different can this be?"

"The difference will be remembering who you really are when you've been pretending to be someone else for months. This requires you to become someone else entirely. Your thoughts, your reactions, your preferences are all calibrated to ensnare your target."

Grace removed her fake glasses, setting them on the table. "I've been doing this my whole life. I'm used to playing a part, hiding my immortality, my strength, my night vision, my hearing, and all the other ways I'm superior to humans. This will just be taking it to the next level. I'll become a professional."

Carol shook her head. "When you play roles at parties, you go home and become yourself again. In this work, you might have to maintain a cover for months, even years. You might have to hurt people you've grown to care about. Can you do that?"

Grace's confidence wavered. "Yeah. For the right cause, I think I can."

"Thinking so isn't enough," Carol said. "You need to know."

Regina finally spoke, her voice barely above a whisper. "I want to matter. This is my chance to do something important. To contribute."

"That's admirable and commendable," Carol said. "But are you prepared for the cost?"

Regina lifted her chin. "Are any of us ever prepared for the costs of our choices?"

It was a better answer than Carol could have come up with herself.

All eyes turned to Greta, who hadn't spoken beyond requesting water. She stared at her untouched glass for a long moment before raising her eyes to meet Carol's.

"I did this in World War II," she said quietly. "Not for the clan, but for the Resistance. I seduced Nazi officers, gathered intelligence that saved some lives and cost others. When it was over, I swore that I'd never do it again."

"Then why are you here?" Carol asked gently.

"Because I'm good at it," Greta admitted, self-loathing clear in her voice. "Because I can compartmentalize in ways that frighten me. Because the clan and the world need me again, and I have the experience. And because..." she paused, seeming to struggle with the words, "Because part of me misses it. The adrenaline, the power, the knowledge that I was making a difference. Fates help me, but I miss it."

Carol knew the feeling well. She still missed her courtesan days, and if she weren't mated, she would have jumped at the opportunity to effect change in a way only she could.

"Thank you for your honesty," she said. "All of you. Now, let me share something about my experience." She tucked a curl behind her ear and took a sip of water. "As most of you probably know, I was a courtesan for many years, and I developed these methods through trial and error, without anyone coaching me. I was a natural at it—reading people, becoming what they needed me to be, extracting secrets along with pleasure. The difference was that I was doing it for fun, not to change the world, but to exercise my power, not as an immortal who can thrall men to fulfill her every wish, but as a female. Some of you will find that you're naturals at this, too. You'll slip into roles like comfortable clothes, lose yourself in the game, and find a thrill in the deception that's almost addictive.

Others will struggle with every moment, fight against the false persona, and count the days until you can be yourself again."

"Which is better?" Teresa asked.

"Neither," Carol replied. "Both have advantages and dangers. The naturals risk losing themselves to the game. The strugglers risk breaking cover because the strain becomes too much. You need to find balance, and that's what I'm here to teach you."

She returned to her seat. "But first, let's see what we're working with. I want you all to observe each other for five minutes in complete silence. No talking, no deliberate communication. Just observation. Then you'll tell me what you've learned." She smiled. "People reveal a lot nonverbally if you know how to look."

The women knew each other, which was less than optimal for this exercise, but their familiarity was superficial, and Carol was certain that hidden layers could be uncovered with focused attention.

At first, the women were self-conscious, trying to project certain images. But as the seconds ticked by, natural behaviors emerged.

Marlene's confident posture never wavered, but her fingers traced small patterns on the table—a self-soothing behavior that suggested her confidence was at least partially restored.

Teresa's analytical gaze moved systematically from person

to person, cataloguing and filing information with an efficiency that spoke to years of experience.

Grace smiled several times, trying to make eye contact, seeking connection and approval even in silence. When others didn't respond, micro-expressions of hurt flashed across her face before being quickly erased.

Regina kept touching items on her body, her earring, her necklace, twisting her ring, and dropping her hands in her lap in frustration. She had a hard time controlling the physical manifestations of her anxiety despite being aware of them.

Greta sat perfectly still, her expression neutral, giving nothing away—except that such perfect control was revealing in itself. No one was naturally that still unless they'd trained themselves to be that way.

"Time," Carol announced. "Marlene, tell me about Regina."

Marlene nodded. "She touches her jewelry when she's nervous. She's aware of it, tries to stop, but the anxiety wins. She's also left-handed but tries to use her right hand as if she's right-handed. She reaches with her left first, then corrects."

"Good observation," Carol said. "Teresa, what did you notice about Grace?"

"The smile is a mask," Teresa said without hesitation. "She uses it to deflect, to seem harmless and friendly. But if you watch her eyes when she smiles, you can see that they don't always participate. She's performing happiness more than feeling it."

Grace flinched, and Carol saw hurt flash across her face before the smile returned.

"It's not criticism," Carol said gently. "We all wear masks. The point is recognizing them in ourselves and others. Grace, what did you observe about Greta?"

Grace studied the female. "She's containing something. Rage, maybe? Or grief? Her stillness isn't natural. It's a cage she's built around something that wants to escape."

Greta's jaw tightened, but that was her only response.

"Regina?" Carol prompted. "Tell me about Marlene."

Regina hesitated, then spoke quickly. "She's performing with confidence, but there's something underneath. The way she traces patterns on the table—it's like she's writing something over and over. A name, maybe? A mantra?"

Marlene's hand stilled on the table.

"And, Greta," Carol said, "what did you learn about Teresa?"

"She's cataloguing exit routes," Greta said. "Her eyes went to the door, the windows, even the air vents. She's also noting potential weapons—the letter opener on the side-board, the heavy-looking vase. Old habits from a dangerous life."

Teresa chuckled. "University politics are more cutthroat than people realize, but I wasn't cataloging the items as potential weapons. I just pay attention to what's around me."

"You've all done well," Carol said. "You're observant, analytical, and aware of what people reveal unconsciously. But this is just the beginning. Your targets will be trained politicians, diplomats, and power brokers. They're used to being watched, so they know how to control what their bodies might reveal. It will take you longer to catch them in moments when their defensive walls are lowered. You might also be the catalysts for that."

She stood again, this time moving to the sidebar where she'd placed a stack of folders.

"Now that you have a better understanding of the undertaking, I'm giving you a chance to reconsider. Once we truly begin, you're in. No backing out because it gets uncomfortable. No quitting when you realize the cost. I'll ask you again in a week, give you a last chance to withdraw, but I hope none of you will drop out. The clan needs you, and I know each one of you has what it takes. With proper training, that is."

"What happens if we want to leave now?" Regina asked.

"Nothing. You go back to your lives with our thanks for giving the project your serious consideration," Carol said. "No judgment. This work isn't for everyone, and recognizing that about yourself is wisdom, not weakness."

The room fell silent. Carol could almost hear their thoughts—weighing desires against fears, potentials against costs.

Marlene spoke first. "I'm in."

"I'm in too," Teresa said. "My mind needs more than civilian life offers."

Grace nodded. "I've been waiting for something interesting to come up my entire long life. Maybe this is it. I'm in."

Regina's hand went to her earring, stopped, and dropped to her lap. "I'm terrified," she admitted. "But I'm more terrified of living another century without contributing anything meaningful. I'm in."

Everyone looked at Greta.

"During the war," she said quietly, "I seduced a Nazi colonel. Gathered intelligence from him for seven months. He fell in love with me, wanted to leave his wife and marry me. He wasn't a monster—he was a bureaucrat who'd gotten caught up in the propaganda."

She paused, and Carol saw her hands tremble slightly before she clasped them together.

"I got the intelligence that led to his unit being ambushed. Seventeen men died, including him. He was holding the picture I'd given him of myself when they found his body." She looked up, meeting Carol's eyes. "I can still see his face when he told me he loved me. I can still remember feeling nothing but satisfaction that my mission was succeeding."

"And yet you're here," Carol observed.

"Because that colonel, despite not being a complete monster, was still part of a machine that was demonic.

Those seventeen men might not all have been evil, but they were enabling it." Greta straightened. "Perhaps if I'd gotten involved earlier, if others had realized where the rhetoric was leading and that appeasement was not the answer, millions of lives could have been spared. I don't want to sit on the sidelines and watch the world spiral into the same hell. If my skills can help stop that, then I'll carry more ghosts in my head. I'm in."

Carol nodded, feeling a mixture of pride and sadness. These five women were strong and brave, and they were going to pay for their sacrifice instead of being rewarded for it.

Perhaps the Fates would take pity on them and at least reward them with truelove mates.

"Then we begin," she said, returning to her seat. "Your first real assignment is to create a persona. Not for a specific target, but a practice identity. Someone who could exist in Los Angeles, with a full background, habits, preferences, fears, and dreams. You have one week to become her so completely that you could wake up from deep sleep and respond as her."

"How do we know if we've succeeded?" Grace asked.

"I'll test you," Carol said. "I'll create scenarios, challenges, situations where your real self would respond one way and your persona another. If you break character, you fail."

"And what then?" Marlene asked.

"Then we try again," Carol said. "And again. Until you can maintain a false identity indefinitely. Because in the field, failure doesn't mean trying again. It means exposure, capture, possibly death—and not just for you, but for anyone associated with your mission."

The truth and gravity of this statement settled in. These weren't games or exercises; they were preparation for operations where lives would hang in the balance.

"I'll send you each a packet tonight with more detailed instructions," Carol continued. "Create your persona's background, but more importantly, understand her psychology. What shaped her? What drives her? What are her unconscious habits, her tells, her dreams? If you need help, I'm here for you. Text me, email me, call me. I'm at your disposal."

"This is intense," Regina murmured.

"This is just the beginning," Carol corrected. "Next week, we'll start working on voice modulation, body language alteration, and emotional control. You'll learn to cry on command, to project emotions you don't feel, to maintain arousal with someone you find repulsive."

Several of the women shifted uncomfortably at that last point.

"I won't lie to you," Carol said. "Some of what you'll learn will feel violating, like you're betraying your own body and mind. But these are tools, and like any tools, are morally neutral. It's how you use them that matters."

"For the greater good," Teresa said, as if reminding herself.

"Yes," Carol agreed. "The information you gather and your influence could prevent wars, expose corruption, and save lives. Hold on to that when things get dark."

10

RUVON

Ruvon pushed open the door to Ingrid's design center, holding a box of pastries. The sweet scent of baklava and rosewater cookies wafted up through the cardboard, mixing with the showroom's usual perfume of fresh fabric and furniture polish.

Arriving with offerings improved his chances of getting useful advice, and today he needed all the help he could get.

Besides, his daily purchases at The Pearl were his way of getting to know Arezoo's mother and aunts better. At first, they'd welcomed him with forced smiles, but nowadays those smiles were genuine. He was a good customer, and he was always courteous. Maybe that's why he had been invited to a Friday dinner with the family.

It was a great opportunity to ask Soraya for her blessing, but he had no idea how to go about it, which was why he was bothering Ingrid again for advice.

She looked up from her design table, where she'd been arranging what looked like a hundred different shades of blue fabric, and gave him a welcoming smile, but he wasn't sure if that smile was for him or for the pastries.

"Are those for me?"

"Who else?" He put them on the edge of the table, away from the swatches of fabric.

"You are going to make me fat."

He chuckled. "If Atzil didn't manage that, I doubt I will."

Her partner was a chef, and Ingrid had told Ruvon that Atzil had won her heart with baked goods.

Ingrid rose to her feet and smoothed her hand over her dress. As always, she was elegance personified, the cream-colored dress fitting her generous curves perfectly. It was paired with heels of the same color that looked dangerous to walk in.

"These pastries should be consumed with tea." She walked to the kitchen, which was part of the original house before it was converted to her design center. "I assume you came with a bribe because you need my advice?"

"I won't deny it. You are the best advice giver when it comes to matters of the heart."

Ruvon knew that Ingrid would love the compliment.

"I don't know about that." She filled a kettle with water from the filter and put it on the stove.

As he waited for her to prepare the tea, he looked around the studio. Bolts of fabric leaned against walls, wood samples hung from hooks, and catalogs as thick as phone books filled several low bookcases.

"So, what is it about?" She started clearing a space at her consultation table by sweeping aside paint chips and fabric samples.

"Arezoo," he said. "It's always about her."

"Naturally." She ducked into the kitchen and a few minutes later returned to the showroom with two big cups of tea. "Tell Aunt Ingrid all about it." She put the mugs on the table.

Ingrid had become an unexpected confidant. She was easy to talk to and knew a lot about what women wanted.

"I'm having dinner at Arezoo's Friday evening, and I intend to ask her mother for her blessing."

"And you're terrified." Ingrid selected a piece of baklava with the concentration of someone defusing a bomb, holding it with the tips of her long fingernails before taking a tiny bite.

"Soraya is intimidating." He winced. "She always gives me a haughty look that implies she knows I'm up to no good, but she tolerates me because Arezoo likes me."

Ingrid laughed. "And I thought she only gave me that look. She's judgmental. That's for sure."

"Why would she give you the look?" He lifted the teacup. "It's not like you are dating one of her daughters."

"I don't know. Maybe she doesn't approve of how I dress, or my makeup, or whatever doesn't sit well with her. Some people find fault with everyone."

He shook his head. "I don't think she's that bad. Maybe she's just looking at you and wondering how you pull off such a polished look. Not many women have your talent."

"Oh, Ruvon." She leaned over and patted his arm. "That was such a sweet thing to say. Especially since I know it was what you actually thought and not something you came up with to flatter me."

"It's true. You are always so elegant."

"Well, thank you." She patted her light blonde hair that was arranged in some kind of updo. "But the same is probably true for you. She's not looking at you and finding you lacking in any way. She is just trying to determine if you are the right man for her daughter."

"That's the problem." He took a rose cookie from the box. "What if she thinks that I'm not the right man for Arezoo?"

"You need to stop doubting yourself. Project confidence even if you have to fake it."

"Easier said than done."

"You can do it." She took a delicate bite, somehow managing not to scatter crumbs despite the baklava's flaky layers. "Soraya isn't your enemy. She's a mother who wants her daughter to be happy. Your job is to convince her that you're the man who can do that."

"How?" He gestured at himself. "I'm not smooth or charming. I don't know how to say the right things."

Ingrid chuckled. "Could have fooled me. A few moments ago, you gave me one of the nicest compliments anyone has ever given me."

"That's because I wasn't trying to compliment you. I just said what I believed."

"And that's precisely what you need to do with Soraya. But since I don't know her very well, I might be wrong." Ingrid took a sip of tea. "You should talk to Kyra, Soraya's sister. She knows the family dynamics." Ingrid pulled out her phone and scrolled through her contacts. "I can give you her number or call her for you." Her finger hovered over the call button.

"Wait. I'm not prepared—"

She sighed. "Yes, you are. You came to me for advice with a box of pastries as a bribe. You can do the same with Kyra. I'll text her and ask if she has time to meet with you. I bet she'll know what this is about."

Ingrid was probably right.

"Okay."

She smiled. "That's my brave guy." Her fingers flew over the screen as she typed the message.

The reply came only seconds later.

"Kyra is heading to the café. She says you can meet her there."

Arezoo was working in the grocery store today, but he would have still preferred a more private setting for his talk with Kyra.

Ingrid closed the box of pastries, stood, and offered it to him. "Take the pastries to Kyra."

He shook his head. "These are from The Pearl. Kyra can get as many as she wants from her sisters. I brought them for you."

His resolute tone must have convinced her that he wasn't going to budge, and she took the box back. "Fine. Have it your way." She smiled. "Good luck, Ruvon. Tell me how it went."

"I will."

As he walked toward the café, Ruvon wondered how Ingrid always managed to steamroll him into action.

The female was a force of nature, and Atzil was lucky to have her even if they weren't fated truelove mates. They had love, the regular kind that wasn't mystical, and it worked just fine for them.

Were he and Arezoo fated for each other?

It certainly felt that way, but since it was the first time either of them had been in love, neither knew the difference between regular love and the fated kind.

Finding Kyra sitting at the back of the café enclosure, he was grateful for her choosing a spot that would afford them some privacy.

"Ruvon," she greeted him, gesturing to the empty chair. "I ordered coffee for you. I hope it's okay."

"Thank you for the coffee and for agreeing to see me so quickly." He sat down and reached for the paper cup so he would have something to do with his hands.

"Of course. You are practically part of the family."

That surprised him. "Am I? I don't think your sister thinks that I am."

Kyra smiled. "I assume that you mean Soraya. She can look intimidating, a mama bear, but she's not as terrifying as she seems. Well, she is, but it comes from a place of love."

"I know she loves her daughters. That's what makes this so intimidating. She sees me as a threat."

Kyra didn't bother to refute his statement. "Arezoo is young and inexperienced, and Soraya worries that she chose you because you chose her. She needs proof that you are worthy of her daughter."

"But how do I prove that? I can't even give her grand gestures or flowery speeches. I have plenty of money, but I don't think that she is concerned about that."

Kyra lifted her hand to stop him. "What Soraya wants to hear is not platitudes or the size of your bank and investment accounts. She wants to know that you'll love her daughter more than anyone else ever could. That you'd give her the moon if she asked for it."

At her words, Ruvon's anxiety spiked. "But I can't actually give Arezoo the moon. That's impossible. And I don't know how to talk like that."

Kyra laughed. "It's not meant literally, Ruvon. It's a figure of speech that means to convey the depth of your feelings. When someone says they'd give you the moon, they mean they'd do anything within their power to make you happy."

"Oh." He was relieved. "Still, I'm not good with metaphors or those kinds of declarations."

"You don't need to be a poet. You just need to be honest." She leaned forward, looking into his eyes. "Tell me something. Why do you love Arezoo?"

The question caught him off guard. "I... she's beautiful, obviously. And smart. And—"

"No." Kyra shook her head. "Those are facts, not feelings. Why do you love her?"

Ruvon was quiet for a moment, thinking. "She makes me feel like more," he said finally. "When I'm with her, I feel stronger, smarter, like I could face anything. She sees something in me that I don't always see in myself. And she..." He paused, searching for words. "She makes ordinary moments feel important. Just sitting with her, talking about nothing important, are the moments I treasure most. I want thousands of these moments, millions, I don't want to be away from her."

"Better," Kyra said with approval. "That's what Soraya needs to hear. Not rehearsed speeches, but truth."

"It still feels inadequate."

"Honesty, even raw and unpolished, is better than the best rehearsed speech." She took a sip of her coffee and leaned back. "I don't remember our childhood because those memories were stolen from me by an evil male. But I know Soraya now, and I know that she trusts Arezoo's judgment more than she lets on."

"Really?"

"Really. But she needs to test you, to push and see if you'll stand firm. It's not cruelty, and it's not because she thinks you are unworthy or untrustworthy. It's caution."

"I would never hurt Arezoo," Ruvon said immediately.

"I know that. Arezoo knows that. But Soraya needs to know it too, and words alone won't convince her. She'll be watching everything—how you look at her daughter, how you interact with the family, whether you show respect without being obsequious."

"No pressure," he muttered. "Any practical advice? Should I bring flowers?"

"Definitely bring flowers for Soraya. Not red roses, though, those are too forward. Not white, that's for mourning. And definitely not yellow."

"What's wrong with yellow?"

"Betrayal, supposedly. Don't ask me why but avoid them. Pink roses are safe, or a mixed bouquet. Something that shows thought without being overwhelming."

Ruvon pulled out his phone to make notes, then stopped. "This feels ridiculous. I'm a grown man, and I'm terrified of a dinner conversation."

"You're not terrified of the dinner," Kyra said. "You're terrified of not being enough, of being rejected. That's universal. Every person who's ever loved someone has feared not being worthy of that love."

11

ELUHEED

The military transport vehicle bounced over rough terrain, taking Eluheed deeper into a part of the island he'd never seen before. Through the windshield, he caught glimpses of training fields stretching toward the mountains, obstacle courses constructed from logs and rope, and rows of low-slung buildings that looked more functional than aesthetic. This was where Navuh's army lived and trained, far from the luxury of the mansion and seemingly at the opposite side of the island from the opulent harem.

"Civilians never get to see this sector," Navuh said from beside him, his voice carrying that particular tone of satisfaction he got when revealing something he considered impressive. "The military installations are kept confidential."

Eluheed kept his expression neutral as he catalogued every detail. Guard towers at regular intervals. Cameras mounted on poles. Warriors running drills in perfect formations despite the oppressive heat. "It's extensive," he offered because Navuh expected him to say something.

"Over ten thousand warriors are stationed here at any given time," Navuh said. "Though that number fluctuates depending on deployments." He gestured toward a massive concrete structure built into the hillside. "The main barracks are underground. Those flying overhead won't see anything of interest out here. They are also easier to keep cool that way.

The vehicle descended a ramp that led beneath the earth, fluorescent lights replacing sunlight as they went deeper. The air grew cooler, but it didn't turn stale. The space was properly ventilated, but it wasn't as cool as in the harem.

"The ventilation system is ingenious," Navuh continued, clearly enjoying showing off to someone new who was seeing parts of his hidden empire for the first time. "When I bought this island in the 1920s and began construction, air conditioning wasn't widely adopted. Mechanical cooling was unreliable and expensive to maintain on an island. So, I used the gods' proven systems instead. Well, not just any gods. My grandfather was a genius who found simple solutions to complicated problems, like how to make life bearable for people who couldn't tolerate the intense sunlight or the heat it produced."

After the driver parked in an underground garage, they got out and Navuh led Eluheed through a heavy steel door into a wide corridor. The walls were unpainted concrete, utilitarian and harsh, but the air was surprisingly comfortable given that there were no compressors pumping cold air into the submerged space.

"Diagonal ventilation shafts," Navuh explained, pointing to grates set high in the walls. "They create natural convection currents. Cool air is drawn from deep underground while warm air rises and exits through vents in the hillside. The barracks are comfortable even without air conditioning. The only structure I had air-conditioned from the beginning was the harem." He smiled. "My ladies always got the best accommodations."

They walked deeper into the complex, passing dormitories with rows of bunk beds visible through open doors, communal bathrooms, and a mess hall that could seat hundreds. Everything was clean and organized and typically military in its austerity, with no personal touches anywhere. These warriors lived like tools in a toolbox, stored efficiently until needed, but that was not much different than what soldiers contended with in other armies.

"The detention facility is new," Navuh said, leading him through another security checkpoint, where guards looked at Eluheed with frowns but said nothing while bowing to their lord. "We converted part of the original barracks after the rebellion to create a secure detention center. Before that, I just had troublemakers executed, but I need the enhanced ones for future testing, and the regular soldiers acted under coercion, so I decided to spare them."

He sounded so magnanimous, as if it were a huge act of mercy on his part to spare those soldiers.

The corridors grew narrower as they continued, and Eluheed noticed additional cameras here, with overlapping fields of view that eliminated any blind spots. The air grew heavier somehow, though the temperature remained constant.

"The regular soldiers who joined the rebellion are housed together," Navuh said, stopping at a reinforced door with a small window. Through it, Eluheed could see a large room filled with bunk beds, with perhaps forty men sitting or lying on them. "They were followers, not leaders. Susceptible to the influence of the enhanced soldiers but not autonomously rebellious." Navuh moved on, leading him down another corridor. "The enhanced soldiers are kept in isolation. Solitary confinement."

They reached a heavy steel door marked with two guards standing outside, both holding automatic weapons. At Navuh's nod, one entered a code into a keypad, and the door clicked open.

Beyond was a corridor lined with cells, each with a small window and a food slot. The silence here was oppressive. There were no voices, no movement, just the hum of ventilation, but Eluheed felt something else, a pressure against his mind that made his skin prickle.

"Thirty-nine enhanced soldiers," Navuh said. "They receive food and water, but they don't go out, so there will be no interaction with each other or the other soldiers."

"What if they compel the other soldiers to release them?"

"They can't," Navuh said, but not with his usual conviction. "Their one compeller is entombed in the tunnel leading to my bunker at the mansion, and so far, none of the others have developed compulsion ability. It's still possible that one or more will, so I'm waiting to see what will happen. In the meantime, they are suffering from withdrawal symptoms and are quite miserable."

"Dr. Zhao didn't leave any drugs for them?" Eluheed asked.

"He did, and we even have his formulas, but I'm still waiting for my people to find a replacement for Dr. Zhao. In the meantime, we are rationing what he left among the soldiers to keep them from going insane."

Navuh was in an uncharacteristically chatty mood, and Eluheed was committing to memory everything the lord was revealing. He didn't know if he would ever find any use for the information, but it might somehow prove valuable.

He walked over to the first cell's window and peered inside. A man sat on a narrow cot, his eyes closed, his lips moving as if in conversation with someone invisible or with himself.

"His name is Nahil, but he calls himself Transcendent," Navuh said with derision. "He was one of the leaders, but he's obviously insane. He claims he can hear the voice of the universe itself."

"Do you want me to touch him?"

"That's why you're here, but we need to secure him properly first, so let's continue walking until they prepare him for you."

Eluheed had a bad feeling about that. "How are they going to subdue him?"

Navuh chuckled. "With enough manpower."

As they continued down the long corridor, Eluheed first heard the sounds of the door opening, then the sounds of struggle, followed by the rattle of chains, and eventually the low whine of the beat-up soldier that was more like a wounded animal's than a man's.

He abhorred violence, and he couldn't help but empathize with the man's pain, but then he remembered Tamira trembling in his arms, terrified of what the monsters would do to her.

Regrettably, he couldn't dismiss it as irrational panic. She'd had good reason to be terrified. Men like that, enhanced soldiers, even in human form, did unspeakable evil to women when they conquered a territory and killed the men so there were no protectors left.

"We can turn around now," Navuh said. "He's secure."

"I figured as much," Eluheed murmured.

"I need to know if they're truly communicating telepathically or if they're simply insane. I thought that your ability could give you an insight."

The truth was that Eluheed was curious about that himself, but he was also afraid of touching the man if it was true that the thirty-nine could communicate telepathically with one another.

It would be a jumbled mess that might pull him under.

As the door opened again, the enhanced soldier opened his one good eye and looked directly at Eluheed. The other eye was glued shut and purple, but the color was already turning yellow, and in moments it would be as good as new.

That didn't matter. What mattered was that he was chained to a chair that was bolted into the concrete, and it was safe to approach him.

"A new player enters the game," the enhanced one said, his voice rusty from disuse. "Which side do you play for, human?"

Eluheed kept his mental shields up in case these soldiers could not only access each other's minds but also those of other immortals.

"I'm not on anyone's side. I'm here to understand what's happening to you."

"Understanding requires opening your mind," Transcendent said. "But yours is barricaded. How are you going to understand when you are not willing to open your mind?"

That was a valid question, and Eluheed hoped that the vision would come without him having to lower his mental shields. He couldn't allow these creatures into his mind and into his secrets.

They would hold him hostage, threatening to tell Navuh that his human pet was actually an immortal from another world.

"The visions come when they will," Eluheed said. "I need to touch you for them to come. Will you allow it?"

"Do I have a choice?"

"Not really, but it's polite to ask."

Nahil snorted. "There is nothing polite about my situation but go ahead. Touch me. See what we've become."

Eluheed hesitated. Every instinct warned him against making contact, but Navuh expected results. He put his hand on the soldier's forearm.

The world exploded.

No, it expanded.

Eluheed was suddenly pulled into something vast and interconnected, a web of linked minds that were trying to create a whole and act as a hive, but their efforts were chaotic, their thoughts jumbled. Not all of the time, though. They were like streams feeding into a river, but the river was muddy, not clear.

Eluheed tried to pull back, but he was drawn to the connection. He could feel their emotions, access their fragmented memories of the enhancement process, Zhao's drugs flooding their systems, the moment when the barriers in their minds dissolved, and they touched each other, and also something more infinite. They were losing their minds, but they weren't completely insane.

Not yet. They were like individual drops of water, suddenly aware they were part of an ocean.

Aware of him.

Panic flooded through Eluheed.

He wrenched back his consciousness, reinforcing his mental walls and flooding his mind with the persona of Elias, the humble shaman. But the knowledge remained. He now knew how to access their network, how to slip into that stream of connected consciousness.

The physical world crashed back into focus, and Eluheed found himself on his knees, Navuh's hand on his shoulder, Nahil watching with a knowing smirk on his swollen lips.

"What did you see?" Navuh demanded.

Eluheed's mind raced, sorting through what he could safely reveal. "They're... connected," he managed in a shaky voice that he didn't need to fake.

"Is it telepathy?" Navuh asked.

"It's more than that." Eluheed rose to his feet on unsteady legs. "It's like...imagine if consciousness itself was an ocean, and we're all droplets in it. We think we're separate, individual, but underneath we're all part of the same water."

Navuh's eyes sharpened with interest. "Let's get out of here." He motioned for Eluheed to step out of the cell. When they were out of the section, he waved his hand. "Now you can continue."

"I'm just hypothesizing here, but I think that whatever Zhao did to their brain chemistry with the enhancement process dissolved some kind of barrier. A filter that normally keeps us separate." Eluheed was breathing hard, still recovering. "They can access that underlying ocean directly, and that's how they communicate, not by sending thoughts to each other but by meeting in that shared space. They are still new to this, and it's a mess in there, but they need to be watched because they are learning how to navigate these waters."

"Can they be blocked?" Navuh asked. "Separated?"

Eluheed shrugged. "I don't know. I'm not a scientist, and I don't know whether what Zhao did is reversible."

"This collective consciousness," Navuh said once they were back on the surface. "Could it be a delusion?"

"It didn't feel like a delusion." Eluheed rubbed the back of his neck with a shaky hand. "Some think that consciousness is the foundation of the universe, with the material world being derivative. But to me, it sounds too esoteric, too abstract to be taken seriously."

"Why couldn't consciousness be primary?" Navuh asked, again surprising Eluheed with how open-minded he seemed to be.

"Because if everything emerges from some universal consciousness, then why is there suffering? Loss? Pain?" Eluheed voiced doubts he'd carried for centuries. "What universal consciousness would choose to create such a harsh world?"

"Perhaps it's a feedback loop," Navuh said. "The universal consciousness creates the material world, but then that world becomes independent of it. It develops its own rules, its own patterns. And the experiences generated—joy, suffering, discovery, loss—feed back into the unified mind, and then the mind creates more material worlds."

"You make it sound like a game," Eluheed murmured, forgetting for a moment that he was addressing the lord of this place.

"Because it is a game." Navuh's smile was cold. "The consciousness divides itself into players, sets rules, and watches what unfolds. Some players win, others lose, but the game itself continues."

"Then what's the point?" Eluheed asked, his frustration bleeding through his words. "If life is just a milestone in some larger game, why does any of it matter?"

"Because we're still playing." Navuh grinned maniacally. "And in every game, there are winners and losers. I'm obviously a winner. Perhaps somewhere there's a great scoreboard, tallying the points over countless life cycles." He trained his dark, intense eyes on Eluheed. "I would love to see my status on that cosmic scoreboard."

12

NAVUH

The shaman was more resilient than most humans, recovering pretty quickly from what must have been an overwhelming experience. But then again, Elias had always been different. His visions, his insights, his ability to navigate the dangerous waters of Navuh's court without drowning.

"Perhaps somewhere there's a great scoreboard, tallying the points over countless life cycles," Navuh said, laughing at his own observation. "I would love to see my status on that cosmic scoreboard." The idea amused him that there was some sort of cosmic accounting of wins and losses, victories and defeats, tracked by a universal consciousness that cared about the outcome of its own game.

But as entertaining as it was to engage in a philosophical discussion with the shaman, it didn't solve his immediate problems. He had enhanced soldiers who might be able to coordinate with others like them who were scattered across the globe, and a clan that had somehow known exactly where to find and eliminate his cells.

"This hive mind," he said, stopping next to the transport. "Can they communicate with others like them across the ocean? I need to know if they can contact the enhanced soldiers I have stationed in other locations."

Elias rubbed his temples, his face still pale following the psychic contact. "It's chaotic in there, my lord. Busy and maddening. Thirty-nine minds are trying to merge into one consciousness but failing to achieve true unity. It's no wonder they're going insane."

Navuh studied the shaman's face. The man was deflecting, answering around the question rather than addressing it directly. It was a skill politicians and courtiers perfected, but Navuh had five thousand years of experience of reading right through such evasions.

"That's not what I asked," he said, his voice carrying just enough edge to convey his displeasure without seeming threatening. "Can the enhanced soldiers here communicate with those abroad? It's a simple question, Elias, with a yes or no answer."

The shaman met his eyes, and Navuh saw uncertainty there. "I'm not part of their hive mind, my lord. What I experienced was just a glimpse, like looking through a window into a storm. I could feel the chaos, the connection between the soldiers, but I couldn't discern any details, not about the number of connected minds or their locations. It would be like asking someone who glanced at the ocean to describe what kinds of fish are swimming in its depths."

It was a reasonable answer, but Navuh wasn't satisfied because he didn't get the answer he needed. That didn't mean the shaman was lying, though.

He seemed sincere.

"I have other ways to test it," he said. "If they can communicate globally, that changes everything about how I deploy them."

As they climbed into the transport vehicle, Navuh considered his next move. The enhanced soldiers were both an asset and a liability. Their strength and coordination made them formidable, but their instability and resistance to his compulsion made them dangerous and limited their usefulness.

"The philosophical implications are fascinating," he said as the vehicle started moving. "But I'm more concerned with the practical applications. I don't particularly care what happens after my consciousness reunites with the universal one, if such a thing even exists."

The thought of that hypothetical reunion with his father brought an unexpected chill. If consciousness did persist, if there was some form of existence after the body died, he would eventually have to face Mortdh again. And his father's scorn would be eternal, his disappointment infinite. Then again, some claimed that everything was forgiven on the other side of the veil and that it was a place of unconditional love.

Boring. Uninspiring. He'd rather go to hell because it would at least be interesting in there.

"The enhancement program will continue," he said, more to himself than to Elias. "But with better controls."

"That seems dangerous, my lord," Elias said, bold now that he'd been allowed unprecedented freedoms.

Navuh let it slide. He needed the shaman to speak freely. "Every new invention and every new weapon goes through several iterations before it becomes viable. The same is true for the next leap in human evolution." He turned to Elias. "The drugs might work just as well on humans as they do on immortals. I wonder what the differences would be. If I can turn average humans into super-soldiers, I will be unstoppable. There is an unlimited supply of humans, but a very limited supply of immortals."

Elias looked horrified. "Those drugs would surely kill humans. The immortals barely survived it."

"The formula will need to be adjusted." Navuh watched the familiar landscape roll by, the manicured grounds giving way to rougher terrain, then back to cultivation as they approached the more developed part of the island. "Progress requires risk."

His phone buzzed with a message from Losham. Three more potential scientists had been identified but extracting them would be complicated. One was in a Chinese military facility, another worked for a pharmaceutical company with heavy security, the third was in a

Russian psychiatric hospital—as a patient, apparently, though his research before his commitment had been brilliant.

A mad scientist to work with mad soldiers. There was a certain poetry to it.

Get the Russian. He typed a message back. *Contact Gorchenco. He can get him out without us having to do a thing.*

Brilliance and madness were often the two faces of the same coin. They could surround the Russian madman with psychiatrists and psychologists and other biochemists to contain the mad element and encourage the brilliance.

"Are we returning to the mansion, my lord?" the driver asked.

Navuh had been so absorbed in his thoughts that he'd forgotten about his passenger. "No. Take us to the harem. Elias needs to get back."

He hadn't planned on visiting Areana in the middle of the day, but it would be nice to surprise her and have lunch with her and the other ladies. He had gotten used to dining with them twice a day, breakfast and lunch, and now dining alone seemed too quiet, too orderly. He had breakfast and dinner with Areana alone in their harem apartment, but his lunches were taken in the mansion's large dining room, which now felt odd since he was the only one there.

The driver adjusted their route without comment. The

harem was on the opposite side of the island from the military installations, a deliberate separation.

Navuh leaned back, getting comfortable. "When you touched the soldier's mind, did you sense fear?"

"No, my lord. They're beyond fear, which is part of their madness. They believe they've transcended human limitations, touched something divine. They feel superior."

"Delusions of grandeur," Navuh mused. "Or perhaps actual grandeur. The line between madness and genius has always been thin."

"Some would say there is no line at all."

Navuh chuckled. "Careful, shaman. That sounds dangerously close to philosophy, and we've already established that I'm more interested in practical matters."

The road curved, bringing them past the mostly vacant resort hotel. It would reopen to guests soon, once the last of the rebellion's damage was repaired. The loss of revenue was not an issue, but the lack of extorting material was more problematic. With no guests, there were no embarrassing recordings of them in compromised situations to hold over their heads if they didn't promote his agenda.

Just one more thing to deal with.

After the coordinated strikes in California, which would have destabilized governments and triggered conflicts, had failed thanks to the clan's interference, he needed to come up with new plans.

"I'm curious about something," he said. "You mentioned the chaos in their shared consciousness. What would happen if one of them achieved actual clarity? Became a focal point for the others?"

Elias shifted uncomfortably. "I don't know, my lord. Perhaps they could bring order to the chaos, create a true hive mind instead of the fractured thing they have now."

"Or perhaps they could extend their influence beyond their immediate group—reach out to the others." Navuh watched the shaman's response. "

"It's possible," Elias admitted. "Consciousness is not restricted by space, and some say that it's not restricted by time either. If they found the right frequency, the right resonance, they'd connect." The shaman smiled. "But that's another philosophical discussion, my lord. I thought you wanted to avoid them."

Navuh didn't respond to the reference. "The enhanced ones could become a network." Navuh smiled at the thought. "A global nervous system of operatives, all connected, all coordinated. No need for communication devices, no time lag between observation and response."

"But uncontrollable," Elias pointed out. "If they're truly connected at that level, traditional command structures become meaningless."

"Unless the commander is part of the network." The idea was taking shape in Navuh's mind. "What if the next enhancement program included a hierarchy? Soldiers who could connect to the hive mind but also maintain individual will? Generals who could direct the collective without losing themselves to it?"

The shaman was quiet for a moment. "Are you thinking about enhancing yourself, my lord?"

"Am I?" Navuh kept his tone neutral, but inside, he was evaluating the possibility. His existing compulsion ability suggested his mind already operated on frequencies others couldn't access. Perhaps he was already halfway to what the enhanced soldiers had become.

But the risk was enormous. If the process drove him mad, if he lost himself to the collective consciousness, everything he'd built would crumble. Areana would be left vulnerable, and the Brotherhood would fragment.

No, he needed others to perfect the process first. Let them pay the price of experimentation.

As the harem grounds came into view, guards snapped to attention and opened the gates.

The driver stopped the vehicle at the harem's main entrance, and Elias reached for the door handle, then paused.

"My lord, may I ask something?"

Navuh nodded.

"If consciousness is truly fundamental, if we're all part of some vast game, what do you think the prize is? What does winning actually mean?"

It was a good question. "Power," he said. "The ability to shape reality according to your will. Gods create worlds, immortals shape civilizations, mortals struggle for control over their brief lives. The prize is always the same—dominion over your domain, whatever that might be."

"What happens at the end of time, when the game ends?"

"It never ends," Navuh said. "It just transforms. New board, new rules, same players in different configurations."

13

AREANA

The breeze from the ocean below was a blessed relief from the heat, and as Areana sat on her usual stone bench at the lookout point, she took a moment to gaze at the dark, churning water below. The cliff's edge was mere feet away, a sheer drop of hundreds of feet to the rocky shore beneath, and while most would find the precarious perch terrifying, to her it was a lifeline to the outside world.

Tula sat beside her, gazing into the distance with a longing that Areana couldn't decipher. Did she crave freedom?

They all did, but how was today different than all the others that came before it?

Areana pushed the thought aside. She had more important things on her mind. Today was Wednesday, her scheduled call with Annani, and there was so much she needed to pack into those short minutes. The easy part would be telling her sister that the harem had been restored, and their Wednesday calls would resume as usual. A hard part of the conversation would be asking about Darien and whether he was one of the men who had escaped with Kalugal. The hardest part, though, would be what to do with the information, and it didn't even matter whether she got good or bad news.

Even if the answer was that Darien was alive and well and living in the village among Kalugal's men, Areana couldn't tell Tamira about it because her communication with Annani was her most guarded secret.

Only Tula knew, and it was best that it stayed that way.

If this mode of communication were severed for whatever reason, losing her only connection to her sons and her sister would devastate Areana.

"Keep watch," she murmured to Tula.

"I always do." Tula turned so that she was sitting on the bench sideways, giving her a clear panoramic view of anyone approaching, allowing her to sound the alarm.

Areana pulled the earpiece from a hidden pocket in her purse and put it in her ear. The second part of the device was hidden in the pendant she wore under the neckline of her dress, and she pulled it out as well. Ironically, the pendant had been a gift from Navuh, and now it hid the means by which she communicated with his archenemy.

She wasn't betraying him because she never told Annani anything that could undermine Navuh, but if he ever found out, he would see it that way.

"Lady Areana," William said as soon as she activated the connection. "It's good to hear from you again. I'm patching you through to your sister."

The relay was almost instantaneous.

"Dearest sister of mine," Annani said. "I am so glad that you can finally call me. How are you?"

"I'm well." Areana kept her voice low, even though the wind and the sound of the crashing waves would mask her words. "The ladies and I are back in our quarters in the harem. The restoration is still in progress, but most of the structure is habitable."

"What remains in need of restoration?"

"Books, furnishings, some of the artwork, but let's not waste our time talking about that. How are you, Annani?"

"Over here, everything is fine. It is you I worry about."

"Thank the merciful Fates, things are back to normal." Areana put a hand over her heart. "And how are my sons?"

"They are excellent. Lokan and Carol were put in charge of a group of humans with paranormal abilities, and Lokan is inducing the men. So far, no one has transitioned, but we are still hopeful."

It was good that Lokan had been put in charge of the project. After finally severing his connection to the Brotherhood and escaping his father for good, Areana worried about him finding a place in Annani's clan.

"Did Kalugal arrange for Lokan to get the position?" she asked.

"Oh, no. I believe Lokan volunteered."

"Good." Areana let out a breath. "I'm glad he has something to do. By the way, do you know the names of Kalugal's men? I'm particularly interested in someone named Darien."

"I know all of them, and none of them go by that name."

Areana's heart sank. "Are you sure? Darien is the son of one of the ladies."

"I am sure that none of those residing in the village is called Darien, but it is possible that some adopted new names. Also, several of the men who escaped with Kalugal left the unit. Some wanted to explore the world, others sought independence. Kalugal did not try to stop them. Whoever wanted to leave was allowed to."

"Could you ask Kalugal what happened to Darien?" Areana's fingers tightened on the pendant. "Or perhaps I should call him directly next week?"

"I can ask him," Annani said. "Whose son is he?"

"Tamira's. I didn't know that Darien served under Kalugal, or even that he retained the name she'd given him. The ladies and I visited the beach, and one of the guards who was assigned to us told her that he knew Darien. He immediately saw the resemblance. He told her that Darien served under Kalugal and was part of the unit that defected. Now she thinks that I knew about it and kept it from her. Naturally, I had no idea. Navuh told me that he believed that Kalugal survived and that he'd escaped, but he never mentioned the names of the men who went with him."

"Oh." Annani's voice carried understanding and sympathy. "That must be difficult, especially since you cannot tell her anything, even if Kalugal sheds light on what happened to Darien. I will call him as soon as we are done."

"Thank you." Areana touched her earpiece, a nervous habit when she was emotional.

"Lady Areana!"

Tula's sharp call made her blood freeze. She looked back to see Tula standing to shield her from view, and beyond her, still distant but approaching, was an unmistakable figure.

Navuh.

"I have to go," Areana whispered urgently into the pendant.

"Be safe," Annani said, and the connection died.

Areana's hands trembled as she quickly pulled the earpiece from her ear and tucked it into the hidden compartment of her purse. The pendant required no adjustment, looking like an innocent piece of jewelry, but she still tucked it under the neckline of her gown.

"Ready?" Tula asked in a barely audible voice.

"I am. Thank you." Areana pulled out the ribbon she was embroidering and tried to thread the needle, but her fingers trembled too badly, and she stabbed herself instead.

A drop of blood welled on her fingertip, and she immediately put the finger in her mouth.

"Let me," Tula said, taking the needle and thread. With steady hands, she threaded it and handed it back just as Navuh's footsteps became audible on the gravel path.

Areana forced herself to make a stitch, then another, creating the illusion that she'd been sitting there peacefully embroidering while enjoying the morning air.

"Areana," Navuh's deep voice carried a note of surprise. "I didn't expect to find you out here."

She looked up, composing her features into a pleased smile. "This is when I usually sit out here. The morning breeze cools the air, and the ocean is relatively calm. This is the best time of day to be here."

He moved closer, his dark eyes studying her face with an intensity that made her want to fidget. After five thousand years together, he could read her moods with uncanny accuracy.

"You look perturbed," he observed, sitting on the bench beside her. His presence was overwhelming, as always—not because he was a large male, but because of the force of his personality, the power that radiated from him, and the intensity. "What's troubling you?"

"It's nothing," she said, then caught herself. Navuh hated it when she dismissed her own concerns. "I just had an upsetting thought."

"About what?" His tone was patient, but she knew that his patience had limits.

Areana set down her embroidery, using the moment to gather her thoughts. She needed something believable, something that would genuinely upset her but wouldn't invite further investigation.

"The enhanced soldiers," she said, meeting his eyes. "I was thinking about what might have happened if they'd succeeded. If they'd gotten into the basement during the rebellion."

His expression softened, but not by much. He wasn't a soft male, and he never pretended to be anything other than who he was. "I would never allow anything to happen to you, and that's not an empty promise. I would have fought them with my own hands if I had to."

Areana felt the tension ease from her shoulders. "I know." She leaned and kissed his cheek, even though Tula was standing behind them. "My imagination sometimes runs away with me. Sitting here, looking at this drop, I was thinking about how we're always perched on the edge of disaster. One wrong step, one failure of vigilance, and everything falls apart."

Navuh was quiet for a moment, his gaze moving from her face to the cliff's edge. "The enhanced soldiers are contained. They won't threaten you again."

"I'm surprised that you didn't have them executed." She let curiosity color her voice.

"They're too valuable to waste." He leaned back. "I took Elias to see them today. His insight was interesting."

Areana felt Tula shift slightly behind them.

Navuh had told her about the shaman's special abilities, but Tula wasn't supposed to know, and Areana was surprised that he was telling her about this when Tula was within earshot.

"Was it wise to let Elias near them?" she asked. "That seems dangerous."

"It was a risky move." Navuh sounded smug. "But it was productive. He confirmed what I suspected. The enhanced ones are connected, able to communicate through some form of shared consciousness. The enhancement process broke down barriers in their minds, allowing them to access something beyond individual awareness."

"That sounds...terrifying."

"Or revolutionary." His eyes gleamed with the kind of fervor that always made her nervous. "Imagine an army that needs no communication devices, no chain of command in the traditional sense. They could have perfect coordination through shared thought."

"But you can't control them," Areana pointed out. "That's the most important thing. What good is a weapon that does whatever it wants? It's worse than useless. It's like sitting on top of a volcano and boasting about being its king." She stopped herself from continuing to say that the volcano was the true ruler and would consume the foolish human, immortal, or even a god sitting on its summit.

"The first iteration had flaws," Navuh admitted. "But that's the nature of progress. The next version will be better. More stable. Perhaps even hierarchical, with less enhanced soldiers at the bottom and generals who can connect to the collective but maintain individual will without losing themselves."

Areana suppressed a shudder. Sometimes she forgot how differently they saw the world. To her, the idea of minds merged into a collective was nightmarish. To him, it was just another tool to be perfected and wielded.

"What did Elias say?" She deflected from her own discomfort.

"When he touched the soldier, he was pulled into their shared consciousness briefly. Lesser minds would have been overwhelmed, but he managed to maintain his identity and extract useful information."

"That's remarkable," Areana agreed.

"Indeed. I hope Tamira bears him a child," Navuh said. "The offspring of a female of her intelligence and a man with Elias's gifts would be exceptional. I could use more clever minds in my command structure."

"They seem well suited," she offered, glad to change the subject. "As are Tula and Tony." She glanced at Tula, who was still standing behind them.

"I'm less certain about the potential of their offspring," Navuh said with no regard for Tula's feelings. "Tony is intelligent in his narrow field, but he lacks broader vision."

Behind them, Tula remained perfectly still, but Areana could feel her tension.

"Not everyone can be a general," Areana said mildly. "Or should be."

"True." Navuh stood, offering her his hand. "Come, my mate. It's nearly time for lunch."

Areana packed her embroidery carefully, aware of him watching her.

"You pricked yourself?" He looked at the black ribbon, and as Areana followed his gaze, she noted the slight red smear she hadn't noticed before.

"The needle slipped." She smiled. "I was distracted by my foolish worries."

He took her hand and kissed her fingers. "Your worries aren't foolish. Vigilance is what keeps us safe. But you're protected, Areana. I would burn the world before I let harm come to you."

The declaration should have been romantic. Instead, it chilled her. Because she knew he meant it literally—he would indeed burn the world for her and count the ashes of all that had been consumed a small price to pay.

"I know," she said, and let him lead her back toward the harem.

14

TIM

Tim stared at the television screen without really seeing what was playing. He sat on one end of Hildegard's couch, hyperaware of the careful distance between them—not quite at opposite ends, but far enough apart that there was no chance of accidental contact.

Hildegard sat with her legs tucked under her, a bowl of popcorn balanced on the middle cushion between them, like a buttery barrier. She wore yoga pants and an oversized t-shirt that said, 'Nurses Call the Shots,' her dark hair pulled back in a messy bun. She looked comfortable, relaxed, and entirely at ease with their arrangement.

Which was the problem.

They'd been sharing the house for three weeks now, three weeks of this careful dance of roommates who might be something more but probably weren't. They watched TV together most evenings, went on walks around the village, and shared meals. But he slept in the guest room, she slept in hers, and the space between them might as well have been an ocean.

The doorbell ringing made them both look up.

"That must be Magnus." Hildegard paused the documentary. "He said he might stop by after work."

Tim felt annoyed and slightly embarrassed.

He'd actually texted Magnus earlier, asking if he could come over, but Magnus hadn't replied, and instead, had told Hildegard that he was coming.

Tim would have preferred to do this when she wasn't home.

He needed to talk to someone, and Magnus was probably the closest thing he had to a friend in the village. Well, besides Andrew, but Andrew didn't seem interested in being friends. He had a little girl who was the center of his universe, and he preferred to spend every free moment with her and his wife. Tim couldn't blame him for that. The guy had his priorities straight. Then there was Roni, but he was so busy in the tech lab that he barely had time to eat, let alone entertain an old acquaintance.

Hildegard opened the door, and Magnus's elegant frame filled the doorway. As always, the guy was dressed to the nines.

"Good evening, Hildegard," Magnus said warmly, then nodded to Tim.

"Can I get you something to drink?" Hildegard offered. "Beer? Wine? I think I have some of that mead you like."

"Mead would be perfect, thank you."

"Tim? Another beer?"

"Sure," he said, though he'd barely touched his first one.

Hildegard disappeared into the kitchen, and Magnus settled into the armchair.

"You look good," Magnus said. "Hildegard must be working you hard."

"She is." Tim glanced down at himself.

He'd grown four inches and put on muscle mass that would have taken years of gym work to achieve as a human. His clothes had all had to be replaced, and he sometimes still misjudged his new strength.

"It feels weird," Tim admitted. "I broke three coffee mugs in the first week."

Magnus chuckled. "I still remember that phase, even though it was a long time ago, and I was a teenager at the time. The key is to always assume things are more fragile than you think, and it's especially important to remember when being intimate with human ladies."

Tim wasn't intimate with anyone, human or immortal.

Hildegard returned with their drinks, handing Magnus a large mug of mead and placing a fresh beer in front of Tim.

"I will leave you boys to talk," she said. "I'll watch the latest romcom in my room." She cast Tim a smile. "I didn't want to subject you to the torture of having to watch it with me."

He dipped his head. "That's much appreciated, but I wouldn't have minded at all. Would have given me more material to make fun of."

She laughed. "That's why I didn't want to watch it with you. Some things are not supposed to be made fun of."

"I disagree."

"I know." She continued walking and waved at them before disappearing into the corridor.

Tim waited until he heard her door close before slumping back against the couch.

"That bad?" Magnus asked, taking a sip of his mead.

Tim groaned. "We live together, but we're like a couple of polite roommates. I don't even know if she's interested in me that way."

Magnus studied him for a moment. "Have you tried talking to her?"

"And say what? 'Hey, Hildegard, I know you invited me to live here out of pity because I had nowhere else to go after my transition and needed physical therapy, but I have feelings for you?' That's so romantic that she will right away fall into my arms and kiss me breathless." He batted his eyelashes.

Magnus set down his mug. "Hildegard doesn't do

anything out of pity. If she invited you to stay, it's because she wanted you here."

"As a roommate."

"Maybe. Or maybe she's waiting for you to make a move." Magnus leaned back, the chair creaking ominously. "What was your experience like with women before your transition?"

Tim felt heat rise to his face. "Not extensive."

Magnus waited, patient as a mountain.

"Fine. Nearly nonexistent," Tim admitted. "I went on a few dates in college, none of which led to a second date. After that, I threw myself into my work and pizza." He patted his flat stomach. "I'm glad that's at least fixed. I never liked to watch what I ate." He picked at the label on his beer bottle. "I actually looked into those companion robots. You know, the really sophisticated ones from Japan? I figured if I couldn't connect with a real woman, maybe an artificial one would be better than nothing." He snorted. "The best part about them is that you can put them in the closet when you are not interested in their company. I pity men who have to listen to their wives' nonstop gabbing."

He was such a liar. He would have gladly listened to endless gabbing from a woman if she actually gave a damn about him. It would have been music to his ears.

"I didn't know those kinds of robots were for real." Magnus's expression didn't change, which Tim appreciated.

"They are, and I even saved up for one," Tim continued. "I had the money set aside and everything. Then this happened." He gestured vaguely at himself. "Now I'm this, whatever this is, living with an incredible female who treats me like a pleasant but sexless houseguest."

"You've never been much of a ladies' man," Magnus said. It wasn't a question.

"That's the understatement of the century. Several centuries, in your case."

Magnus was quiet for a moment, seeming to consider something. "Have you heard of Perfect Match?"

"The dating service?"

"It's more than that. They offer romantic fantasy adventures, immersive experiences that can teach you about romance and help you build confidence. Think of it as practicing in a safe environment."

Tim frowned. "I wanted to try that, but not as a learning experience. More out of necessity and frustration. Your angle is interesting, though."

Magnus lifted his jug in a sort of salute. "Just think about it. You can learn how to read social cues, practice conversations, and even experience different types of romantic situations. Several of those, and you will become a Don Juan."

"It's expensive."

"It's free for clan members," Magnus said. "The downside

is the waiting list. We only have four machines, and everyone wants a turn."

Tim couldn't imagine the flawless immortals needing practice in romantic situations, but Perfect Match offered much more than just romantic encounters.

He would probably be the only one requesting that sort of thing.

"It seems kind of pathetic, doesn't it? How am I even going to explain what I want?"

Magnus shrugged. "I never went on a virtual adventure, but I heard that there is an extensive online questionnaire. Do you really care what the artificial intelligence thinks about you?"

"No. That makes things easier, sort of. What am I going to tell Hildegard?"

"Here's a thought," Magnus said. "Hildegard is an adventurous sort. She likes trying new things."

"Your point?"

"Maybe she'd be interested in going with you. She could be your romantic instructor without knowing that's what she's doing. You could frame it as an adventure, something fun and different to try together. If she says yes, you'll have your answer about whether she's interested. If she says no, at least you'll know where you stand."

"And if she laughs at me?"

"She won't. I've known Hildegard for a long time, and that's not the kind of woman she is."

Tim took a long drink from his beer, thinking it over. The idea terrified him, but so did the thought of spending the next few decades or even centuries living in limbo.

"What would I say to her? 'Hey, want to go on a romantic fantasy adventure with me?' sounds like a pickup line from someone who doesn't know how pickup lines work."

Magnus chuckled. "Fair point. Has she mentioned anything she wants to do? Places she wants to see?"

Tim thought about their conversations during their walks. "She mentioned wanting to see the Northern Lights someday. And she's curious about wine tasting in France, but now that Gertrude is mated, Hildegard has no one to go with. She said she'd feel awkward going alone because she doesn't know anything about wine."

Magnus gave him a knowing look. "That sounds to me like a big fat hint that you've missed completely."

"You think she wanted me to offer to go with her? I can't leave the village yet, so that doesn't make sense."

"She might have been testing you, but don't worry. You can still salvage the situation. As far as I know, Perfect Match offers a Paris vacation. You can suggest that."

"That's...actually not terrible advice."

"I have my moments." Magnus finished his mead, stood, and headed toward the door, then paused. "You are no longer the same person you were a month ago, and I don't mean just physically. Take a look in the mirror and have a serious talk with the new Tim. You need a new script for your self-talk."

After Magnus left, Tim sat in the living room for a while, staring at the paused image of a bird of paradise mid-display on the TV screen. The male bird had its wings spread, showing off spectacular plumage in an elaborate dance designed to attract a mate. It looked ridiculous and magnificent at the same time.

He heard Hildegard's door open and her soft footsteps coming down the hall.

"Did Magnus leave already?" she asked.

She'd changed into pajamas that he was well familiar with by now. The fleece pants had cartoon sheep on them, the pink tank top had a white fluffy sheep on its front, and it always made him smile.

"Yeah, just now."

She sat back on the couch in the same spot as before. "Want to finish the episode?"

"Actually," Tim said, his heart suddenly pounding, "can I ask you something?"

She turned to face him, pulling one knee up on the couch. "Sure."

"Have you ever tried a Perfect Match virtual adventure?"

"I did. Solo sky diving. It was much more terrifying than I expected. Going in, I knew it wasn't real, but once you are inside, you don't know that it only happens in your head, and I nearly peed my pants."

"No, you didn't. You are the brave Hildegard, and you would never pee your pants. That's more up my alley."

She tilted her head. "Why the sudden interest in Perfect Match?"

This was it—the moment where he either took the leap or retreated into safe, comfortable limbo. "Magnus mentioned it, and then I remembered what you said about wanting to see the Northern Lights and wine tasting in France, and I thought that we might do that together inside a Perfect Match adventure. That way, I don't have to wait until my transition is complete so that I can leave the village."

She grinned at him. "Are you asking me on a romantic fantasy adventure in France, Tim?"

There was no point dissembling now. "Yes?"

She was quiet for a moment that stretched like eternity. Then she laughed—not mockingly, but with what sounded like genuine delight.

"It took you long enough," she said.

"What?"

"I was starting to think that the transition changed you in more ways than one. After all that talk about me being a fifteen on your scale of hotness, I was expecting more initiative."

"I didn't know if you..." He stopped, processing what she'd said. "You've been waiting for me?"

She rolled her eyes. "I invited you to live with me. I spend my evenings watching TV with you instead of going out with friends. I go on walks with you every day, and I supervise your physical rehabilitation. What did you think was happening here?"

"I thought you were just doing your job and being super nice about it."

She shifted closer on the couch, close enough that he could smell her shampoo. "I'm not that nice, Tim. In fact, I'm quite naughty."

15

KALUGAL

Kalugal set down his phone and stared at it for a moment. The summons from the Clan Mother worried him. She rarely did that unless it was an urgent matter, but he'd known better than to ask her the reason for the summons over the phone.

Protocol was important to Annani, and she was perfectly entitled to be treated with the utmost respect as befitting her station. He could contain his curiosity for the few moments it would take him to walk over to her place.

Hopefully, nothing had happened to his mother.

It was Wednesday, which was when she usually called her sister, but Areana hadn't done so for the past month because she and the other harem ladies had been evacuated to his father's mansion.

Were they back in the harem?

Did she have pertinent information about the enhanced soldiers?

Nah, she wouldn't share it with Annani. Areana was loyal to Navuh, and she wouldn't divulge anything that might harm him. It was a delicate dance she and Annani engaged in, balancing their love for each other with the security needs of their other loved ones.

As Kalugal walked toward Annani's house, people nodded and waved and he responded in kind, pretending that nothing was amiss. By the time he'd walked up to his aunt's door, he'd cycled through a dozen scenarios, but none of them made sense given the players involved.

Ogidu opened the door with his customary bow. "Good afternoon, Master Kalugal. The Clan Mother is expecting you."

"Thank you." Kalugal followed the butler to Annani's reception room, where he found her sitting on the couch with a tea set already in place on the coffee table.

"Good afternoon, Clan Mother." He dipped his head.

She smiled, which eased some of his tension. "I'm Aunt Annani to you, Kalugal."

"I know." He walked over to her, bent down, and kissed the cheek she offered. "But I prefer to address you first as the Clan Mother. It's a good habit in case we are in public."

"Oh, well. Have it your way." She patted the spot next to her. "Would you like some tea?"

He sat where she indicated. "I would love some. Thank you."

"I spoke with your mother this morning." Annani leaned forward to lift the carafe and pour tea into two dainty teacups.

"Is she well?"

"She sounds fine. They are back in the harem, and she is re-establishing her old routines, so we can expect calls every Wednesday from now on." Annani handed him a cup. "She asked me about someone who might have served under you. A soldier named Darien."

Hearing the name surprised Kalugal, causing a pang of hurt. He rarely thought about Darien or the others who had chosen to go their separate ways after he had brought them to America. He tried very hard not to regard their departure as betrayal, especially Darien's, but it was always in the back of his mind despite having given them his blessing to leave and pursue their dreams.

They had acted selfishly, repaying what he had done for them with abandonment.

"He was among the men who followed me out of the Brotherhood, but he left early on to pursue his own path."

"Do you know if he is still alive?" Annani asked gently.

"I assume he is." Kalugal took a sip from his tea. "After my men and I dropped off my father's radar, using the chaos in the aftermath of the bombing of Hiroshima and Nagasaki to disappear and escape to America, we spent two years moving constantly, always looking over our shoulders, waiting for my father's retrieval teams to find us."

He recalled those years with vivid clarity—the constant worry, the weight of responsibility for the men who had trusted him to join him in exile, but also the overwhelming sense of freedom and possibility that had enveloped them like a potent drug.

"All my men thrived on the freedom, the adventure, but some were tired of being part of a group and wanted to venture out on their own."

"I assume Darien was one of those?"

Kalugal nodded. "He was one of the first to leave. For a while, I kept in touch with those who didn't stay, but eventually they disappeared. I guess they didn't want any ties to their former lives. Or perhaps they feared that their connection to me might endanger them. I didn't try to stop anyone, and I wished them all the best of luck." He turned to look at her. "Why the sudden interest in Darien?"

Annani put down her teacup. "His mother has recently found out that he served with you, and she accused Areana of knowing about it and hiding it from her. Of course, Areana could not have known that because your father never told her who had been serving with you when you defected. What surprises me, though, is that Darien served with you at all. Navuh does not like his sons working together, so they will not have the opportunity to combine forces and plot against him."

"That's true, but only to a certain extent." Kalugal leaned back. "The senior sons usually don't serve in the same departments, and Navuh likes to switch them around so none will amass too much power. But they have to work in coordination with one another. The Brotherhood is a big organization, and if each department worked completely independently, it would create chaos. Darien was very close to my age, which meant that he was a nobody in the Brotherhood. I was exceptionally gifted, which was why I was made a commander at such a young age." It was true, but Kalugal was well aware of how it sounded. "Naturally, my father didn't know about my compulsion ability, so he assumed that I was a born leader."

Annani smiled indulgently. "Do not attempt to be modest, nephew of mine. It does not suit you. You are exceptional in every way, and your father was wise enough to recognize that and promote you ahead of your older so-called brothers."

Kalugal stifled a satisfied smirk and bowed his head instead. "You flatter me, Aunt Annani. Thank you."

She waved a hand in dismissal. "I am just stating facts. Now, what about Darien, and why was he placed under your command?"

"Oh, yes, Darien." Kalugal refilled his teacup and took a sip. "Darien was a smart fellow, but he wasn't a military genius by any stretch of the imagination. Navuh should have assigned him to work under Losham, but he wanted all his sons to have the ability to command. He placed Darien with me so he could watch me and learn."

"Did he?" Annani asked.

Kalugal laughed. "He could probably write a book about my style of command and the different strategies I employed and taught my men, but I doubt he had it in him to lead men into battle."

"So, he was the scholarly type?"

Kalugal paused to think and reflect. "He was an observer. Someone who enjoyed watching and listening but didn't like to participate. I didn't know back then that we weren't related by blood, and I hoped for a relationship with him, but he was always a little aloof."

"His loss," Annani said softly. "Having you as a friend would have been a valuable asset to him."

Kalugal nodded. "That being said, none of Navuh's sons were close to each other. They were competitors, so Darien didn't trust me even after I freed him from Navuh's compulsion and told him my plans. I think he only started to trust me when I let him go and didn't try to stop him. I promised my men freedom, and that included freedom to choose their own paths. They were not obligated to stick with me, but most chose to stay."

"Do you know where Darien went?" Annani asked.

"He said that he wanted to travel the world. I told him to stay away from countries my father had influence over, but I know that he didn't listen. He called me from Iran right when the revolution was happening, and the place was probably crawling with members of the Brotherhood. After I scolded him for being irresponsible, he stopped calling."

Annani nodded. "He did not want to be told what to do. Would you be able to locate him?"

"If he kept the same fake name I bought for him, I might be able to do so, especially if he returned to America. But if he's still roaming the world, I doubt it."

"Would you give it a try? It would mean a lot to your mother, even though she can't tell Darien's mother about it. As you know, no one on the island other than Tula is privy to our secret communication."

"I'll do my best to find him," Kalugal said. "Or at least what happened to him. For my own curiosity as much as for my mother's."

Darien had been smart, capable, and determined. If he'd wanted to disappear completely, he would have succeeded. But he might have retained the fake identity Kalugal had secured for him. It hadn't been cheap, and it had come with a US passport. Darien would have been a fool to discard it.

After leaving Annani's home, Kalugal pulled out his phone. "Call Preston," he told the device.

The phone rang three times before a cultured British voice answered. "This is Preston King. How can I help you?"

"Hello, Preston. This is Professor Gunter. How have you been?"

"Professor!" Preston's voice lost its formal tone. "I haven't heard from you in years."

"Indeed. I think the last time we worked together was over a decade ago. I need your services again."

"Of course. Anything for you."

Kalugal stifled a chuckle. He'd never met Preston face to face, but he'd used his services several times and had provided generous bonuses when the people he had been looking for had been found quickly. The promise of those bonuses ensured that Preston would drop any case he was working on at the moment to work on whatever Kalugal needed from him.

"I'm looking for a guy who used to go by the name of Darien Croft. I will email you a copy of his passport when I get back to my office, but I'm not sure he is still using that identity. I don't know what he does for a living these days, but he might be working as a translator or a historian."

He couldn't give the detective more information without the guy becoming suspicious of Darien's age. As it was, Kalugal would have to explain why he was looking for someone who was supposed to be seventy-seven by the date of birth listed on his passport but looked twenty-five, exactly the same age that he was when the passport had been issued in 1952.

The other option was to give the task to Roni, but the guy was always swamped with work, and it would take him a while even to start the search.

16

TAMIRA

The moment Eluheed closed the door to Tamira's room, she attacked the buttons of his shirt, but instead of responding in kind, he placed a gentle finger over her lips and leaned close to her ear.

"We need to talk," he whispered.

Nodding, she climbed onto the bed, pulling him with her. They lay facing each other, heads close on the same pillow, creating an intimate cocoon where whispers could be exchanged under the cover of lovers' passion.

"What is it?" she breathed against his ear, her hand resting on his chest where she could feel his heartbeat.

"I found it," he whispered back, his lips grazing her ear. "The tunnel entrance is hidden behind a bookshelf in Navuh and Areana's bedroom."

Her heart skipped a beat. They'd known about the tunnel's existence not only from his vision but from figuring out the practicality of Navuh traversing the distance between his mansion and the harem every day without passing through the gates.

"Did you go inside?" she asked.

"I didn't dare. I figured out where it was and then went to Hassan's office and examined the architectural plans. The spot is marked as a support column, but the dimensions don't match. It's definitely a concealed entrance."

She pressed closer, nuzzling his neck. "What stopped you from entering?"

His hand came up to stroke her hair, the gesture allowing him to speak directly into her ear. "I'm sure there is an alarm system. Pressure sensors, infrared, and who knows what else. If we trigger it, we're dead."

It wouldn't even be vindictive. Navuh wouldn't allow anyone with the knowledge of where his escape tunnel was to live.

"I need to find out what kind of security is on that door," Eluheed murmured. "And if there's an alarm, how to disable it, what triggers it."

Tamira pulled back slightly to look at his face, keeping her expression soft and adoring for any cameras that might be watching. "I'll get it out of Areana."

His eyes widened. "How? We can't allow her to suspect what we are planning."

"She won't." Tamira traced a finger along his jaw. "She feels guilty about keeping secrets from me. About Kalugal and my son. I know how to use that to my advantage."

"We'll find out what happened to Darien," Eluheed promised, cupping her face with his hand. "Once we're free, we'll search for him."

"First, we need to get free." The doubt crept into her voice despite her efforts to stay positive. "Even if I can get the information about the alarm from Areana, there's still the problem of the submarine. We don't know for sure that it exists, or how to operate it. According to your vision, it can only seat two or three people. I can't leave without the others." She grimaced. "And I don't count Areana among them. I know she would never leave Navuh."

"One problem at a time," he murmured, pressing his forehead against hers. "First, let's see if we can even get into the tunnel."

She nodded, then pulled back to study his face. Even whispering about escape felt dangerous.

"I need to figure out how to approach Areana about this," she said. "I can't just ask her about security systems."

"You're clever. You'll find a way." He stroked her cheek with his thumb. "Maybe express worry about her safety after the rebellion? Ask about emergency procedures?"

"Maybe." She considered the angles. "Or I could ask about the restoration work. Hassan has been everywhere fixing things. Surely he's been in their quarters. I could wonder aloud about privacy, about whether workers disturbed things or activated alarms."

"That could work. Make it seem like idle curiosity."

"Nothing's ever idle with Areana. She notices everything." Tamira felt a wave of frustration. "Five thousand years of playing these games. I'm so tired of it."

"I know." He pulled her closer, and this time it wasn't a pretense. She could feel his desire for her. "Soon. We'll find a way out."

"Do you really believe that?"

"I have to. The alternative is accepting this forever, and I can't do that. Not for me, and not for you."

The words warmed her despite her own doubts. She'd lived for millennia, but these past months with Eluheed had made her feel more alive than in centuries before them.

"I keep thinking about what Areana said during lunch about you," she whispered. "Navuh's impressed with your insights about the enhanced soldiers, and he hopes we'll have a child together."

Eluheed's expression darkened. "He thinks of us as livestock, breeding his superior specimens to produce brilliant generals for his army."

She smiled. "At least he thinks of us as superior. It's better than being generic livestock." Her smile wilted. "He wants another boy to steal from me and turn into a warrior."

"That won't happen," Eluheed said. "We'll be gone long before that. And if we are blessed with a child, we'll raise him free. I promise you that."

She wanted to believe him, but he was making promises he might not be able to deliver, and they both knew that.

Then again, Eluheed had special abilities, and there was a chance they could use them to escape.

"What did you see when you touched one of the enhanced soldiers?"

Eluheed was quiet for a moment. "It was overwhelming. All of their minds are trying to merge into something greater but failing. They're connected but chaotic, like instruments playing different songs simultaneously."

"Can they communicate with the others? Those who are off island?"

"I don't know. Maybe, if they could achieve focus. Right now, they're too fractured, too insane." He paused. "Navuh thinks they're the future of warfare. Soldiers who need no communication devices, enjoying perfect coordination through shared thought."

"That's terrifying."

"It's also unrealistic. They can't be controlled, and they think they are gods."

She chuckled. "In a way, they are. They are the descendants of gods. I wonder how many experiments the gods went through before perfecting their formula."

He frowned. "They weren't naturally immortal and powerful?"

"That was what they claimed, but who knows? Maybe they were created like these enhanced soldiers." She nuzzled his neck as she whispered. "Is there any way you can conceive of that we might use these men to help in our escape? If you can access their minds, you might be able to command them."

Eluheed gave her an incredulous look. "Didn't you hear what I just said? They are chaotic. Besides, I need to touch them to make contact."

Tamira glared at him. "I'm trying to think outside the box. I'm desperate."

"I'm sorry." He deflated. "I shouldn't have snapped at you."

"It's okay. I'm not really mad." She cupped his cheek to prove it and kissed him on the lips. "What do you think? Should we make love and provide the perverts who are watching us with a show?"

His whole demeanor changed instantly. "We could move things to the bathroom."

That was what they'd been doing since their return to the harem, and Tamira was a little tired of lovemaking in the shower or the tub. She wanted a comfortable bed.

"Perhaps we can find a room in the servants' quarters that is private."

"I wish." He cupped the back of her head. "But it's not allowed. The rest of the harem staff still thinks that Navuh makes use of all of his ladies and that he's just a little kinky and likes to watch them with other men."

"Really? Did they tell you that?"

He snorted. "They didn't tell me anything, but that's what I would have assumed if I were suddenly invited for an interlude with one of the ladies."

Tamira pursed her lips. "In theory, that sounds kinky, but I'm not built that way. I can't get excited while thinking that he's watching me."

"How about someone else?"

"Anyone." She pulled away. "I wonder if the enhanced soldiers share intimate moments with each other. If they have any, that is. They are probably savages."

Eluheed's grimace was all the answer she needed.

"How many more of these monsters does he intend to produce?"

"As many as he can. He's looking for new scientists to continue the project and perfect the process."

"We need to get out of here before that happens." The urgency felt more pressing to her suddenly. "The next rebellion might not be as easily quashed. Not that this one was easy. But you know what I mean. They might take longer to plan, coordinate better, and have contingencies. Nowhere on this island will be safe."

"I can't argue with your logic. I tried to point out how dangerous it is, but Lord Navuh is enamored with the idea of creating an unstoppable army."

She sighed. "I'll talk to Areana tomorrow and find out about the security."

"Be careful," he repeated. "If she suspects anything—"

"She won't. I've known Areana for five thousand years. I know how to navigate her moods, her guilt, her need to be both Navuh's perfect mate and our protective older sister. Those contradictions create openings."

"You sound like you're planning a military campaign."

"That's because I am."

"My warrior queen." He kissed her, soft and sweet, and for a moment, she let herself forget about tunnels and alarms and escape plans. Let herself just be a woman in love with a man who loved her back. *Not a man,* she reminded herself. *An immortal.*

It suddenly occurred to her that his contact with the enhanced ones could expose him.

"What if they sense what you are?" she asked.

"They were too caught up in their own chaos to probe deeper into my mind. Besides, I keep my mental shields up when I'm with them. Even more so than what I do with Navuh. Frankly, I'm more worried about him. He's much more dangerous than they are."

"Everything here is dangerous." She shifted, laying her head on his chest where she could hear his heartbeat. "I used to think I was safe here. Now I realize we're all just prey waiting for the predator to decide our fate."

"Not prey," he corrected. "Survivors. There's a difference."

"Is there?"

"Prey accepts its fate. Survivors find a way to change it."

She wanted to believe him, wanted to embrace that hope. But five thousand years of captivity had taught her that hope was not a plan.

"Make love to me," she whispered. "I'm tired of talking about escape plans that might kill us. Tonight, I want to forget everything except you."

17

ELUHEED

Eluheed often wondered about the memories stored in the walls of rooms, well lived or ill lived, for that matter. Had Tamira's room recorded the soft thud of his boots when he set them by the wardrobe? Or the beautiful sound of Tamira's laughter in rare moments of levity? Did it know where he kept a knife under the mattress? And what about the pouch of dried lavender that sat on Tamira's makeup table and filled the space with calming aroma?

The mattress, for sure, stored the shape of them together—the perfect fit of their bodies, the way their souls connected in the middle.

They were alone, the door bolted, the night lamp turned low, but the walls had hidden cameras, and it was a form of art to make love while pretending the watchers weren't there.

Thankfully, the four-poster bed had curtains that afforded them some privacy, but the sounds of passion couldn't be muffled by the sheer panels of fabric, and staying silent proved impossible.

Tamira lay on her side, facing him, hair spilling dark and heavy over the pillow.

"Are you with me?" she asked softly, her palm resting on his chest.

He pressed his hand over hers, holding it there, heartbeat to palm, a steady drum. "I am always with you. Even when I'm not."

"Are you sure?" Her eyes searched his. "You seem distant. Are you still troubled by the memory of touching the enhanced soldier?"

She always saw him so clearly. "It shook me, and the effect lingers, but I'm here with you now." He let her see the memory recede as he focused on her face, her mouth, the deep blue of her eyes.

"Then take off your shirt," she said.

He obeyed without question.

Tamira had already taken care of most of the buttons, and it was the work of a moment to free the last remaining two. As the fabric fell from his shoulders, she placed her warm hand on his skin and stroked him from collarbone to sternum, tracing a pattern down the line of muscle that had borne the weight of stones and the heft of trees and had rarely experienced such a gentle touch.

She leaned in and kissed his mouth. He tasted salt and the ghost of the fruit she'd eaten at dinner and the particular sweetness that belonged to her alone. He deepened the kiss gradually, drawing it out until he felt the last of the day burn away in the heat of her, until his mind was filled with the simple miracle of a woman opening up to him because she wanted to, because he had earned her trust, because she loved him.

He cupped her face and kissed the corner of her mouth. "Do you want me?" he asked, a ritual that was never rote.

"Yes." Her voice was low and sure. "Always and everywhere."

He traced her profile with his fingertips, the arc of her cheekbone, the slope of her jaw, the soft place under her ear where her pulse ran, and as he slid his hand down the column of her throat, she arched into his touch. He tugged at the tie at her shoulder, and the silk loosened, the gown sliding down and pooling at her waist. He paused, looking his fill. He did this every time, worshiping the body of his goddess.

"You are so beautiful," he said, and the words rang true because they came from his heart, his mind. They were not the hollow compliments men showered women with as a form of seduction.

Her mouth softened. "Come here, my love."

She was careful not to call him by his true name even when they were alone, but he wanted her to own everything that was his. "Say my name," he murmured against her lips. "Own me."

Her breath hitched. "Eluheed," she whispered. "My Eluheed."

"Always." His hand covered her breast, gentle at first, thumb circling until her nipple tightened beneath his palm.

She shivered, and he did it again, pressing a fraction harder. Her hand slid to the back of his neck and held him close while he kissed down her throat, over the slope of bone, across the rise of her chest. He carefully took the swollen peak between his lips, then a little less carefully when she arched and pushed more of it into his mouth.

"More," she whispered, and he obliged, mouth and hand working in unison.

As her fingers dug into his shoulder, his breath became unsteady, the ragged sounds she made stoking something primal in him. He loved that he could undo her like this, coaxing pleasure from her with such ease. Her body was so responsive to his touch, so eager for it.

He lowered himself, kissing the line of her ribs, the hollow of her belly, the soft curve where her thigh began. She spread for him without hesitation, confident in what she wanted and accepting of his offer. He breathed her in, that warm musk that was hers alone, and a sigh escaped him before he could stop it. She caught the sound with a smile and slid her fingers into his hair. He nuzzled the inside of her knee and felt the tremor move through her.

"Tell me what you want me to do," he said, and when she

didn't answer right away, he lifted his head to look up her body at her face.

Her eyes were dark and clear. "You know what to do," she said. "Don't stop."

The command in her voice was an aphrodisiac.

He parted her with his thumbs and put his mouth on her, tasting, learning yet again the precise patterns that made her gasp and the angle that pulled a breathy curse from her lips. He had memorized her responses over the course of their time together, but he was mindful of not treating her like a schematic he'd learned and followed blindly.

Each time was like a new beginning, and each time he paid attention to the subtle changes in her mood. Tonight, her body wanted a slower rhythm at first, a coaxing, and then a hungry push into speed that made her thighs tighten around his ears and her heels drag at the sheets.

He rode that change with her, responsive, relentless when she asked it wordlessly with her grip in his hair.

When he eased two fingers inside her, her head tipped back, and a sound escaped her that would have carried if not for the overhead fan's steady swallow. He curled his fingers just so, and her hips lifted. He then stroked again until he felt her begin to climb. He kept the pace even as her muscles fluttered around him, even as his own desire threatened to crest before it was time.

He wanted her to go first because he loved the way it remade her, the glow that came over her skin, the looseness that meant she would take him without him having to modulate his hunger.

"Elu—," she began, cut herself off because saying his name out loud was dangerous, then abandoned caution. "Eluheed—yes—"

He smiled into her, tasted the sharpness of her readiness, and did not stop until she took what she wanted. It came on a long, shuddering breath as she bit the back of her wrist to keep the sound in.

She went tight around his fingers and trembled against his mouth, and he stayed with her through it, easing when she needed him to, pressing when her body begged for that last, exquisite push into release.

When the tremors softened, he kissed the inside of her thigh and breathed her in again.

She threaded her fingers in his hair and tugged. "Come here," she said in a voice roughened by pleasure.

He slid up her body and kissed her slowly and deeply, letting her taste herself on his mouth. She made a delighted sound and bit his lower lip, a sweet sting. He settled over her, careful on his forearms so he wouldn't crush her, but she hooked her leg around his hip and pulled him closer.

He pressed the head of his shaft against her and closed his eyes, steadying himself with the taste of her kiss. She was slick, hot, and yielding, and as he slid the first inch, the sharp blast of pleasure nearly undid him. He exhaled and opened his eyes to look at her face, then eased forward until he was fully seated. The perfection of their fit undid him every time. It was like they had been created for one another.

Her hands smoothed down his back. "You feel so perfect inside of me."

He drew back and slid in again, a measured stroke that found the angle he knew she liked most. Her breath hitched. He did it again, a little deeper, adjusting the tilt of his hips until he felt the catch inside her that meant he had found it. He set a rhythm then, deliberate, grounding, each thrust stronger than the last.

She met him, body rising to his, never passive. She learned his timing and then played with it. He buried his face in her neck and breathed her in, that wild little smile curving against his jaw as she moved.

"Look at me," Tamira whispered, and he lifted his head.

She held his gaze, deep blue eyes wide open. He felt naked in a deeper way than skin, deeper than he had allowed himself to be exposed in a thousand years, and he loved her for demanding everything he had, everything he was.

He changed their angle, shifting her knee higher against his side, and she cried out as he hit that place inside that made her shake. He did it again and again, steady, tender, ruthless in his determination to give her everything.

The bed groaned under them, but he ignored the sound. Let the watchers look and listen and covet what they would never have.

Heat climbed, coiling at the base of his spine, insisting on being released. He drove slower to hold it at the edge and felt her respond, her body taking him deeper, little muscles inside gripping him in pulses that made his vision blur. When her fingers slid down to where they joined and circled that most sensitive spot on her body, he bit off a curse and lost a measure of control. He thrust harder, and she made a noise that was a better reward than any medal or accolade he could have ever won.

"Now," she gasped, and he obeyed her again, letting go of restraint. He pushed into her with a rougher rhythm, the slap of skin against skin quickening, the strain in his muscles making him quake. She came first, a sudden convulsion that locked him inside her, her mouth open, breath caught, eyes open and wild.

The sight and feel of it dragged him over the edge. He groaned into her mouth and spilled deep, hips jerking as pleasure tore through him.

For a long moment, he couldn't do anything but breathe. Her hands moved on his back, soothing, stroking lines across muscles that had gone tight with effort and sleek with sweat. He eased his weight down carefully, chest to chest, heart pounding into her palm where she had slipped her hand. He kissed her shoulder, the hollow of her throat, the sweat that had gathered at her hairline.

She laughed softly, breathless and pleased. "How do you do that?"

"Do what?"

"Make each time better than the last?"

"It's not me. It's you."

They lay tangled, catching their breath, the room settling around them. Eluheed felt himself soften inside her, the leisurely slide as his body began to relinquish its claim, but only temporarily.

They were immortals, and one time was never enough.

He kissed her again and rolled to his side, bringing her with him, keeping them joined a few heartbeats longer before slipping free. She made a noise of protest and then curled into his chest, leg thrown over his hip possessively.

"Tired?" she asked teasingly.

"I just need a moment."

They drifted on the edge of sleep, not ready to cross. He traced slow circles on her back and let his mind wander aimlessly, which was a mistake. The swirling abyss of the enhanced ones' shared consciousness surfaced, threatening to pull him into its vastness.

"Tell me about the ocean of minds," she said as if she could read his thoughts.

He tensed, and she noticed, her hand soothing him. "You don't have to."

"It's vast and tempting," he told her. "It promises connection and offers drowning. I don't want it in here with us."

"It's not here," she said. "You left it outside the door."

"I did." He imagined doing exactly that, leaving the memory of that connection outside the door.

When their breathing slowed again, she tipped his chin up with two fingers. "Ready for once again?" She smiled like a woman who knew exactly what she wanted and did not intend to accept no for an answer.

Eluheed laughed. "Greedy."

"For you, always."

He moved down her body again, learning the new map of her afterglow, which was softer, more fluid. He drew another climax out of her with his tongue and fingers and watched the heat rise under her skin. When she pulled him up with a strong hand and guided him inside, he went easily, their bodies finding the path faster this time, slick and sure, heat exchanging, breath mingling. He set a lazy rhythm at first, then switched them around and let her ride him, her palms pressed to his chest as she took what she wanted, pace building, hair wild, a queen remaking the night.

He came with her again, slower, deeper, both of them groaning into each other's mouths, the pleasure this time a heavy tide that lifted and set them down in perfect tandem. He held her hips until the aftershocks eased, then tugged her down to lie flat against him.

18

TAMIRA

Eluheed slept the way men at peace with their world slept—deep and unguarded.

Chin propped on her hand, Tamira watched him, committing to memory the way the corners of his mouth curled up in almost a smile, the way his lashes cast shadows on his cheeks, the proud line of his nose, and the burn mark on his right pectoral that looked almost like a symbol of something.

He still refused to tell her about it, saying that it had been part of a shamanic ceremony and that he had vowed not to reveal it. She traced it with her fingertips, feeling him tense beneath her touch, but he didn't wake up. Somehow, she knew that the burn mark had something to do with his immortality, which was also connected to his secretive shamanic tradition.

Eluheed kept so many secrets from her, secrets that had been burned into his mind with vows as strong as the fire or acid that had marked his flesh. He would never be able to reveal them to her because his vows didn't come with an expiration date.

It was frustrating, especially to someone like her who thrived on solving mysteries, but if that was the only obstacle in their lives together, she would count herself lucky. They needed to find a way to escape the island before Navuh realized that Eluheed wasn't aging, or he would torture his secrets out of him.

Perhaps her wish to take her sisters with her was selfish.

Eluheed had to be her priority, and if the submarine could only take the two of them, so be it. It would break her heart to leave the others behind, but life was full of compromises, and no one ever got everything they wanted.

Not even Navuh.

The sudden sputtering of the air conditioning as the power went out again proved that the master of this island didn't have everything under control.

When the power returned and with it the cool air, Tamira thought of Areana's lie and the ache that had dulled from a knife wound to a bruise and stayed there, a reminder that love and disappointment often came wrapped together.

Would that be how her sisters felt when they realized she'd escaped with Eluheed and left them behind?

Tamira slid from the bed without waking him and crossed to the balcony doors, drawing the curtain just wide enough to look out at the indoor garden. The artificial lighting had been programmed to follow the cycle of the sun, but since it was still nighttime, the lighting was subdued, mimicking what the moon was doing aboveground.

Behind her, the sheets rustled. "Tamira," Eluheed said in a sleep-rough voice that made heat lick low in her belly, and then he reached for her blindly, eyes still closed, hand finding air where her hip should have been.

"I'm here." She walked back to the bed, amused by the very apparent immediacy of his need. She slid under the sheet and lay on her side facing him.

He blinked, focusing his blurry eyes on her, and smiled in that quiet, devastatingly handsome way that seemed designed to make her melt.

"I was afraid you left." He kissed her forehead in the precise spot he always did.

"Where would I go?"

"Breakfast?"

She chuckled. "It's still night."

"Then why are we awake?" He pulled her closer to him.

"I can't sleep," she admitted. "I want to speak to Areana today, and I need to devise a strategy."

She wasn't ready to tell him what she'd decided only moments ago. It was a difficult decision, and it hadn't settled in her heart yet. She might still change her mind about leaving her sisters behind.

"Did you come up with any ideas?"

Tamira twisted a curl around her finger and studied its give. "I can employ two tactics," she whispered next to his ear. "One is to pretend that I'm still fearful and ask about security measures and alarms and whether I could find sanctuary in her quarters in the case of an attack. I can then flat-out ask her if there are alarms anywhere. Even if she deflects and says that there are none, I will know by her body language if she's hiding something.

Eluheed canted his head. "Are you sure you know Lady Areana that well? Living with Navuh and navigating his moods and his bouts of madness, she must have become an exceptional actress. She probably lets you see what she wants you to see."

She regarded him with somber eyes. "Is that what you do?"

"Not with you, but with others, I have no choice. My survival depends on it."

For a long moment, she just looked into his eyes. "I bet you couldn't hide anything from me even if you tried. I wouldn't know what you're hiding, but I would know that you're doing so."

He nodded. "That's because you see me so clearly."

"I see her just as well," Tamira said with more confidence than she commanded.

Eluheed was right about Areana having to become exceptional at manipulating Navuh, and since he was probably the most difficult person on Earth to manipulate, Areana could do that to anyone.

He reached up and touched the curl she had been playing with, winding it around his finger, loosening it, and winding it again. "Do you want me hovering nearby when you talk with her? I can be your silent encourager."

"I appreciate the offer, but no. She might not open up to me when others are present. But I can tell you one thing. Tonight, I want you to be exactly where you are now."

"Where else would I be?" The words arced between them like an electrical current.

He drew her in, rolled her beneath him, and kissed her slow and deep. His weight was welcome, the length of him settling between her thighs with a thrilling familiarity. She loved that he did not rush, even when her body offered him a dozen reasons to. He moved his mouth slowly down her throat, over the curve of her breasts, and then lower, spreading her with patient hands, kissing her with a focus that made her thoughts unravel.

There was no point in arguing that she was ready, that he didn't need to devote so much care and attention to her pleasure, or that not every encounter needed to be a five-course meal, and that sometimes a quick snack was all that was needed.

Eluheed didn't do anything halfheartedly.

Instead, Tamira sighed, lacing her fingers into his hair and letting her legs fall wider in an unabashed welcome.

He teased first, light strokes of his tongue that woke every nerve, and then settled into the pressure and rhythm that took her apart. She lifted, seeking more, and he gave it, eagerly, as if her pleasure was what he lived for.

"So good," she breathed, and felt his answer in the increased insistence of his mouth.

He slipped his fingers inside her, curling just right, and she tipped into sensation with a sound she swallowed in the curve of her arm. The release shook her, rolling through in waves that eased and then surged again when he didn't let up. She rode his mouth until the edge softened, and she let out a long, shaky exhale.

When he came up smiling, mouth slick and eyes bright, she tugged him up by the hair and kissed him long.

"I want you inside of me," she commanded.

"Yes, my lady." He slid into her in one smooth stroke that made both of them groan. He filled her completely, and she wrapped her legs around his waist, holding him there and loving his weight on top of her.

He started slow and deep, and she met him easily, rolling her hips to keep the angle, to drive him into that sensitive spot inside her sheath that made her see stars.

"Look at me," she whispered, because seeing his eyes when he was inside her was a privilege she never wanted to squander.

He lifted his head at once, his breath catching and his gaze locking with hers, and then he pushed deeper, and her body clenched around him in welcome.

Tamira climbed again, faster than she had expected. The lingering sensitivity from his mouth and tongue, layered with the thick, steady friction, gathered heat quickly. She pressed her heels into his solid buttocks, slid her hands down to grip his hips, and urged him harder. He answered, still in control but close to losing the battle with his need to climax. The strain in his neck, the way his breath shortened and turned ragged, spoke of the unbearable pressure that was about to erupt.

She timed her movements to meet him in a series of quick thrusts that tumbled them into a shared inferno. She came first, biting back a cry. He followed with a rough groan against her neck, his hips stuttering, and the hot rush inside her made her shiver with a second, smaller after-climax that left her boneless.

He stayed inside her, breathing hard.

She smoothed his hair back and kissed his cheek, the tender act an instinct she didn't examine. He nuzzled her palm and turned his head to kiss it.

When he slipped out, she made a small sound of protest and then laughed at herself. He laughed with her, the kind of hushed, delighted sound that felt like sunlight through leaves.

Eluheed fetched a cloth from the bathroom and returned to clean her with infinite care. She drew him down and did the same for him, trailing the cloth lazily over warm skin until the lazy became intent and he caught her wrist, playful warning in his eyes.

"We need to sleep sometimes," he murmured.

"Sleep is highly overrated," she teased, feeling way too energized to just surrender to slumber. "Besides, it's almost time for breakfast, and I'm hungry."

"Of course you are." He got out of bed and returned with a tray of cheese and grapes that they'd brought from the dining room. "We can't have you starving for a whole hour until breakfast."

They nibbled on the cheese and popped the succulent grapes into their mouths, and as juice ran down his wrist, she licked it clean. He went still, pupils widening, and she grinned, pleased by how easy it was to undo him.

"Tell me," he said quietly as he offered her another succulent grape. "If Areana names security features you've never heard of, what will you do?"

"I'll admit that I'm clueless and ask her to show me," she whispered back without missing a beat. "That would be perfect because I'll get to see how to disarm it."

He shook his head. "You are dangerous."

"Not really, but I'm learning to be." She put the tray on the nightstand and turned to pull him into her arms. "We should wash up, get dressed, and head out to the dining room."

19

CAROL

Carol surveyed the penthouse dining room one last time, checking that everything was in place for the first real training session of her spy team. The cameras were positioned at multiple angles, notebooks and pens laid out at each seat, and she'd even set up a small area near the windows with various props—hats, scarves, different styles of glasses, things they'd use later when Eva arrived.

When the doorbell rang at precisely nine in the morning, she opened it to find all five women standing there once more, looking ready for battle.

"Morning, ladies. Ready for today's lesson?"

"Ready as we'll ever be," Marlene said, striding in with confidence that looked innate rather than a mere façade. She'd dressed more practically today—dark slacks, a simple blouse that wouldn't restrict movement, and low kitten heels that were comfortable but still looked fashionable and polished.

Carol approved.

They filed in and took the same seats as before, which told Carol they were already creatures of habit. That would need to change.

"First rule," Carol said, remaining standing. "Never sit in the same place twice. Patterns make you predictable, and predictable makes you vulnerable."

Teresa immediately stood and moved to a different chair. The others followed, some more reluctantly than others.

"Better," Carol said, taking a seat herself—not at the head of the table this time, but along the side. "Today we're focusing on observation. It's the foundation of everything else you'll learn. You can't become someone's ideal woman if you don't know what they're looking for, and most people never say what they really want. Sometimes they don't even know that themselves, but you will learn to puzzle it out by observing their behavior."

Grace raised her hand. "We did observation exercises last week."

"That was just for demonstration. This is the real deal." Carol pulled out a tablet and tapped the screen. "I'm going to show you a thirty-second video. Watch it once, then tell me everything you observed."

The wall-mounted screen came to life, showing what appeared to be a coffee shop. A man in a business suit sat at a corner table, typing on a laptop. A woman walked past with a dog. Two teenagers argued near the counter. A barista called out an order. Then the video ended.

"What did you see?" Carol asked.

"Man working on his computer, probably a businessman based on the suit," Marlene said. "The woman with the dog was wearing designer clothes—wealthy neighborhood."

"The teenagers were arguing about money," Teresa added. "One claimed that the other owed him twenty dollars, but the other was saying that he's already repaid it."

"The barista called out an order of soy latte with extra foam and caramel," Grace contributed.

Regina spoke up hesitantly. "The man kept touching his wedding ring. Twisting it."

Carol smiled. "Good catch, Regina. What else?"

Greta, who'd been silent, finally spoke. "The businessman wasn't typing. His fingers were moving, but if you watched the screen's reflection in the window behind him, it never changed. He was pretending to work while watching the woman with the dog."

"Excellent," Carol said. "What else did everyone miss?"

They looked at each other, uncertain.

"The teenagers weren't customers," Carol explained. "Neither had drinks or food. They were there for another reason—probably dealing drugs based on the quick hand exchange that happened when one 'bumped' into the other. The woman with the dog? She was casing the place. Her eyes swept every corner and noted the camera positions. The dog was a prop to make her look harmless. And the businessman? He wasn't wearing a wedding ring. Regina saw what she expected to see based on his demographic, not what was actually there."

Regina flushed. "But I saw him touching—"

"It was his class ring. Different finger, different meaning. He was nervous, yes, but not about infidelity. Watch again." Carol replayed the video, and this time they all saw what she'd pointed out.

"This is what I mean by observation," Carol continued. "You need to see what's actually there, not what you expect or assume. Your targets will be powerful men who've spent their lives learning to hide their true intentions. You need to see past their masks."

"How do we learn that?" Teresa asked.

"Practice. Constant, deliberate practice." Carol switched to another recording. "I recorded this earlier on the street below. Pick a person and tell me their story—not what you imagine, but what you can actually observe and reasonably deduce."

"There." Marlene pointed. "The woman in the red dress. She's walking fast but checking her phone constantly. She's late for something but expecting an important call or message. The dress is wrinkled on one side, so she might have slept in her car or someone else's bed."

"Possible," Carol said. "But look at her shoes."

"Flats," Grace observed. "She's carrying heels in that bag."

"So, she changed shoes for the walk, which suggests planning, not a spontaneous overnight. The wrinkles could be from a long flight. The phone checking might be waiting for an Uber. See how the story changes when you notice more details?"

They spent the next hour watching clips of random people that Carol had recorded at different places doing everyday things. She was pushing them to look deeper, to question their assumptions. Regina, surprisingly, began to excel at it. Her natural anxiety made her hypervigilant, and once she learned to channel that into observation rather than worry, she caught details others missed.

"That man is favoring his left side," Regina pointed out about a pedestrian. "Old injury, probably military, based on his bearing. But he's trying to hide it, which means he doesn't want to appear vulnerable. It might be something that is innate, or he's going to a job interview or an important meeting where he needs to project strength. I would need to observe him in different situations to know which is true."

"Good," Carol said. "Knowing when you need more clues is just as important as observing what you can at first glance."

When the doorbell rang, Carol stopped the recording. "That must be Eva."

The female didn't require introductions as everyone knew her and was familiar with her work.

When Carol opened the door, she found her carrying two large cases and wearing all black, which wasn't her usual style. Eva preferred flowy long skirts and pretty blouses that made her look feminine and obscured her ruthless nature.

"Let me help you with that." Carol reached for one of the cases.

Eva gave her a haughty look. "I can manage. Where to?"

"The dining room."

"Ladies," Eva greeted as she set down her cases. "I'm here to teach you the art of disguise. You will learn how to become someone else and how to be unrecognizable."

"Isn't that the same thing?" Grace asked.

"Not at all." Eva opened the first case, revealing an array of products. "Becoming someone else is psychological. Not being recognized as yourself is physical. They require different skills."

She studied each woman in turn. "Marlene, your cheekbones are your most distinctive feature. We'll need to minimize those. Teresa, your eyes are beautiful, very memorable. Regina, your nervous habits are more identifying than your face. Grace, you have perfect posture, which is rarer than you think. And Greta..." She paused. "You've done this before."

"A long time ago," Greta admitted.

"The bones remember even when the mind forgets." Eva pulled out what looked like a simple makeup compact.

"This is theater putty. With this and some basic contouring, I can age you twenty years or take off ten. Change your race, your social class, your entire presence."

She demonstrated on herself first, adding subtle shadows under her eyes, changing the shape of her nose slightly, and adjusting her jawline. Within minutes, she looked exhausted, older, beaten down by life.

"But makeup only goes so far," she continued, wiping it off with a makeup-removing towelette. "True disguise is about changing how you move, how you hold yourself, how you occupy space."

"Show them the walk," Carol suggested.

Eva smiled. First, she walked across the room with her natural gait—confident, smooth, slightly predatory. Then she adjusted something in her posture and walked again. This time, she seemed smaller, hesitant, her feet barely making a sound. A third pass and she strutted, taking up space, her heels clicking authoritatively.

"Same shoes, same clothes, same person," Eva said. "But would you recognize me as the same woman if you saw these three versions on the street?"

"No," Regina said, looking fascinated. "The middle one especially—you seemed to shrink."

"That is why some women complain about being invisible," Eva explained. "When you make yourself small and unthreatening, your presence doesn't even register. It's extremely useful for a spy who wishes to be overlooked, and you should practice this until you master it. The opposite is true when you need to command attention and respect."

She had them practice walking, adjusting their natural gaits. Marlene struggled at first—her confidence was so ingrained that making herself seem meek was difficult.

"I can't," she said after her fifth attempt. "It just makes me depressed. It feels wrong."

"Because you're doing method acting and trying to think of yourself as small and insignificant. That can work for some, but not for you. Think of it as choosing to be underestimated. There's power in being overlooked—you see everything while no one sees you."

That reframing helped, and Marlene's next attempt was better.

Regina excelled at physical transformations. She could shift from nervous to confident to invisible with remarkable ease.

"You're a natural," Eva told her. "You already understand how to modulate your presence."

"Years of trying not to be noticed at parties," Regina admitted with a self-deprecating smile.

They moved on to surveillance detection—how to know if they were being followed, how to lose a tail without seeming to notice it.

"The key is natural movement," Eva explained. "Window shopping to check reflections. Tying your shoe or rubbing the back of your foot if you are wearing heels, to see who stops. Taking an elevator up, then immediately back down. But these only work if they fit your cover. A rushed businesswoman wouldn't window shop. A fitness enthusiast wouldn't take the elevator."

"This is incredibly complex," Grace said, looking overwhelmed.

"It becomes instinct," Carol assured her. "Like driving a car—at first you have to think about every action, but eventually it's reflexive."

Eva pulled items from her second case. "Now, practical disguise elements. These are things you can carry that completely change your appearance with minimal effort."

She laid out reversible jackets, collapsible hats, magnetic jewelry that could be reconfigured, and glasses with removable tinted lenses.

"The goal isn't to become unrecognizable to someone who knows you well," Eva explained. "It's to be forgettable to strangers or not to match a description. If someone reports a blonde in a red jacket heading north, you need to be a brunette in blue heading south within minutes."

They practiced quick changes, ducking into the penthouse bathroom and emerging transformed. Teresa showed unexpected talent for this, managing complete appearance shifts in under ninety seconds.

"I used to do theater in college," she explained when complimented. "I'm very well practiced in quick changes between scenes."

As the morning progressed, Carol watched her students absorb the information with varying degrees of success. Marlene's natural confidence made her excellent at commanding attention, but she struggled with invisibility. Teresa's analytical mind excelled at spotting surveillance, but she overthought the physical changes. Grace tried too hard to please, making her performances feel forced.

Greta's experience showed.

Regina was the most striking revelation, though. The woman who'd arrived weeks ago, touching her jewelry nervously, had found her calling. She absorbed every technique, every observation, channeling her anxiety into hyperawareness, and her need to please into perfect mimicry.

"Watch this," Regina said during a break. She walked to the corner of the room as herself—shoulders slightly hunched, one hand near her throat where her necklace usually sat. Then she straightened, dropped her hands to her sides, lifted her chin, and walked back. The transformation was remarkable—she moved like Marlene, all confident and commanding.

"Have you been practicing?" Carol asked.

"My entire life." Regina let her shoulders slump back to their usual position. "It's exhausting to project confidence and attract attention when you prefer to lock the front door to your house and curl up with a book."

"The introvert's curse," Eva said. "You can console yourself with the knowledge that introverts are better spies. Since they hate attracting attention, they are very good at observing others, and this is what a spy's job is all about."

"Which brings me to the next segment of today's class," Carol said. "I'm going to play a video of a man at a restaurant. I want you to observe him for five minutes and then tell me how you'd approach him. What persona would you create? How would you dress? What would you say?"

The video showed a well-dressed man in his fifties dining alone at an upscale restaurant. He had silver hair, wore an expensive watch, and spent most of his time on his phone.

After five minutes, Carol paused it. "Marlene?"

"Wealthy, obviously. Probably divorced—no wedding ring but a tan line where one used to be. The way he's sitting, slightly to one side, suggests he's used to having someone across from him. I'd approach as a sophisticated divorcee myself, someone who understands his situation. Commiserate about the challenges of dating again after ending a long marriage."

"Teresa?"

"He's not texting. Look at his thumb movements—he's playing a game. Probably bored, killing time. The restaurant is near the financial district, so he's likely waiting for a business meeting. I'd be a young professional seeking advice, flattering his expertise."

"Grace?"

"His shoes don't match his wealth level. Everything else is expensive, but the shoes are mid-range and comfortable.

He cares about appearance but values comfort more. I'd be approachable, down-to-earth, someone who makes him feel relaxed."

"Regina?"

Regina studied the frozen image. "He's left-handed, but his watch is on his left wrist. That's unusual unless the watch has sentimental value and he wants to keep it visible. The way he holds his phone—see how his pinky supports it? That's an old injury, probably from sports. I'd create a persona with a similar injury, something to bond over. Maybe mention physical therapy, see if he relates."

Carol was impressed. "Greta?"

Greta was quiet for a long moment. "I wouldn't approach him at all. He's security. Look at how he's positioned—back to the wall, clear view of all entrances. The phone game is a cover for surveillance. That's not a businessman waiting for a meeting. That's someone watching someone else."

They all looked at the screen again and suddenly saw what Greta had noticed. The man's eyes flicked up from his phone regularly, scanning the room. His position was indeed tactical.

"Very good," Carol said. "This is why observation is critical. Approaching the wrong person with the wrong persona doesn't just mean failure—it means exposure."

20

LOKAN

The keep's gym smelled of cleaning solution and perspiration, a combination that reminded Lokan of the exclusive gym in the Beijing high-rise he'd been living in for the past two years.

But this was different.

Instead of bored business executives hoping to maintain their health by paying their dues on the long row of treadmills, the participants in tonight's ceremony hoped to join the ranks of the immortals by facing one of them on the wrestling mat.

The paranormals filed in with expressions ranging from nervous to excited. Jeremy led the group, elected as their unofficial leader. Behind him came Spencer and Dylan, who were also trying one more time to be induced. James and Mollie entered holding hands, while Abigail, Sofia, and Naomi walked in chatting among themselves and looking nervous.

The door opened again, and Kian entered with Anandur and Brundar flanking him like bookends of opposite temperaments—one grinning broadly, the other wearing his usual stoic expression. Carol followed, catching Lokan's eye and giving him a smile that could melt ice.

Kian took a bag from Anandur that Lokan hadn't noticed him carrying and pulled out a bottle of wine. "I've been thinking about why the inductions didn't work before. Maybe we've been too casual about it and offended the Fates. We shouldn't have skipped the ritual. It has always been part of the process."

"You surprise me." Lokan took the sleeve of paper cups that Anandur handed him. "You're usually too pragmatic and skeptical to believe that a ceremony might change the outcome."

Kian set the wine on a bench and started separating the paper cups. "Over the past five years, I've gradually changed from a skeptic to a believer. If there's even a sliver of a chance that the ceremony is what's been missing, it's worth the few extra minutes it will take."

Anandur clapped his hands together, the sound echoing in the gym. "Any excuse for a party, right? Even a small one with crappy sweet wine in paper cups."

"It's not crappy," Kian protested. "It's ceremonial wine."

Anandur shrugged. "That doesn't make it taste any better, and it still goes into paper cups."

Lokan studied Kian's face, wondering if Carol had told the boss about his crisis of confidence after his failures to induce the paranormals. He'd started to believe there was something fundamentally wrong with his venom, despite everyone's assurances that being three-quarters god should make it the most potent available.

But Kian didn't look like he was humoring anyone. He seemed genuinely convinced that the wine and the traditional words would make a difference. Lokan didn't want to mention that the Brotherhood never bothered with a ceremony or wine. The induction ceremony at thirteen years of age was a brutal and humiliating affair, and the young dormant males subjected to it still managed to transition to immortality.

Lokan had been born immortal because his mother was a goddess, and so had Kalugal, but Navuh had manipulated everyone to believe that they'd gone through a privately held induction ceremony like all his other so-called sons.

"Alright, everyone, gather round," Kian said. "We're going to do this properly this time."

The paranormals formed a loose semicircle, their partners standing beside them.

"Before we begin," Kian said, pouring wine into the small cups Carol was distributing, "I want to make something clear. Whether this works or not, you've all shown tremendous courage by coming here, trusting us, and being willing to go out on a limb."

"Hear, hear," Anandur boomed, already holding his cup high.

Kian cast him a reproachful look and then cleared his throat. "We are gathered here to present these brave three souls to their elders." His voice carried a formal cadence. "They stand ready to attempt transition into immortality, if the Fates will it. I vouch for each of them as being worthy of the honor."

The atmosphere in the gym shifted, became charged with something that hadn't been there during the previous attempts. Even Anandur seemed to stand straighter, taking the ceremony seriously.

"Jeremy, please come forward," Kian continued. "Who volunteers to take on the burden of initiating Jeremy into immortality?"

"I do." Anandur raised his hand.

Kian nodded. "Jeremy, do you accept Guardian Anandur as your initiator? As your mentor and protector, to honor him with your friendship, your respect, and your loyalty from this day forward?"

Jeremy glanced at Naomi, who squeezed his hand encouragingly. "I do," he said.

"Does anyone have any objections to Jeremy becoming Anandur's protégé?"

Silence filled the gym, but it was supportive rather than awkward.

"Then let's seal it with a toast." Kian raised his paper cup. "To Jeremy and Anandur."

"To Jeremy and Anandur," everyone echoed, taking sips of the ceremonial wine.

Lokan had to admit that the ceremony made a difference. Before, there had been a clinical efficiency to the induction—get in, inject the venom, wait for results. This had weight to it, a meaning beyond two guys on the mat, one with fangs and the other without.

"Now then, ready to dance, Jeremy?" Anandur asked, his grin tempered with purpose. "I promise I'll go easy on you."

"Define 'easy,'" Jeremy said, managing a nervous laugh.

"I won't break anything important."

Carol moved to stand beside Lokan as the others cleared a space for the two combatants. "Was this your idea?" he asked quietly.

"Not at all. It was all Kian."

"He truly thinks the ritual will make a difference?"

"It can't hurt." Carol shrugged. "The ceremony creates a bond between the initiator and the initiate. Perhaps the psychology of it matters as much as the physicality."

Lokan watched as Anandur and Jeremy circled each other, the Guardian moving with deliberate slowness to let the human track him.

"You know, the key to a good fight is not thinking too much," Anandur said conversationally as they moved.

"Jeremy, my friend, you're thinking so hard I can hear the gears grinding from here."

"Hard not to think about my upcoming demise when someone your size is about to attack me," Jeremy replied.

"I'm not attacking. I'm initiating. That's a completely different thing." Anandur feinted left, and Jeremy jerked back. "See? You're anticipating. Don't anticipate. React."

"Easy for you to say."

"Actually, it took me about two hundred years to learn that lesson, so no, not easy at all."

The exchange continued, Anandur keeping up a steady stream of instruction and encouragement while gradually increasing the pace. Jeremy was sweating, breathing hard, but there was a determination in his eyes that hadn't been there during the first attempt.

Anandur finally made his move, a lightning-fast grab that caught Jeremy's arm. They went down in a controlled fall, Anandur's fangs extending as he bit down on Jeremy's neck.

Jeremy gasped but didn't cry out, his body going rigid as the venom entered his system.

"Well done," Anandur said as he released the guy. "He took that like a champ."

"Did it work?" Naomi rushed forward, dropping to her knees beside Jeremy.

"We won't know for a few days," Kian said.

"My turn?" Spencer asked.

Kian nodded and lifted the wine bottle again. "Who volunteers to be Spencer's initiator?"

"I do," Brundar said, stepping forward.

"Spencer," Kian continued after refilling everyone's cups. "Do you accept Guardian Brundar as your initiator? As your mentor and protector, to honor him with your friendship, your respect, and your loyalty from this day forward?"

Spencer studied Brundar for a long moment. Where others might have been intimidated by the Guardian's silence and intensity, Spencer seemed to appreciate it. "I do."

"Does anyone object to Spencer becoming Brundar's protégé?"

Again, supportive silence.

"Then we toast. To Spencer and Brundar."

The contrast between the two sparring pairs couldn't have been more pronounced. Where Anandur had been vocal and encouraging, Brundar was silent and intense. But Spencer seemed to understand the Guardian's style, matching his quiet focus with equal concentration.

They moved like dancers who'd rehearsed together, despite this being their first real encounter. Spencer, like everyone else in the government paranormal program, had military training, and it showed in the way he moved and his ability to read Brundar's intentions.

When Brundar struck, it was swift and precise. Spencer's jaw clenched as Brundar's fangs pierced his skin, but he didn't cry out.

Once he was taken off the mat, Kian turned to Dylan. "Lokan has volunteered to be your initiator again. Do you accept him as your mentor and protector, to honor him with your friendship, respect, and loyalty?"

Dylan met Lokan's eyes, and Lokan saw his own uncertainty reflected there. But then Dylan nodded. "I do."

"Any objections?" Kian asked.

The silence felt heavier this time, and Lokan wondered if everyone was thinking about his previous failures. But no one spoke against it.

"Then we seal it. To Dylan and Lokan."

As the wine touched his lips, Lokan felt something shift. This wasn't just about successfully inducing a transformation anymore. He'd just taken responsibility for this man, ceremony or not, success or not.

"Ready?" he asked Dylan as they moved to the sparring area.

"Are you?" Dylan countered, and there was understanding in his voice.

"No," Lokan admitted quietly. "But that has never stopped me before."

Dylan smiled. "Good enough for me."

They circled each other, and Lokan found himself talking like Anandur had, partly to calm Dylan but mostly to calm himself.

"You know what the interesting thing about the transition is?" he said as they moved. "It's not really about the venom. I mean, yes, the venom is necessary, but it's just a catalyst. The real change comes from within. The venom just gives your body permission to become what it always had the potential to be."

"Provided that the potential is there," Dylan said, maintaining his guard.

Lokan struck then, not giving Dylan time to tense up in anticipation. His fangs pierced the skin cleanly, venom flowing from his glands.

When Dylan passed out, Jeremy started waking up, and Spencer followed a few minutes later.

"What now?" Spencer asked, sounding as if he were drunk, still loopy from the venom effect.

"Now we wait," Kian said.

21

TAMIRA

Tamira walked the familiar route—left at the tapestry, down past the arch where the plaster still wore a water stain. She passed two maids sharing gossip and smelling of cleaning solution. They bowed and scurried past her, then resumed their excited conversation as if it had never been interrupted.

She let their chatter wash over her. It steadied her.

As she opened the doors leading to the indoor garden, she found Areana sitting on a stone bench, the fountain's music filling the silence with sounds that couldn't replace what nature sang aboveground.

"Care for some company?" Tamira asked.

"Yours? Always," Areana said.

It was such a nice thing to say, but Tamira doubted Areana meant it, especially after the spat they had over Darien and whether Areana knew that Darien had escaped with her son.

"Thank you." Tamira sat down. "We should head to the library soon."

"Yes," Areana acknowledged. "I just needed a few moments alone here."

She usually had breakfast with Navuh in their apartment, and after he departed, she often came here or joined the other ladies for breakfast, sharing a cup of coffee with them. Navuh was intense, so Tamira could understand Areana's occasional need to recuperate and center herself after spending time with him.

"I wish we could have birds here," she said, just to start the conversation. "But I wouldn't want to do that to the poor creatures."

"No, I guess not." Areana glanced upward, acknowledging the watchers without mentioning them. "Did you come just to keep me company, or do you have something you wanted to discuss?"

Tamira sighed. "I feel anxious all the time. Ever since the rebellion, even the harem doesn't feel safe. I can't fall asleep, and when I finally do, I can't stay asleep. I keep waking up."

Areana smiled knowingly. "You have a handsome male sharing your bed. I'm sure he has something to do with your lack of sleep."

"He distracts me as much as he can." Tamira leaned back. "But when he sleeps, I'm left alone with my thoughts and fears."

It was true, but she knew Areana would interpret that as Eluheed's human need for many hours of sleep and Tamira's reduced need.

"What are you afraid of?" Areana asked.

Tamira canted her head. "Isn't that obvious? The enhanced soldiers. I know that they are being contained, but fears are not rational. I was so terrified in Lord Navuh's basement that I haven't managed to return to normal. I jump at every noise. Elias can't defend me from these enhanced warriors, and it's up to me to defend both of us, but I have no training, no weapons, and I feel helpless." She leveled her gaze at Areana. "You probably don't feel any of that because you have a powerful compeller sleeping next to you at night. You don't feel the danger as acutely as I do."

Areana nodded. "I fear too, but not as acutely. Having Navuh sleep next to me helps, but he's not there every night."

That was something Tamira hadn't known. "How come? He never goes off island, so what reason can he have for not spending the night with his truelove mate?"

"Sometimes he works late at night, communicating overseas across many time zones, and then he just spends the night at the mansion."

That was the opportunity Tamira had been waiting for to ask what she came for. "The ladies and I have been wondering for years how Lord Navuh comes to you at night and leaves in the morning without anyone knowing.

We are guessing that he has a secret tunnel leading between your rooms in the harem and his mansion."

Areana laughed. "I wondered when one of you would have the guts to ask me about that."

Tamira widened her eyes in pretend shock. "So, there is a tunnel?"

"Of course. How else do you think he gets to my rooms? Flying on a magic carpet? Even that could not bring him underground."

Tamira leaned closer to the goddess. "Have you ever been in that tunnel?"

Areana shook her head. "I know where it is, and I know how to open the secret passage without triggering the alarms, but I've never actually stepped inside of it. Navuh told me to use it only in an emergency, when the harem is attacked or on fire."

So, Eluheed was right, and the entrance to the tunnel was rigged.

Tamira assumed an offended expression. "That kind of information should be shared with all the ladies. What if there is a fire and you are unconscious from smoke inhalation, and we can't evacuate you through that tunnel because we don't know where it is? What if you leave and we remain trapped?"

Areana had the decency to look uncomfortable. "You are right. I've never thought of it that way. Knowing how to open that door could be lifesaving. I guess I could show you how to open it without showing you how to disable the alarms. Navuh would have my head if I did that. But in case of an emergency, you can just use the escape route and trigger the alarm. If there is a fire or the defense parameters are breached, all the other alarms would be blaring anyway."

That was less than ideal, but maybe Areana would open the passageway for Tamira to see, and she could memorize what needed to be done to disarm the alarm.

"So, Lord Navuh has to disarm that door every time he enters or leaves?"

Areana nodded. "He uses an application on his phone. But since I don't have a phone, I use the manual sequence."

"That's another thing I wanted to ask you about. Why don't we get phones? They can be for on-island communication only, but they could also be a lifesaver in an emergency."

Areana looked exasperated. "Don't you think I know that? Don't you think I tried to get us phones or even walkie-talkies with just one channel? Everything is an endless negotiation, and I need to be careful not to press too hard or he shuts down completely. It's a delicate balance, and every little concession is a victory."

"I understand." Tamira put her hand on Areana's arm. "I'm sorry for dumping all of this on you at once, but we were all wondering about those things, and you are the only one who could get us those concessions."

Areana nodded. "Do you want to see it now?"

"The entrance to the tunnel?"

"Yes. We can stop by my suite before we head out to the library."

"What about the others?"

Areana smiled indulgently. "I'm not about to lead a guided tour. One at a time is better, and since the other ladies are at the library already, this is the perfect time to show you."

"Then lead the way." Tamira pushed to her feet.

She followed Areana through the corridor and then the staircase to the first level, their footsteps muffled by the thick carpets. The opulence here always made her slightly uncomfortable—not because she envied it, but because it felt like a gilded cage within a cage.

Areana's suite was sprawling. They passed through the sitting room with its silk-covered walls and entered the bedroom, where the massive four-poster bed dominated the space. Tamira's eyes went immediately to the shallow bookshelf Eluheed had described, built into the north wall. Then her eyes darted to the ceiling, and the ornate drapes covering the doors that led to the balcony overlooking the interior courtyard.

"There are no recording devices in here," Areana said, noticing Tamira's scan. "Navuh values our privacy."

Tamira nodded and smiled, but she wasn't convinced. Navuh could have easily installed devices without telling Areana, turning them off only when he visited. But she kept that thought to herself.

Areana walked to the bookshelf and ran her fingers along the spines. "The sequence is important," she said, positioning herself so that her body partially blocked Tamira's view, or at least it appeared to do so. "I must do it exactly right, or the alarms will be triggered."

As Areana moved through the disarming sequence, her positioning was carelessly ineffective. Tamira could see everything clearly, as if Areana were only pretending to conceal it.

"First," Areana said, pressing down on a specific spot on the floor with her heel. A soft click sounded. "The pressure plate beneath the rug."

Her foot hovered over the spot long enough for Tamira to memorize the exact location. It was the third pink rose from the left in the pattern, about one-third of a meter from the wall.

She moved to the bookshelf. "After the plate comes the books." She reached for a leather-bound volume on the second shelf and as she pulled it out halfway, another click sounded.

Herodotus's Histories, Tamira memorized, wishing she could write it down. Areana repeated the same process with *Plato's Republic* on the third shelf, then *Marcus Aurelius's Meditations* on the first, and finally, *Ovid's Metamorphoses* on the very top shelf that required her to stretch on her tiptoes. But this one she pushed rather than pulled out.

A deeper click resonated through the wall, and a section of the bookshelf swung inward on silent hinges, revealing darkness beyond.

"The pressure plate resets after thirty seconds," Areana continued, still making a show of blocking Tamira's view while actually demonstrating everything perfectly. "So, the book sequence must be completed quickly. On the way back, it needs to be done in reverse. The books first and the pressure plate last."

Tamira committed it all to memory: the third rose, a third of a meter out. Herodotus, Plato, Marcus Aurelius, Ovid. Pull, pull, pull, push. It wasn't difficult to memorize the classics, but the sequence was a little trickier. She would have to devise a mnemonic. H, P, M, O. Three pulls and then one push. Heroes Plot Military Overthrows. That needed work, but it would do for now.

"What if you make a mistake?" Tamira asked.

"The alarm sounds throughout the complex. Guards converge from every direction." Areana's expression was serious. "Navuh would assume an intruder, and because it's in my quarters, the response will be fast and forceful."

Tamira peered into the darkness beyond the opening. "How far does it go?"

"All the way to the mansion. Navuh told me that it's wide enough for a compact vehicle. The tunnel has emergency lighting that activates with motion, and in an emergency, I'm supposed to just run and get as far away from the harem as I can."

Tamira peered into the darkness but saw nothing, even with her enhanced immortal vision. "Haven't you ever been tempted to explore it?"

Areana shrugged. "Not really. I'm not a fan of spiders and other creepy-crawlies that I have no doubt this tunnel is full of. And speaking of those unsightly creatures, I'd better close this door before any get in." She went through the sequence in reverse. Ovid pulled out, then Marcus Aurelius pushed back in, Plato, and then Herodotus. Finally, she stepped on the pressure plate again—not the same spot, but a different rose in the pattern, the fifth from the left, same distance from the wall.

"That locks it again," she explained. "Without that final step, the door remains accessible to anyone who pushes on it."

Tamira nodded, her mind running through the sequence again. When the time came, she could get herself and Eluheed through, but the guilt of abandoning her sisters sat heavily in her stomach.

"Thank you for showing me," she said. "This could save lives one day."

"Indeed." Areana smoothed her dress. "We should get to the library before the others send a search party for us."

As they left the suite, Tamira wondered if Areana knew exactly what she'd done. The goddess was far too smart and cautious to accidentally reveal such crucial information. But whether it was a gift, a test, or a trap, Tamira couldn't say.

22

ELUHEED

The morning sun beat down on Eluheed's back as he knelt in his herb garden, but he didn't mind. There was something so soothing about being surrounded by rows of fragrant herbs, the scent of fertile earth, the buzz of insects, the distant sound of waves, and about dipping his hands in the rich soil. Tony worked beside him, less enthusiastic about the dirt under his fingernails but surprisingly still eager to learn about growing things in general and medicinal plants in particular.

"Is this the one you gave me for my headaches?" Tony held up a sprig of feverfew.

"It was one of the herbs." Eluheed patted soil around a newly transplanted sage plant. "It's good for other things as well, but the preparation matters as much as the plant itself. Too strong and you'll cause more problems than you solve."

They'd been working for a couple of hours already, taking advantage of the cooler morning hours, but they would need to call it a day soon, wash up, and join their ladies.

It wasn't a bad life, and if Eluheed didn't have a vow to fulfill and Tamira didn't have a son she wanted to find, there would have been no urgency to find a way to escape this island. It would take many years before people started noticing that he didn't age. His charges could wait as well, and yet Eluheed felt in his bones that time was running out and that he needed to hurry up with the escape plans.

The sound of approaching footsteps made him look up, and he saw a guard striding toward them with purpose.

"The lord requires your presence, shaman," the guard said.

Eluheed set down his trowel. "Right now?"

"Immediately."

"I need to change first." Eluheed gestured at his soil-stained clothes and lifted his hand to show the guard the dirt caked under his fingernails. "Give me five minutes to clean up."

"There's no time. The lord is waiting, and if you know what's good for you, you won't make him wait a second longer than necessary."

"Right." Eluheed rose to his feet, brushing the worst of the dirt from his pants. His hands were hopeless, though, with soil ground into every crease and embedded under each nail.

Tony shot him a sympathetic look. "I'll finish here."

Eluheed nodded, then followed the guard toward the double fence while trying to clean his hands on his already-dirty pants. That only made things worse.

The guard noticed and seemed amused. "The lord couldn't care less about what you look like, shaman."

"I care," Eluheed murmured under his breath.

The guy shrugged and motioned for him to keep going toward the waiting vehicle beyond the second fence.

The driver of the jeep was an immortal, but he wasn't enhanced.

Music from the radio filled the awkward silence, the island's station broadcasting popular tunes that were occasionally interspersed by praises to the magnificent Lord Navuh.

The ruler of this island certainly lived large and had one hell of a god complex.

Eluheed was just grateful that he and the rest of the harem seemed to be exempt from the constant indoctrination bits.

Absentmindedly, he watched the scenery passing by, the beautiful greenery that covered every unclaimed portion of the island, and the construction crews that were still working on the damaged buildings, but his mind was on what Navuh expected him to do.

One option was that the lord wanted a personal session and a vision concerning his future, and the other was that he wanted Eluheed to touch one of the enhanced ones again.

As the jeep entered the underground military complex, the temperature dropped the further down they descended. The fluorescent lights made the dirt on Eluheed's clothes look even darker, more pronounced, but he forced himself not to think about it.

It was what it was.

Navuh waited inside the detention facility, immaculate as always in his black attire. His eyes took in Eluheed's appearance with one sweep, and his mouth twisted in distaste.

"Forgive my appearance, my lord. The guard said that you wanted to see me urgently."

Navuh waved away the apology. "Your appearance is of no consequence. My time is."

"Of course, my lord." Eluheed bowed his head. "Your time is priceless."

"It is." Navuh turned to look at the long row of detention cells. "I need you to take another look at their shared collective. They are still not talking, but they are twitching less and eating more. I wonder if the withdrawal symptoms have eased."

Wouldn't it have been easier to just ask them?

But Eluheed didn't say that. Instead, he dipped his head again. "As you wish, my lord."

Their small procession passed the communal cell where the regular soldiers were kept. These men played cards and talked quietly, seemingly resigned to their imprisonment. But in the isolation wing, the silence was absolute. It was as if there was no one in those cells.

"I want to monitor what's happening with them," Navuh said, stopping at an interrogation room. "And since they are not communicating with their guards or each other, you are the only one who can tell me whether they're planning something or if they're simply escaping somewhere in their heads that we can't access."

Through the reinforced window, Eluheed could see guards preparing the space—bringing in the reinforced chair, checking restraints. His hands clenched involuntarily, driving dirt deeper under his nails.

"The same precautions as before?" he asked.

"Yes. But this time, it's a different soldier. His name is Malak." Navuh gestured to the guards, who left to retrieve the prisoner. "I've learned that he was one of their strategists. Perhaps his mind will be more organized than Nahil's."

When they brought Malak in, the soldier didn't resist the chains, didn't even seem aware of them. His eyes were open but unfocused or perhaps focused on something only he could see.

"He's either in their shared space or his brain is fried," Eluheed observed.

He approached the guy slowly, noting how Malak didn't track his movement. The soldier's breathing was deep and regular, almost hypnotic in its rhythm.

"Malak," Eluheed said.

There was no response.

"I'm going to touch your arm now."

Still nothing. Malak might have been carved from stone.

Eluheed placed his hand on the soldier's forearm, prepared for the violent pull of consciousness he'd experienced before.

Instead, he found himself slipping into something that felt almost peaceful. The transition was smoother this time, like slipping into water instead of being pulled under. The chaos he'd encountered before had evolved into something more organized—still turbulent, but with patterns, currents, and an underlying rhythm.

Another visitor, one of the voices in the void, said.

The bounded one, another said.

He brings the earth with him.

That last thought made Eluheed freeze. In this space, everything about him was more exposed—not just his thoughts but the essence of what clung to him.

Soil. Growing things. Life and death and life again.

He tends the gardens.

More than that. The earth knows him.

The attention of multiple consciousness turned toward him, drawn by something in the soil under his nails, the plant oils on his skin. In the physical world, these were just dirty hands. Here, they carried stories, and these men were hungry for something to occupy their shared mind.

Eluheed reinforced his mental shields, trying to pull back, but the curious presence from before was there again, stronger now.

An old dirt. Much older.

From another place. Not Earth.

Eluheed severed the connection, jerking his hand away from Malak's arm.

The interrogation room slammed back into focus, harsh lights reflecting off concrete, the astringent smell of industrial cleaning products tickling his nostrils.

"What happened?" Navuh demanded. "You pulled away violently."

Eluheed's heart was racing. "It's much less chaotic in there, and they are perceptive." He looked at his hands. "Malak shared with them that he smelled earth on me, and they wanted to find out more. They are bored and hungry for stories."

Navuh's eyes sharpened. "What kind of stories?"

"Anything. They were fascinated by the idea that I work with plants. That I tend gardens." It was true enough, though incomplete. "One consciousness in particular is very curious about external stimuli. It latched on to these details and tried to construct a picture of who I was."

"Could they have learned anything they were not supposed to know?"

Eluheed shook his head. "I disconnected before they could go deeper. But they're definitely evolving. The isolation is allowing them to explore their connection without distraction."

Navuh began his characteristic pacing—three steps one way, three back. "So, they're using the imprisonment to grow their abilities."

"In a way. Without external stimuli, they're turning inward. Or rather, toward each other. If you don't want them to keep doing that, perhaps playing music or showing them movies could be a distraction."

Navuh regarded him with thinly veiled amusement. "I know that you don't believe that. They can tune out exterior stimuli."

Eluheed let out a breath. "Forgive me, my lord. I wasn't thinking clearly. You are absolutely correct. They've found each other in a space where physical conditions are largely irrelevant."

"Then what do you recommend?"

That was a loaded question, and he didn't want to give Navuh an answer that would result in the execution of these men.

The truth was that they were dangerous, and the prudent thing to do would have been just that, but it wasn't Eluheed's responsibility to determine their fate.

"There isn't much to do except to frequently monitor them. They're in a process of becoming, and I assume you would like to understand what they're becoming before the process is complete."

He might have just bought these poor souls a few more days to live.

"Could you do this daily?" Navuh asked.

The thought made Eluheed's gut twist. Each contact risked exposure, especially now that they were becoming more perceptive and more intrusive in their pursuit of entertainment.

"Every other day would be safer, my lord. Repeated exposure might allow them to map me, for lack of a better term. To understand my mental architecture well enough to predict and possibly manipulate it."

Navuh considered this. "You're concerned they could influence you?"

"It's possible. They're learning to work as one mind. Against that unity, an individual consciousness, especially a human one, might be vulnerable."

The lie was wrapped in truth. He was vulnerable, just not in the way Navuh assumed.

"Every other day then," Navuh agreed.

"Thank you, my lord." Eluheed bowed again.

As they walked back through the facility, Navuh seemed contemplative. "What did you mean when you said they wanted stories of the earth you carried?"

Eluheed chose his words carefully. "It was like they were trying to read a book written in a language they only partially understood. They could sense there was meaning there but couldn't quite grasp it."

"Meaning in dirt?"

"Everything carries information, my lord. The soil contains minerals from specific locations, pollen from certain plants, and microscopic life unique to particular environments. To a consciousness that has expanded beyond normal limitations, these details might be significant."

On the drive back to the harem, Eluheed stared at his soil-caked hands and thought about the answer he'd given Navuh. The enhanced soldiers had sensed something about him that was more than skin deep. Somehow, the dirt on his hands created a bridge to his past, which was why he'd ejected so quickly, severing the connection.

He couldn't allow them to find out that he was not human.

23

LOKAN

Lokan stood outside Jeremy's bedroom, watching through the open door as Julian checked the man's temperature.

"It's 102.6," the physician announced, not looking up from his tablet where he logged the second reading he'd taken in the last hour. "It's slowly climbing, but it's not at a level that justifies moving you into the clinic. I can monitor you here until we are sure that you are transitioning."

Jeremy lay propped against a pile of pillows, his face flushed and glistening with sweat, but his eyes were alert and excited. Sitting beside him on the bed, Naomi held his hand, her thumb stroking across his knuckles.

This morning, when Jeremy woke with a headache, no one was sure it was a sign, but by noon the fever had started and everyone's hopes had gone up.

"This is good, right?" Jeremy sounded hopeful and scared

simultaneously. "The fever could mean that I'm transitioning, right?"

It had been just one day since the induction ceremony and Anandur's venom bite, but Jeremy was acting as if he'd been waiting forever for the transition to start. Then again, this hadn't been his first time, so he might have counted the days after the previous attempt.

"It's most likely the start of your transition," Julian said. "But we need to give it more time. Sometimes a simple flu or cold can manifest in the same way."

Lokan shook his head in disbelief. Why had it worked with Anandur's bite and not his? Anandur was just a simple immortal, several generations removed from the source, while Lokan was a three-quarters god. Was it really the ceremony that had made all the difference? Or was there something wrong with his venom?

"Can't you check?" Naomi asked Julian. "I mean to rule out a cold or flu. Can't you measure antibodies or something like that?"

Julian cast her a smile. "There will be antibodies in either case. It's the body's first line of defense."

She nodded even though she wasn't happy with the explanation. "How long until we know?"

"If it follows the typical pattern, the fever will build for another day or two, and other symptoms will start to manifest. Losing consciousness is the best sign."

Jeremy grimaced. "I've heard that, and I can't believe that I am actually looking forward to it."

"Sometimes it doesn't happen." Julian looked at something on his tablet. "You are twenty-five and in good health, which means that the transition shouldn't be dangerous or too difficult for you. You may or may not lose consciousness." The physician put the tablet aside and turned to look at the large group of people assembled in the living room of Jeremy and Naomi's apartment. "This is good news. Let's hope that Spencer and Dylan will soon follow."

Spencer perhaps had a chance, but since Lokan had been the one to induce Dylan again, he doubted it would turn out differently than it had in the two previous attempts just because Kian had performed the proper ceremony. On the other hand, if it worked for Jeremy, it might work for Spencer.

"Can I come in?" Carol asked.

Jeremy nodded. "Of course."

"I'll get out of your way." Julian rose to his feet and collected his things. "You know where to find me in case you need me."

"Thank you, doc," Jeremy said. "Do I need to stay in bed?"

"Not if you don't feel you have to." Julian paused at the door. "But you need to listen to your body and be careful not to exert yourself. Also, don't take anything for the fever. Let your body fight it naturally."

"Yes, doc." Jeremy saluted.

Once Julian left, Carol sat on the chair he had vacated. "How are you feeling?" she asked.

"Achy and feverish like I've got a nasty flu just without the sore throat and runny nose." Jeremy attempted a smile. "I hate being sick."

"You are not sick. At least I hope you're not. We all hope that this is the start of your transformation, and that your dormant genes are activating, rewriting your biology. Immortality is worth a little discomfort."

Spencer entered the room, leaned against the dresser, and crossed his arms over his chest. "I heard you were showing signs," he said. "I came to investigate."

"Can we come in?" Mollie asked.

"The more the merrier." Jeremy motioned for her and James to enter. "This bedroom is big enough for everyone to join, and you all know how much I love attention."

Naomi chuckled. "We do."

"Still nothing for me," Spencer said, trying for casual and missing by a mile.

"Don't give up yet," Carol said. "Everyone's timeline is different. It has only been one day."

"It might never happen," Spencer said. "We need to face that possibility."

An uncomfortable silence settled over the room. They all

knew that not every suspected Dormant carried the godly genes.

"Are congratulations in order?" Onegus asked from the doorway.

"Onegus," Carol said. "I didn't know you were at the keep."

"I was down in the lower levels and heard that good things were happening up here." He walked in and stood next to Jeremy's bed. "How are you feeling?"

"Hopeful," Jeremy said. "The rest is irrelevant."

The chief had probably come from the dungeon, but the paranormals weren't supposed to know about that level of the keep and what was going on in there.

"It might be just a bug," Lokan said.

"Or not," Spencer muttered under his breath.

Onegus cast him a consoling glance. "If anyone wants to go for another round, I'm volunteering my services."

"I've gone through the induction three times." Spencer shook his head. "I don't think there is any point in trying again."

"Roni had five different inducers," Onegus said. "And that included me, Anandur, and Brundar. The one who finally succeeded was Kian, but it was more thanks to Roni's improved health than the quality of Kian's venom. I know that all of you have gone through health screening, but you never know what else could be preventing the transition from starting. If it doesn't happen for you in the next couple of days, I suggest that you wait a week or two and try again."

Carol shifted in the chair. "Maybe it's not just about the health of the inductee or the potency of the inductor. Maybe it's also about compatibility."

Lokan tried not to glare at his mate. It was sweet of her to try to protect his ego, but her attempt at shifting blame away from him was so transparent that it was embarrassing.

"Is that a thing?" Dylan asked. "Compatibility between venom and recipient? Julian never mentioned it."

"We don't know," Carol said. "But what we do know is that some Dormants who don't respond to one immortal's venom transition successfully with another's."

Spencer glanced between Onegus and Lokan, looking skeptical.

"It's worth trying," Lokan said, pushing down his pride. "What matters is the result, not whose venom achieves it."

Carol cast him an encouraging smile that further annoyed him. He didn't want her pity or her protection. He wasn't a fragile teen who needed his ego stroked by his girlfriend. He was a millennia-old immortal who'd fought in more battles than the chief of Guardians had read about.

Spencer walked over to Jeremy's bedside. "I'm counting on you. Show us it can be done."

Jeremy clasped Spencer's offered hand. "You're next. I can feel it."

It was the kind of baseless optimism that should have annoyed Lokan, but somehow it didn't. This was different than Carol's attempts at protecting his ego. This was about providing hope, even if it wasn't grounded in realistic probability.

24

TAMIRA

The dining room hummed with conversation as Tamira and her sisters gathered for dinner.

Areana was absent as usual, her chair at the head of the table sitting empty like a throne without its queen. Her breakfasts and dinners were taken with her mate, and she only joined them for lunch.

Tula, who always sat on Areana's right, was picking at her food and looking either angry or depressed. Sitting next to her, Tony looked like a clueless male who had no idea how to make his partner feel better and was probably wondering what he had done wrong. Tula had a bit of a temper, or a lot, if Tamira cared to be truthful. She might have gotten angry at something trivial that Tony had done or said, and it wouldn't be the first time.

However, there were also other signs that indicated a much more serious issue. It was the wine glass that sat untouched in front of her, the frequency of her hand landing on her stomach, and resting there for a split second before being quickly removed with an accompanying grimace.

The female was expecting, and by now, all the ladies suspected it, but Tony still seemed oblivious.

Across the table, Sarah and Beulah exchanged a meaningful glance, and Raviki nodded as if to cast her vote alongside them. They all saw it, but none dared speak it aloud.

"The beef smells wonderful," Liliat said, filling the awkward silence as servants placed dishes on the table.

It was at that moment that the lights above flickered, and the hum of the air conditioning stopped. The emergency lights came on right on cue, but then everything came back online, and the meager emergency lights turned off.

"When are they going to fix this finally?" Raviki asked. "It has been going on since we returned to the harem."

Sarah waved a dismissive hand. "It was happening in the mansion as well, but the emergency generator always clicked in before we even noticed it. I don't know why the harem can't have the same generator. The one they installed here is crappy."

"They are replacing it," Tony said. "I spoke with Hassan today, and he said that Lord Navuh managed to secure a big electrical contractor from India. They are going to replace the main transformer and most of the emergency generators on the island. Hassan is excited to see it being done."

Tamira wondered how Navuh was managing the memories of all the contractors and their crews. Half the island needed rebuilding, and more human crews were arriving daily to do the repairs. She hoped Navuh wasn't planning just to kill them all like he had done with the people who had built this island sanctuary a century ago.

Not that she knew for a fact that was what he had done, but she suspected it. Navuh had little regard for human life, and if it were more expeditious and less complicated to kill them off rather than let them go and compel their silence, he would have killed them with no compunction.

Naturally, that wasn't as easy to do these days as it had been then, and crews disappearing wouldn't go unnoticed, so he would have to compel them this time.

"You don't look that good." Raviki frowned at Tula. "Are you sleeping okay?"

"Not really." Tula's response was clipped. "I keep having nightmares and can't sleep. I'm tired and cranky."

That sounded like a reasonable explanation after what they had all been through, but Tamira had a feeling that Tula was lying to cover the real reason for her bad mood and exhausted appearance.

The sound of the dining room door opening had Tamira look up, and as Eluheed walked in, she welcomed him with a bright smile.

"You're late," she admonished.

"I know." He pulled out the chair next to her. "Lord Navuh summoned me straight from the herb garden, covered in dirt and sweat, and I returned only a short while ago, showered, changed, and rushed over here, hoping to still grab something to eat. I'm starving."

"You look exhausted." She took his plate and started piling it with food. "What did he make you do?"

He cast her an apologetic look. "I can't really share that."

She'd forgotten that those kinds of conversations needed to wait for them to be alone.

"Of course." She put the plate in front of him. "My apologies."

"Thank you." He accepted the plate with a grateful nod and attacked the food with gusto.

Unlike Eluheed, Tula was still shoving food around her plate, and Tony kept shooting concerned glances at her. His obvious worry made Tula withdraw further, focusing intently on cutting her meat into increasingly smaller pieces without eating any of it.

"You've done a beautiful job in the indoor courtyard." Liliat looked at Eluheed and then at Tony. "I sat on the bench during our break today, and everything looked so real that I could almost forget that I wasn't outside, and that the sunlight was fake." She chuckled. "The illusion stuttered when the light flickered again. It happens so many times during the day that I barely even notice it anymore, but the indoor garden doesn't have emergency lighting, and I sat in the dark. Luckily, Raviki had forgotten to close the drapes in her suite, and the emergency lighting from her room cast a little light on the garden. The outage only lasted a few seconds, but it was a reminder of the artificial environment we live in."

"Nothing here is real," Tula murmured. "I mean the fake sunlight never looks real."

"The plants are real," Tony offered, trying to be helpful. "They grow and bloom just like they would aboveground."

"Are you sure about that?" Tula's voice carried an edge. "Wouldn't they bloom better if they were out in the real world? Perhaps they can't reach their full potential because they are trapped underground with lamps coaxing their growth instead of real sunshine."

"Are we still talking about plants?" Liliat asked.

"Plants adapt," Eluheed said quietly. "They find ways to thrive even in artificial environments. Life is remarkably resilient and persistent."

Tula let out a breath. "Ignore me. I'm cranky and tired."

Tony reached for Tula's hand, but she pulled away. "Excuse me. I need to take a nap before I destroy everyone's mood." She didn't even wait for Tony before she bolted out of the dining room.

An uncomfortable silence followed her exit.

"Should someone...?" Raviki started.

"Give her time," Sarah advised. "You know how she gets

sometimes. The more you try to talk to her, the more her mood will sour. She needs to be alone."

Tony stood. "I should go to her."

"No," Beulah said. "We've known her for much longer than you have. Tula needs her space. She'll come to you when she's in a better mood."

Tony sat back down even though he could have gone to his own room. He and Eluheed still had their own rooms even though they rarely stayed there, so it wasn't as if Tony didn't have somewhere to go.

The rest of the meal passed in stilted conversation, everyone pretending not to notice Tony's distress.

When they finally retreated to their rooms, Tamira let out a breath as soon as Eluheed closed the door behind them. "That was awkward."

"Does Tula often get like that?" Eluheed asked.

Tamira nodded even though this time it wasn't about Tula's volatile, habitual moods. This time, she had a good reason to be upset.

"Did the lord summon you to connect to the enhanced soldiers?" she asked in a whisper.

Eluheed nodded. "They're evolving rapidly," he whispered back. "The change from when I saw them last is startling." He moved to sit on the couch.

She joined him, taking his hand and putting her head on

his shoulder so she could whisper directly into his ear. "In what way are they evolving?"

"They are becoming more coherent. They also sensed things about me today. The soil under my fingernails fascinated them. They wanted to know more about me. They are bored."

"Well, that's obvious. They are being kept in isolation with nothing to do."

"They are not idle. They keep working on improving their network." He rubbed his face with his free hand. "They're becoming more perceptive. Each contact is more dangerous than the last, and Lord Navuh wants me to repeat this every other day. He wanted me to do it every day, but I managed to convince him to let me rest between encounters."

Tamira squeezed his hand and leaned closer to his ear so he would hear her soft whispers. "We need to leave before they discover what you are. I got Areana to show me how to enter the tunnel. She showed me the disarming sequence."

His eyes widened. "Just like that? How did you convince her to do that?"

"First, I got her to admit that the tunnel existed, then I told her that all the ladies should know about it in case of an emergency, when leaving the harem through the pavilion is not possible. If we are attacked or if there is a fire, the tunnel might save our lives. Areana agreed and took me to show me where the entrance is. She said that if there was an emergency, we shouldn't worry about the alarm, and just open the door, but she didn't put in any real effort to conceal the disarming sequence."

Tamira described the hidden door behind the bookshelf, the specific books that needed to be pulled out, and the pressure plates in the carpet pattern.

"Third rose from the left, a third of a meter from the wall," she repeated. "Herodotus, Plato, Marcus Aurelius, then Ovid pushed instead of pulled. I memorized it as Heroes Plot Military Overthrows," Tamira reiterated.

He smiled. "Clever."

"It is, right? The sequence needs to be completed within thirty seconds of stepping on the pressure plate, so there is no time for hesitation."

"That sounds easy enough. All mechanical triggers instead of electrical ones, which is smart. As we know from experience, electricity on the island is not reliable, and that's even more true in the case of an emergency like a fire or an attack on the harem." He was quiet for a moment. "She really let you see all of this?"

"She made a perfunctory effort to hide it, but I think she wanted me to know the sequence."

"Why would she do that?"

Tamira had been wondering the same thing. "Maybe she just wanted someone else to know in case of emergency."

"Or maybe it's a test," Eluheed suggested. "To see if you'll betray her trust."

That thought made Tamira's stomach clench. "Areana isn't that calculating."

"She's survived five thousand years as Navuh's mate. She has to be calculating."

He was right, of course. Areana's survival depended on navigating Navuh's moods, managing the harem, and keeping everyone safe while maintaining the illusion of perfect loyalty. She was a master manipulator by necessity.

"Even so, we know how to get into the tunnel now."

"Yes, but that only solves one problem." Eluheed's expression darkened. "The tunnel will have surveillance cameras. The moment we enter, Navuh will know."

The brief flame of hope in Tamira's chest guttered out. "Of course. I should have thought of that."

Every step forward seemed to reveal two more obstacles. The tunnel existed, they could access it, but they still couldn't use it.

"There has to be a way," she said, though the words sounded hollow even to her.

"There has to be." Eluheed pulled her against him, but she felt the defeat in his posture. "We will figure it out."

"How?"

His arms tightened around her. "We will find a way."

She knew he didn't mean a word of that and was just saying it to keep her from despairing.

"We will because the alternative is accepting this forever, and I can't do that. Not anymore." She thought of Tula's words at dinner. "This plant wants to experience growing free."

"You will," he said with no conviction at all in his voice.

She had to revitalize him somehow, to offer him hope even if she felt hopeless.

"What if we use the enhanced soldiers?" she whispered. "What if we could somehow use their evolution as a distraction? If they become coherent enough to act, even from their cells, Navuh would have to focus all his attention on containing them."

Eluheed shook his head. "I can't control them. I can barely maintain my own identity when I touch their consciousness."

"You don't need to control them. Just... nudge them maybe? Give them an idea?"

He opened his mouth, then closed it. "That's incredibly dangerous."

"Everything we do is dangerous." She took his hands. "Living here is dangerous. Loving each other is dangerous. Trying to escape is a choice, which is not something we get to do here."

He was quiet for a long moment. "The enhanced soldiers creating a distraction does not solve the problem of the cameras in the tunnel."

"It might. Knowing Navuh, he doesn't let anyone monitor that tunnel so they won't discover his escape route, and if he was busy with some emergency, he wouldn't think of looking at the feed from the tunnel."

"What if there is an alarm as soon as someone enters it?"

"Then we enter as soon as he leaves in the morning. Even with a vehicle, it must take him at least half an hour to get to his mansion, and during that time, someone is in the tunnel."

The despair in Eluheed's eyes turned into calculation. "If the tunnel is narrow, which it probably is, he can't turn around until he reaches the other end. It might give us enough time to escape."

25

ELUHEED

Eluheed had said all the things that Tamira needed to hear, but he hadn't truly believed in them until she started providing real solutions and shaming him into action.

He'd been so affected by the encounter with the enhanced ones that he was starting to suspect they were somehow sucking out his energy. He wasn't the type to give up easily, and yet he'd allowed himself to feel hopeless for a few moments.

Tamira put a hand on his arm. "I've never asked you to do this before because I know how much it takes out of you, and I know it's not fair to ask it of you today, but can you summon a vision about my future the same way you did for Lord Navuh?"

"Tamira…" He turned his gaze up and scanned the walls and the ceiling to remind her that what they said in there wasn't private, and she hadn't kept her voice low enough.

She stood and tugged on his hand. "I feel like soaking in the tub. Care to join me?"

He knew she wanted them to have privacy, and the bathroom seemed safer than the bedroom, although they had no proof of that. The safest was outside, far into the gardens surrounding the harem, but it was obvious that Tamira didn't want to wait until tomorrow. She wanted him to see her future now.

After she closed the bathroom door behind them, he waited for her to start the water for the tub. "That's not how the visions work, Tamira." He sat on the tub's ledge.

"Why not?" She sat on the ledge next to him and took his hands, her grip firm and warm. "You've had visions about others. About Navuh, about the enhanced soldiers. Why not about me?"

Eluheed let out a long breath, feeling the familiar burden of his gift—or curse, depending on the day. "Visions don't work well for loved ones. The emotional connection interferes. It clouds things. What I might see could be wishful thinking rather than true sight."

"Or it could be real." Her fingers tightened around his. "Please, Eluheed. I need something to hold on to. Even if it's uncertain, even if it might be your wishful thinking, I need something positive. To know there's a possibility of something out there for me. For us."

He wanted to say that there was no guarantee his vision would provide anything good, but studying her face and seeing the desperation she was trying so hard to hide behind determination, his resolve faltered.

If he saw something that could lift her spirits, he would tell her, and if he saw their plans failing, he would lie and say that he had seen nothing. To lie went against his religion, but he had already misled people and told untruths so many times since his arrival on Earth over a thousand years ago that one more lie wouldn't matter. As it was, he was guaranteed to end up in the seven hells of purification after he died and not in Sacred Dolis.

"Even if I see something, there's no guarantee that it's a future that will come to pass. Visions show possibilities, not certainties. Sometimes they show what might happen if we do nothing. Sometimes they show what could happen if we act. There's no way to know which."

"I understand." But her eyes said she needed this anyway, needed even the illusion of hope if that was all he could offer.

Eluheed leaned over to release some of the water that had accumulated in the tub so they could keep it running and cover up their conversation. When most of the water had emptied, he closed the drain again and took hold of Tamira's hands. "I need you to be very still and very quiet and wait until I let go of you."

When she nodded, Eluheed closed his eyes and let his consciousness drift, loosening the careful controls he usually maintained. Summoning visions hadn't been part of his shamanic training. It was something that had shown up in his family once in a few generations—a gift from a distant ancestor that had been blessed or cursed with a prophetic ability. Still, the gift hadn't manifested until after he'd been trained as a shaman, the training helping him access the veil between present and future, between what was and what might be, and peer through it.

At first, there was nothing but the familiar darkness behind his eyelids, the sound of Tamira's breathing, the warmth of her hands in his. He pushed deeper, past the surface thoughts that cluttered his mind, seeking that deeper current where visions swam like dreams drifting in the void.

The shift came suddenly, as it always did. One moment, he was sitting on the edge of a bathtub in Tamira's quarters, and the next, he was elsewhere.

The noise hit him first. Not the controlled hum of the harem or the chaos of the island's construction, but something vast and overwhelming. Horns blaring, voices calling out in multiple languages, music spilling from doorways, the rumble of relentless traffic.

The vision sharpened, bringing details into focus.

Massive screens blazed with advertisements, their light turning night into perpetual twilight. Buildings stretched impossibly tall, their windows reflecting the chaos below in fractured patterns. And the people, so many people, streams of humanity flowing in every direction, each absorbed in their own urgent journey, overwhelming, pressing.

Times Square.

He recognized it from movies, though he'd never been there himself. New York City, that monument to human ambition and excess, alive and thriving with more energy than seemed possible.

And there, in the midst of it all, he saw her.

Tamira.

But not as she was now. This Tamira wore modern clothing, dark jeans that fit her perfectly, and a soft sweater in deep burgundy that complemented her olive skin. Her hair was a little shorter, styled in soft curls that spilled below her shoulders but not down her back as it did now.

Her arm was threaded through that of a man who wasn't Eluheed, and she was gazing adoringly at him as he explained something with animated hand gestures.

For a moment, a haze of jealousy threatened to burn through the vision, but then Eluheed noticed that their hair color was identical. When the man turned and looked right at him, or rather, through his vision, Eluheed saw that his eyes were the same shade of dark blue as Tamira's. The resemblance was undeniable, and he realized that he was looking at her son.

This was Darien.

Tamira's son lived, and given the expensive clothes he wore with casual ease, he was thriving. He moved through the crowd with the confidence of someone who belonged there, and when he looked at Tamira, there was love in his eyes. He knew she was his mother, had accepted her, and had chosen to have her in his life.

She was free. They both were.

The vision held for another moment, letting him see the small details. The expensive-looking watch on Darien's wrist, his polished shoes, the ring that some men wore as a symbol of graduating from a certain university or belonging to a certain club or an association—all those were clues that might help them find Darien. Then it began to fade, the lights of Times Square dimming, the sounds muffling, until—

Eluheed gasped, his consciousness slamming back into his body with enough force to make him sway. Tamira's hands gripped his almost painfully, her eyes searching his face.

"What did you see?" she asked.

He had to take several breaths before he could speak, his mind still reeling from the transition. "I saw you and Darien in New York. Times Square, specifically."

Her eyes widened. "I was with my son?"

Grinning, Eluheed nodded. "I saw him, and he was alive and free, living in New York. And you were with him, which means that you are going to get out of here. Our escape is going to work."

The joy that transformed Tamira's face was almost painful to witness. She pressed her free hand to her mouth, tears starting to spill down her cheeks. "Are you sure it was him?"

"The resemblance was unmistakable. The same eyes, the same mannerisms. And the way he was with you—he knew you, loved you. You somehow found each other."

"Oh." The word was more sob than speech. She released his hands to wrap her arms around herself, rocking slightly as she processed what he'd told her. "He's alive. Free. We were together."

Eluheed watched her joy, and he was happy for her, but she hadn't asked the obvious question yet. She would in a moment or two, and then her happiness would diminish.

It came sooner than he'd hoped.

The elation in her expression dimmed, her eyes focusing on his with sudden sharpness. "Wait. You said I was with Darien. Where were you?"

He tried to keep his face neutral, but she knew him too well.

"You weren't there." Her voice had gone flat, all the joy draining away. "In this vision of my freedom, my reunion with my son—you weren't there."

"The vision was about your future," he said. "They usually focus on one person, showing what matters most to them. My absence doesn't mean that I didn't make it out. I could have been somewhere else while you were enjoying New York with Darien."

"Stop." She stood abruptly, pacing away from him before spinning back. "Don't lie to me."

Did she know how grievous an insult it was to hear her accuse him of lying?

She should because he'd told her, but she was emotional right now and thinking in human terms, or rather, immortal terms. Neither had a problem with deception, and some elevated it to an art form.

"I'm not lying," he said as calmly as he could. "I'm telling you that visions are incomplete by nature. They show fragments, moments. I might have been somewhere else in the city. I might have been the one who helped you find him. I might have been fulfilling my other obligations. Don't read too much into this."

Still, even as he said it, he knew she heard the hollow ring in his words. None of them were meant to deceive, and they might have been true, but the vision had felt complete in the way true visions did—not showing everything, but showing what mattered. Tamira and her son, free in the world, building a relationship that had been stolen from them.

Without Eluheed.

He leaned over to drain some of the water again, but before he had a chance to re-plug the tub, Tamira moved to sit on the edge next to him and took his hands. "I won't accept a future without you. If the vision shows me free but alone, then we change it. We make a different future."

"Some things can't be changed," he said. "Maybe my part in this story is to get you free. Maybe that's enough."

"Enough?" Her voice rose with indignation. "How can you think I'd want freedom and a new life without you in it?"

He wanted to comfort her, to agree that they'd find another way, but the vision had felt true in a way he couldn't deny. And perhaps it was better this way. If setting her free cost him his life, wasn't that a price worth paying?

She would have her son, her freedom, a chance at the life that had been stolen from her. But even as he thought it, Eluheed remembered his obligation. His precious charges. His sacred duty to protect them, to one day return them to his people. If he died on this island, who would recover them? Who would complete the mission that had brought him to this world in the first place?

No. He couldn't accept death as the price of Tamira's freedom. Not because he feared it, but because his duty extended beyond this world. His charges were the key to his people's survival. He was their guardian, the only one who knew their location, and the only one who could bring them home.

"I have to survive," he said, the realization hitting him with unexpected force. "I have to complete my mission." He couldn't tell her everything, couldn't break the oaths that sealed his lips about the true nature of his tasks, but he could give her something. "Remember what I told you about why I came to Earth? The sacred treasures I was meant to protect?"

She nodded.

"If I don't make it out of here, they'll remain lost forever. My people need them. Someday, somehow, I have to complete my mission and bring them home, which means that I have to survive, find a way to retrieve what was buried, and find a way home."

She was quiet for a long moment and then nodded. "We both have to survive. We both have to be free. The vision showed me with Darien, but that's just because you were busy somewhere else and the vision you summoned was about me."

"It's possible," he said, but there wasn't much conviction in his voice.

She shook her head. "Remember the first time we spoke? When I willed you to come to me, and my wish manifested?"

He smiled. "I do."

"I will do it again. I will hold this vision you've given me close to my heart and imagine it manifesting, but I will not stop there. I will imagine you bravely searching for your charges and finding them." She stroked her thumbs across his cheekbones. "I'll make it happen."

Despite his reservations, Eluheed believed her. It was impossible not to. That ferocious willpower of hers would make her dreams manifest.

He smiled. "If anyone can make a dream become a reality, it is you."

Her return smile was brilliant. "Darien is alive. He's free. He's living in New York, of all places. That means Kalugal must have helped him establish himself there. It means there's a whole network of escaped Brotherhood members who've built lives outside Navuh's reach. That means we will have help once we get out of here."

Tamira was right. He hadn't considered the implications, but Darien's presence in New York and his obvious comfort there suggested an established life. Resources. Connections.

"If we can find them," Tamira continued, her voice gaining strength, "they can help us find your treasure. Kalugal is Navuh's son, so he must be smart and resourceful. He also knows how his father thinks and how the Brotherhood operates, enough to remain hidden through all these years. He could be invaluable in keeping us safe from Navuh."

"First, we need to escape," he said. "Then we have to find Darien and his friends without Navuh tracking us. Then we have to convince them to help us."

She smiled again. "I'll just add it to my wish list and make it manifest."

He wanted to share her optimism, but the combined challenges tempered his. The enhanced soldiers' growing awareness, their potential ability to penetrate his mental shields, the cameras in the tunnel, and the submarine they might not know how to operate. Those were all serious impediments that might thwart their escape.

26

KIAN

Kian stood with his coffee mug in hand, looking through his office windows down at the village square below, where his people were gathering at the outdoor café. Beyond, the playground still stood empty, the swings and the jungle gym awaiting their little enthusiasts.

It had been peaceful for a while now, and that worried him.

In his experience, a long period of quiet usually preceded a storm of spectacular proportions, and he wondered if Kalugal's ambitious island project would be the catalyst.

Building an army under Navuh's nose, on an island just a little over a hundred miles away from his, was daring to say the least, but Kian couldn't argue with the obvious advantages. With Lokan finally jumping ship, the clan had lost their eyes and ears in the Brotherhood's stronghold, and having a base so close opened up new surveillance possibilities.

Other than that, the paranormal project was still proceeding, albeit with mixed results, but Kian didn't anticipate any problems on that front. The female spy corps that Carol was training showed promise, but since it was just in its initial stages and not operational yet, he didn't expect any trouble from there either.

The unusually quiet period of time allowed him to catch up on piles of neglected work, and he even had made dinner reservations for him and Syssi at By Invitation Only for tonight. Hopefully, nothing would happen to interfere with their plans.

Taking another sip of coffee, Kian watched a group of Guardians emerge from the pavilion and head for the café. They had also been taking it easy lately, which was perfectly fine. They needed a break just like everyone else.

As his phone buzzed on the desk behind him, he turned from the window, and when he picked it up, he saw Kalugal's picture on the display.

"Good morning." Kian put his mug down and sat down behind his desk.

"It is." Kalugal's voice carried its usual mix of dry humor and a tinge of superiority. "But I suppose that depends on one's definition of good. Mine was excellent because Darius gave me a big hug before heading out with Jacki. What made your morning good, cousin?"

"The same." Kian thought about Allegra twirling in her new dress and then running up to him at full speed, knowing he would catch her, and then the triple hug with his wife and daughter. "There is nothing better than family."

"I agree," Kalugal said. "But back to our business, I wanted to tell you that I'll be flying out to the island in three weeks. Jade, Phinas, and Drova will be accompanying me. I wondered if you would like to join us."

Kian was curious, and if Syssi was game, he might take Kalugal up on his offer. Combining a family vacation with work was not a bad idea.

"Where will you be staying?"

"We have most of the buildings renovated by now, and furniture will be delivered by the time we get there. I wouldn't have suggested for you to come if I didn't have proper accommodations ready."

"If I come, it will be with Syssi, Allegra, and a cadre of Guardians. Do you have space for all of us?"

Kian would have liked to invite Turner and Bridget as well, and get their opinion on the island, but that could wait for a later visit.

Kalugal was quiet for a long moment. "If Syssi and Allegra come, I'll bring Jacki and Darius, and that means I will have to bring along a cadre of guards as well."

"We can share the security detail," Kian offered.

"True. Let me check with Jacki, and I'll get back to you on that."

"Same here. I don't know if Syssi can take a break from the university."

Kalugal chuckled. "Her boss is your sister. I'm sure something can be arranged."

"That's not necessarily true. If the lab has important tests scheduled for that time, Amanda might have a problem with letting Syssi go."

"We can fly out Friday night and return Sunday evening," Kalugal suggested. "The jet lag will be bad, though. It's not a problem for us, but the kids might have trouble adjusting."

Darius might struggle because he was still human, but Allegra had already transitioned thanks to Annani's blood, and her sleep needs had changed accordingly. Still, Kian wasn't going to share that information with his cousin. The goddess's blood only helped little dormant girls transition. It didn't work on boys. Darius would have to stay human until he was old enough to fight an immortal and be induced the traditional way.

"Kids are resilient," he said instead. "I wonder about your timing, though. The first human recruits aren't scheduled to arrive for another month. I thought you would want to be there for that."

"I don't. Jade and Phinas are bringing Drova, and she can handle the compulsion with ease. She's as strong a compeller as I am, if not stronger. The three of them will make sure that everything is properly prepared. What I want to do is verify that the living quarters and training facilities are ready for the recruits and get a general feel for the place." He snorted. "Didn't you always want an island like Navuh's? Maybe we can one day turn it into the clan's sanctuary."

"No, thank you." Kian lifted the coffee mug and took a sip. "I don't want my people anywhere near the Brotherhood. What about the exoskeletons? How many are ready for training?"

"We'll have ten functional exoskeleton units ready for testing when the recruits arrive. The training simulators are already installed and operational."

Kalugal was exceptionally efficient. When he put his mind to something, he got it done faster and better than anyone could. It was scary to think that his father was the same way or better.

"There's one problem," Kalugal continued. "The power requirements, which exceed the capacity of what the current facility can generate. We're installing additional generators, but long-term, we need to consider alternative energy sources. Can the firm that installed the mini nuclear reactor in the village install one on the island?"

"I'll check, but we will probably need to provide transportation. It's not something that you can easily put on a commercial ship or even easily export out of the country."

"That's why I'm leaving this to you," Kalugal said. "I don't have the right connections."

Kian chuckled. "And you are admitting that?"

"I have no problem admitting that I need help or accepting it, cousin. That's something that you struggle with."

"I do not." Kian let out a breath. "On some things I do. By the way, have you made any progress finding Darien?"

There was a pause. "Your mother told you about that?"

"Of course. She takes Areana's requests seriously and makes sure they are honored."

"I have an excellent private investigator working on it. Preston King is known as the best, but so far, he has had no luck. Darien must have changed his name and obtained a new identity. We have his old passport photo, and Preston is using facial recognition software to search for matches, but we both know that it is quite easy to manipulate images to avoid detection, especially when someone is deliberately trying to stay under the radar."

"It's to be expected. Darien is probably still hiding from the Brotherhood. Maybe ask William to run the photo through our resources? I suspect that we may have access to better data and software than your guy could ever hope for," Kian offered.

"I didn't want to bother Roni when he's so busy, but I will do that if Preston fails to find him." Kalugal sighed. "The other possibilities are less optimistic. He might have been found by Brotherhood operatives years ago or got killed some other way."

"I hope he's alive," Kian said. "It would mean a lot to both our mothers, even if Areana can't tell Tamira about her findings."

"I know. I'll call you after I speak with Jacki."

"Please do. I'll speak with Syssi."

Kian had barely set the phone down when it rang again, and this time it was Kalugal's brother.

"Good morning, Lokan," Kian answered. "I heard the good news about Jeremy."

"Did Julian call you?"

"He did. He said Jeremy's fever is holding steady and he's showing all the classic signs of transition."

"He's still conscious," Lokan said, and there was something in his voice—relief mixed with something else. Vindication, perhaps? "His temperature has been hovering around thirty-nine degrees Celsius for the past twelve hours. Julian says that's good for someone his age and level of health."

"Excellent. How are Spencer and Dylan taking it?"

There was a pause, and Kian could practically feel Lokan's mood shift through the phone. "Not well. They are disappointed, but not ready to call it quits yet. Onegus has volunteered to induce them, and they both seemed happy to accept his offer."

Kian doubted another attempt would prove more effective than the preceding ones, but he wasn't about to voice that opinion. "It's nice of Onegus to offer. He's a busy guy. When does he plan to do it?"

"He said they should wait a couple of weeks."

"Based on what?"

"He mentioned Roni and how long it took him and how many trials he went through. I think Onegus just wanted to give them hope."

"Hope is important," Kian said, though privately he wondered if false hope was crueler than acceptance. "Let them try again if they want to. We're in no rush to end the program. Keep me updated on the inductions."

"I will."

After Lokan hung up, Kian returned to the window. The square was busier now, with more people arriving at the café, others heading toward their respective duties for the day. A regular Friday morning in their hidden sanctuary, peaceful and productive.

So why did he still feel like he was waiting for something to go wrong?

27

RUVON

As Ruvon strode along the path on his way to Arezoo's home, the box containing the ring felt much heavier in his pocket than it should, its outline too noticeable. He would have to keep his hand in the same pocket at all times to prevent Arezoo and her family from guessing what it was until he was ready to reveal its contents.

It reminded him of another evening just like this one and another jewelry box that had felt like a radioactive rock, even though it hadn't been an engagement ring or anything as presumptuous. That gift had led to a heart-to-heart conversation with Arezoo about their hopes and aspirations, which had in turn prompted him to level up his courtship. He intended to give Arezoo everything she desired, but to do so, their relationship had to become official, and her family needed to accept him.

The problem was that he wasn't sure whether he was

supposed to give Arezoo the ring right after her mother gave them her blessing.

If Soraya gave it.

"Assume the win," he murmured. "She will approve."

Perhaps it would be better to propose to Arezoo on a separate occasion and then give her the ring? He would play it by ear, as the saying went. If it didn't feel right, he would just keep it in his pocket and wait for a better opportunity.

The problem was that he wasn't great at reading cues. He would probably mess it up and pull the ring out at the worst time.

As he stopped in front of Arezoo's house, Ruvon looked at the ridiculously large bouquet of pink roses he was holding with one hand and the paper bag with three bottles of wine in the other. Would three be enough? Arezoo's family was large, but the kids didn't drink wine, so it should be okay.

"Are you planning to stand out here all night?" said a familiar voice from behind him.

Ruvon turned toward its owner, finding Max and Kyra walking toward him. He should have been aware of their approach, but he'd been too preoccupied to notice. Luckily, the village was safe, and he didn't need to fear an ambush.

"I'm gathering courage," he admitted.

Max clapped him on the shoulder. "You've been invited to a family dinner, not a match with a dragon."

Ruvon cocked a brow. "Are you sure about that?" He didn't want to say that facing Soraya felt very much like facing a dragon.

Kyra laughed. "At least Soraya doesn't breathe fire." She looked elegant in a deep blue dress that complemented her dark hair. Despite being the eldest of the sisters, her early transition into immortality made her appear the youngest, which was a little confusing. "Let's go in and not make everyone wait for us."

"We are early," Max pointed out. "There is no rush."

"There is no reason to stand out here either." She walked up to the front door and simply pushed it open without bothering to knock or ring the bell.

Max cast Ruvon a sidelong glance, shrugged, and followed in his mate's footsteps.

Fortunately, Soraya had not materialized at the doorway, so Ruvon felt a little less trepidation about walking in.

The living room of Arezoo's home had been transformed. The couch and chairs had been pushed against the wall to make room for the long dining table that was probably comprised of several smaller ones. Candles flickered along its center, interspersed with small vases of wild-flowers. The entire family was there, from four-year-old Cyra to Soraya herself, who sat at the head of the table like a queen holding court.

Arezoo stood near the kitchen, helping her younger cousin with something, and when she looked up and saw him, her face lit up with a smile that made his chest swell with the first full breath in a while. She wore a green dress he'd never seen before, her dark hair falling in soft waves around her shoulders.

"Ruvon!" Several of the younger children called out his name, having gotten used to his presence over the past months. "What did you bring?"

"Flowers for the lady of the house and wine for everyone else who is over eighteen."

Their small faces fell.

"Nothing for us?" Rohan asked.

"Not today, but I promise to get you something the next time."

"I'll take these," Arezoo offered. "Although I don't know if we have a vase large enough to contain them."

"You can split them into two," her mother suggested, then shifted her gaze to Ruvon. "Come, take a seat." She motioned to the chair on her left. The one on her right was not occupied, and Ruvon assumed it was where Arezoo would be sitting.

"Thank you for inviting me to dinner, Soraya."

She always insisted he call her by her given name and not the one belonging to her estranged husband.

She nodded. "You are welcome and thank you for the flowers. They are lovely."

He pulled out the three bottles of wine, put them in equal intervals along the table, and then sat down.

"I want Ruvon to sit next to me!" Rohan pouted.

"You can bug Ruvon after dinner," Yasmin said. "Tonight, Ruvon is sitting next to Aunt Soraya. They have important matters to discuss." She winked at him.

It seemed that everyone knew what this dinner was about. In a way, it was a relief. He wouldn't surprise anyone when he asked Soraya for her blessing.

As everyone settled into their places, Rana and Parisa carried the food out with help from the older children. The spread was magnificent—herb rice with tahdig, kebabs, chicken legs, beef chunks in some sort of fragrant sauce, root vegetables, and several salads, some of them made with fermented vegetables and others with fresh. It was a feast that must have taken all day to prepare.

"Everything looks and smells incredible," Ruvon said.

"Maman and Aunt Rana cooked all day," Laleh informed him. "Arezoo helped too, but Maman kept making her redo things because she was distracted."

"I was not distracted," Arezoo protested. "I'm just not as practiced as Maman."

"You nearly spilled the rice," Donya pointed out with sisterly glee. "Maman almost fainted."

"I did not," Soraya protested. "We would have just made more."

The familial teasing helped ease some of Ruvon's tension. This felt more like other family dinners at Arezoo's home, warm and chaotic rather than formal and intimidating.

"So, Ruvon," Soraya said as plates were being filled, her tone conversational but her eyes sharp. "Tell us a little about your work."

On Kyra's advice, he'd prepared for this question, practicing his answer until it felt natural. "The field of surveillance equipment keeps evolving, so I need to be on top of things to ensure that Kalugal has the latest and the best. I'm constantly learning."

"That's good," Soraya said. "Success in life depends on the ability to learn new things. Whoever stagnates is left behind."

"A hundred percent." Ruvon reached for the wine bottle next to him and uncorked it. "Wine?"

Soraya nodded. "Yes, please."

Given where they had come from, drinking wine was another small rebellion on the sisters' part, another shackle broken. The changes were not dramatic, but they were constant and progressing.

He poured her the wine, then looked at Arezoo, who nodded.

"Just a little. I don't want my mother to think that you are a bad influence on me."

The table had gone quiet, even the younger children sensing the shift in atmosphere.

"Oops," Donya said from a little further down the table.

Soraya took a long sip from her wine glass. "I'm not an expert, but this is an excellent wine. Ruvon always brings the best for Arezoo."

He nearly fell off his chair.

Had that been praise from Soraya? The same woman who had rarely smiled at him and had been giving him appraising looks that always made him feel not good enough?

"He does," Arezoo agreed quickly, lifting her wrist to show the bracelet he'd gotten her. "And the gifts are always so thoughtful. Ruvon got me this for our three-month anniversary. Just look at the little book charm. Isn't it perfect?"

"Perfect." Donya rolled her eyes, probably having heard Arezoo gushing over the bracelet before.

"It's a very nice piece," Soraya agreed. "But even though gifts are nice and show affection, life is about more than this." She leveled her dark eyes on Ruvon. "Am I right?"

"Absolutely." Ruvon nodded. "Life is made of moments, and none of them should be squandered. I cherish each moment I get to spend with Arezoo."

Soraya smiled. "What are moments usually squandered on?"

No one around the table was breathing, including the little ones. They all knew Ruvon was being tested, and he hoped that they wanted him to pass the test.

"Small and big things," he said. "Even indifference is a culprit. When one partner prefers to scroll the endless feed on some social media platform instead of paying attention to the most important person in his or her life? Why watch meaningless television shows when you could be talking to your loved one? Then there are the big squanders like anger and resentment. I'm not saying that everything always has to be rainbows and flowers but paying attention and communicating is paramount in a relationship."

Laleh sighed. "That's so beautiful, Ruvon. Do you have any friends who think like you?"

"Laleh!" her mother admonished. "You are not allowed to date anyone older than you."

"But there are no boys my age in the village."

"Then you will have to wait." Soraya turned back to Ruvon. "You didn't mention trust."

"Trust is important," Ruvon agreed. "It should be earned, though."

"And how does one earn such trust?"

"Through actions, not words," Ruvon said. "Through being present, consistent, and reliable. Through showing respect not just for the person you love, but for their family, their values, their dreams." He paused, gathering courage. "Through understanding that when you love someone, you're not just choosing them, but everyone they hold dear."

Soraya was quiet for a moment and then turned to Arezoo. "What do you say to this?"

Arezoo reached over and took Ruvon's hand, interlacing their fingers on top of the table where everyone could see. "I say that Ruvon has shown me all of these things. But most importantly, he never doubted me in anything. His trust in me is absolute, and that's precious to me."

Arezoo was right about him trusting her absolutely, but he hadn't known that it was so important to her.

Soraya studied him for a long moment, then looked at her sisters and daughters, each in turn. Some form of silent communication seemed to pass between them, a conversation conducted entirely in glances and subtle expressions.

"Maman," Arezoo said softly, "Ruvon is the one for me. I know it, everyone around this table knows it, and deep in your heart you know that too."

Soraya's expression softened. "You're very young, my Arezoo. Nineteen is too young to make such a commitment."

"You were younger than me when you married Father."

"That was different, and you know it. I didn't have a choice, but you do. You can do whatever you want, choose any path. Why limit yourself?"

Ruvon cleared his throat. "I will never limit Arezoo. She can choose any path, become whoever she wants to be. I just want to accompany her on her journey."

That seemed to break the last of Soraya's resistance, and she reached for his hand, clasping it with surprising force. "Look into my eyes, Ruvon."

He did, his heart pounding. This felt very much like a pronouncement was coming.

"Do you love my daughter?"

"Yes," he said without hesitation. "With everything I am."

"Will you keep her safe?"

"With my life."

"Will you always respect her?"

"Always," he said. "Arezoo is extraordinary and deserving of respect, not just mine but everyone's. She is brilliant, kind, and brave, and just being with her makes me a better person. She's a force of good in this world."

Soraya nodded. "My daughter has chosen you. I see the way she looks at you, the way she lights up when you enter the room. I see the way you look at her, too, like she's the sun and you're the moon orbiting her."

Ruvon nodded, lost for words.

"I won't pretend I'm not concerned. The age difference between you is staggering, even though it is not evident from just looking at you. But there is a certain innocence in you that belies your chronological age."

He chuckled, but it was humorless. "I wish I could just nod and agree, but there is no innocence left in me."

"I disagree." Soraya patted his hand. "You are innocent in love. You've never been in love before." Soraya was quiet for a moment, then she reached up and placed a hand on his cheek, a maternal gesture that surprised him. "You have my blessing," she said.

The room erupted. The children jumped up and down, cheering. Arezoo let out a sound that was half-laugh, half-sob, and her sisters applauded. Max and Arezoo's aunts were grinning.

"Wait," Ruvon said, his voice cutting through the celebration. "There's...there's something else."

The room quieted again, and he could feel Arezoo's eyes on him, confused. "I don't know if this is the right time." His hand found the box in his pocket, and he pulled it out, turning to Arezoo.

Her eyes widened as he dropped to one knee beside her chair. "If you want me to put it back in my pocket and save it for another time, just tell me to stop."

She shook her head. "I don't want you to stop." She pressed both hands to her mouth, tears forming in her eyes.

"I'm not great with words, so I'm just going to say what's in my heart. Every morning when I wake up, you're my first thought. Every night before I fall asleep, I thank the universe for bringing you into my life. You make everything brighter, better, more meaningful. I don't want to imagine a future without you in it."

He opened the box, revealing the ring he'd recognized at first glance as the one for his Arezoo. A simple band with a single diamond, modest but perfect, like his intended .

"Will you marry me? It doesn't have to be anytime soon. It can be years from now. I just want to know that our future is entwined."

For a moment, she just stared at him, then she dropped to her knees in front of him and wrapped her arms around his neck. "Yes, I will marry you, Ruvon."

The room exploded again, but he barely heard it. All that mattered was Arezoo in his arms.

When they finally pulled apart, he slipped the ring onto her finger. It fit perfectly, which he had known it would.

"You're really family now." Soraya pulled him into an embrace that felt genuine. "I would call you son, but given that you are probably much older than me, I'll keep using your name."

He nodded. "So, I guess calling you Mother is out of the question?"

She chuckled. "I prefer you keep calling me Soraya."

"Let me see the ring!" Donya demanded, grabbing her sister's hand.

"It's beautiful," Laleh said, crowding close.

"It's perfect," Arezoo corrected, looking at Ruvon with so much love that he felt weak in the knees.

"Let's make black coffee to celebrate," Rana offered.

"I'll help." Soraya, looking relieved to have something to do, rose to her feet, and followed her sister.

Had she been dreading this as much as he had?

For the first time, it occurred to Ruvon that it had been as difficult for her as it had been for him. Perhaps even more so.

"Congratulations." Max clapped him on his back. "You did better than expected. I thought I would have to rescue you, but you did fine all on your own."

"Surprisingly, Soraya didn't eviscerate me."

"She likes you," Kyra said. "She has almost from the beginning; she just needed to make sure."

28

TULA

Tula stood in front of the mirror, turning sideways as she examined her profile. The loose gown she'd chosen this morning, one of several she'd been favoring lately, was draped over her body in what she hoped were concealing folds. But even the generous fabric couldn't hide what was becoming increasingly obvious. The gentle swell of her belly had grown more pronounced over the past week, and no amount of strategic draping could disguise it much longer.

She'd been so careful for five thousand years, taking every precaution except for turning celibate, but in the end, she couldn't escape the inevitable.

Pressing her hand against her stomach, she felt the firmness there that hadn't existed three months ago. Soon, even Tony wouldn't be able to pretend he didn't notice, because he had to be pretending.

The man held a doctorate, for the Fates' sake.

How could he not realize what was glaringly obvious?

Her breasts were tender and swollen, she was short-tempered and irritable all the time, and wine gave her heartburn. Either he was the most oblivious man on the planet, or he was as terrified as she was, and choosing denial was his coping mechanism.

A knock at her door made her drop her hand and smooth the fabric over her midsection.

"Come in," she called out.

Liliat opened the door but didn't come in. "We're going for a walk in the gardens. Want to join?"

It had been presented as an invitation, a wish to include her in their activity, but she knew it for the ambush it was. They'd been giving her knowing looks and whispering among themselves for days.

Her sisters knew.

The gazebo, deep in the harem's gardens, was the only place where they had any privacy. The trees and distance from the buildings meant that even if there were cameras out there, they were few and easy to spot. Nature wasn't conducive to miniature devices that could be swept away in the breeze or obscured by the slightest movement of leaves.

"I'm coming." She took one last look at herself in the mirror.

There was no point in delaying the inevitable. They all knew.

In the corridor the rest of them waited, their expressions neutral, but she knew them all so well that she could read them easily.

They were concerned for her.

"Where's Tamira?" she asked as they began walking toward the elevator.

"She went to get Areana," Sarah said.

So, it was to be a full intervention then.

In a way, Tula was relieved. Better to tell them all at once than to have the same gut-wrenching conversation twice. And maybe one of them would have an idea she hadn't thought of. Some solution that didn't involve either accepting the unacceptable or taking a permanent leap off the cliff outside the harem and ending her miserable existence along with the life growing inside of her.

The mid-morning sun was already scorching, but the path through the gardens was shaded by the greenery. The air was heavy with the scents of growing things she didn't have the patience to discern, and it made her slightly nauseous.

Everything was making her nauseous lately.

They walked in silence for a while, the only sounds their soft footsteps on the gravel path and the distant hum of construction that never seemed to end these days. The island was still being rebuilt after the rebellion, and according to Hassan, new crews and new equipment were arriving at the island daily.

Tamira and Areana caught up with them just as they reached the gazebo. Areana looked as perfectly composed as always, not a hair out of place despite the humidity, while Tamira looked a bit frazzled, and Tula wondered what that was about.

The gazebo was a beautiful structure, with delicate latticed wood, climbing vines, and comfortable cushioned benches arranged in a semicircle. It was far enough from the harem that conversation felt safer here, though Tula knew that safety was always an illusion on the island.

They all sat, and for a moment, no one spoke. Unspoken questions hung in the air like the morning humidity.

Finally, Tula couldn't stand it anymore. "You all know what's going on with me, so there is no point in keeping up the pretense."

"Know what?" Raviki asked.

"Don't." Tula's voice came out sharper than she intended.

Areana leaned forward, her expression soft with understanding. "How far along are you?"

The direct question, asked with such gentle matter-of-factness, broke something in Tula. She felt tears prick at her eyes, and she blinked them back furiously.

She would not cry.

"Three months, maybe a little longer," she admitted, the words feeling like shards of glass in her throat. "For five thousand years, I've been so bloody careful, and now I'm pregnant."

"And terrified," Beulah added.

"Terrified?" Tula laughed, but there was no humor in it. "That doesn't begin to cover it. If it's a boy, he'll be taken from me before he even knows my face. Nine months of carrying him, hours of labor, a few months of breastfeeding, and then they'll just take him. And if it's a girl?" Her voice broke. "If it's a girl, I get to watch her grow up in this prison, never able to transition, aging and dying while I stay young forever."

"There are other options," Sarah said carefully.

Tula's head snapped up. "If you're about to suggest what I think you're suggesting—"

Abortion was a last resort that none of them had attempted, but some of the servants had.

"It's early enough," Sarah said, not flinching away from Tula's harsh tone. "There are certain herbs that trigger it, as well as other methods."

"No." The word came out with such vehemence that Sarah actually pulled back. "I won't do that. I can't." Tula pressed her hand to her stomach again. "The only way this child dies is if I die with it inside of me. At least then we will meet on the other side of the veil."

"Don't talk like that," Areana said. "We've all been through this and survived. You will survive as well. It will break you, as it has broken us, but we will help you rebuild yourself as we have been doing for each other ever since this started."

"That's not an option," Tula said firmly. "Not for me."

Liliat shifted on her bench, the cushions rustling softly. "Does Tony know?"

Tula snorted. "How could he not? My breasts are swollen, my belly is growing, I haven't touched wine in weeks, and I can barely keep food down. But he keeps acting like everything's normal, talking about the herb garden and asking if I want to go swimming. Either he's completely oblivious, which seems impossible given that he has a doctorate in bioinformatics, or he's as scared as I am and pretending it isn't happening."

"Men can be surprisingly dense about these things," Raviki offered. "Especially when they don't want to see something."

"Or maybe he's waiting for you to tell him," Tamira suggested. "Maybe he doesn't want to pressure you or assume anything."

"Assume?" Tula's voice rose. "What else could it possibly be? I told him that I gained weight, but he sees what I'm eating. He should have seen through the lie."

"You need to tell him," Areana said. "Whatever you decide to do, he deserves to know. He's the father."

"And then what?" Tula stood and started pacing the small interior of the gazebo. "He knows what happens to children born to the harem ladies. If we are lucky to have a girl, at least he would get to see her grow, and he will die before her." She shook her head. "That's depressing to even think about."

"There must be another way," Tamira said quietly.

Everyone turned to look at her, and Tula saw something in her friend's eyes that hadn't been there before. Hope, maybe. Or determination.

She narrowed her eyes at Tamira. "Like what?"

Tamira glanced at Areana, then back at Tula. "Things are changing. The rebellion showed that Navuh's control isn't absolute. There might be possibilities we haven't considered before. We need to think creatively."

"What kind of possibilities?" Sarah asked.

"I don't know," Tamira said. "But we are all smart, and if we put our heads together and take into account that things are not the same as they used to be when our children were taken away from us, we might come up with something." She turned to Tula. "You need to have faith."

Areana's expression had gone carefully neutral, which told Tula that she suspected where Tamira was going with that, and she didn't like it.

"How long can I hide it?" Tula asked, changing the subject because she couldn't bear to hope for something that might not happen. "How long before it becomes impossible to conceal?"

"With the right clothing, maybe another month or two," Beulah said, studying Tula's figure with a practical eye. "We can help with that. Looser gowns, different styles. Lord Navuh rarely sees us, and when he does, he pays attention only to Areana. He won't notice until it's impossible to miss."

Tula wasn't sure of that. Navuh noticed everything, but it was true that they rarely got to see him, and it wouldn't be too difficult to avoid him. The problem would be concealing the pregnancy from the staff, and someone would inform Navuh.

"He'll be pleased when he finds out," Areana said. "So, he won't be too angry about no one telling him about the pregnancy. Another child for his army or another daughter for the harem is pure gain for him."

"And a loss for me," Tula whispered.

"Not necessarily," Tamira said, that strange hope still shining in her eyes.

"Stop being so cryptic," Raviki said with frustration. "If you know something, tell us."

"I don't. Not yet, but we will come up with something, and in the meantime, I don't want Tula to do anything drastic." Tamira looked at Tula with pleading eyes. "Please, just don't lose hope."

Tula let out a sigh. "Don't worry. I don't have the courage to throw myself off the cliff." She looked at Areana and wondered if her oldest friend thought the same thing she did.

Carol had thrown herself off the cliff, but it had been a ruse. Annani's clan came to rescue them, but Areana had refused to leave Navuh, and Tula had refused to abandon Areana.

Things were different now, though. Loyalties had shifted. The child growing in her belly took precedence over her loyalty to Areana.

Would they come for her, though?

Would Areana ask Annani to send help?

Tula doubted that. She was a nobody, a servant girl who had grown into a lady of the harem only because she was an immortal and Navuh needed to maintain the fiction of having relations with all his immortal concubines.

The tears she'd been fighting finally won, spilling down her cheeks in hot streams. "I don't know what to do. I don't know how to protect this child."

Suddenly she was surrounded, her sisters wrapping their arms around her in a group embrace that smelled of different perfumes and felt like a safety net, even though it was an illusion.

The only one who could help her was Areana, and Tula doubted the goddess would come through for her.

After all, why did Tula deserve a better fate than her mistress or the other ladies of the harem? They had all been forced to give up their sons. What gave her the right to demand something different for herself?

When they finally pulled apart, Tula wiped her eyes with the back of her hand. "I need you all to keep this secret," she said. "At least for now. I need time to figure out what to do, how to deal with this."

"Of course," Liliat said, and the others nodded their agreement.

"But you need to tell Tony," Areana said gently. "He has a right to know, and you'll need his support."

Tula nodded, though the thought of that conversation made her stomach turn. She was stifling so much anger, not just at the situation but also at Tony. How could he be so oblivious or so cowardly?

He claimed he loved her, but his actions didn't confirm his words.

Seeing Elias with Tamira put Tony's behavior in stark relief. Tony was selfish, and he cared about his survival and his comfort above all. Elias would lay down his life for Tamira. Tony would not do that for Tula.

Tamira stepped closer, and Tula saw tears in her friend's eyes. For a moment, she thought it was pity, and she started to pull away. She didn't want pity. But Tamira's expression stopped her.

"I know what it's like," Tamira whispered. "To carry a child for nine months, to hold him and love him for a few precious months, and then to have him taken away. I know the emptiness that follows, the ache that never really goes away. But that short experience is worth having." She looked into Tula's eyes. "I know you won't believe me, but if I had to do it again, I would. I'd rather create that life and carry it inside of me for nine months, fall in love with my child, and nurse him for a short while, than not have that at all. The time you have, however brief, is precious. And who knows? The future isn't written yet."

29

TAMIRA

Tamira stood at the balcony doors of her room, watching Eluheed and Tony toil in the indoor courtyard. The automated lighting system was sophisticated enough to mimic the gradual color shifts of real twilight, but it was still just an imitation and couldn't compare to the real thing.

The conversation in the gazebo kept replaying in her mind. Tula's tears, the desperation in her voice, the way she'd pressed her hand over her belly while speaking of the child's doomed future. It was one thing to suspect a pregnancy, and another thing to hear Tula confirm it. The anguish in her voice had torn an old wound open in Tamira's chest.

She knew that pain intimately.

The memory of holding Darien in her arms, his beautiful eyes locked on hers, the expression of ultimate trust on his little face that she'd been forced to betray, it was all still as vivid in her mind as the day she'd first held him, the sweet scent of him, the way his tiny fingers had wrapped around hers with such strength. Nine months of feeling him grow inside her, those precious few months of nursing him, and then the empty ache that never truly healed.

But Tula didn't have to suffer the same fate. Not if Tamira could help it.

With a sigh, she turned away from the glass doors and crossed the room to sit on the couch. Once Eluheed returned, she would tell him that Tula was coming with them.

When the door opened sometime later and Eluheed entered, she smiled up at him. "Are you guys done?"

"Not yet. Every time we think that we've got all the broken pipes replaced, we find another section that's leaking and needs replacement." He headed toward the bathroom but stopped before entering. "You look troubled. What happened?"

"It's Tula." She put a hand on her belly, knowing that he would understand.

He nodded. "That's not a surprise. We've all been suspecting it for a while."

"Yeah, but today she confirmed it. Go wash up, and we'll talk. Do you want tea?"

"Yes, please. The jasmine with ginger." He entered the

bathroom, and a moment later, she heard the water running in the shower.

Their talk needed to remain private, so they would have to drink the tea in the bathroom. It was far from perfect, but it wasn't as if they could have tea in bed under the blanket, which was their other mode of secret communication.

When she brought it to the bathroom, she found Eluheed standing in front of the vanity with a towel draped over his hips, and wet hair still dripping water droplets all over the tile. For a moment, she forgot what she wanted to talk to him about.

He turned around and reached for one of the cups. "So, Tula confirmed it." He leaned against the vanity. "How far along is she?"

"Three months more or less." Tamira took a sip of the aromatic tea, closing her eyes for a moment as the rich flavors hit her tongue. "She's understandably devastated and terrified." She sat on the edge of the tub.

"Tony doesn't know?"

"She says that he's either oblivious or pretending not to notice, which makes it worse in my opinion. She needs his support, but if he's either clueless or too cowardly to acknowledge what's happening, he's not the type of partner Tula deserves." Tamira shook her head. "She spoke of throwing herself off the cliff. I know she would never do that, but it's an indication of how desperate and alone she feels."

Eluheed moved to sit next to her on the edge of the tub. "She's distraught. She will come to terms with the situation. It's not like she can do anything about it."

"I know the pain she's feeling, and I can't watch her go through what I had to." She leveled her gaze at him and leaned closer. "We need to take her with us," she whispered. "In the submarine."

Eluheed's eyes widened. "Tamira."

"Just listen to me." She leaned and turned the water on. "We have to do it. It would be incredibly selfish of us to leave her behind in her situation."

Eluheed shook his head. "Even if we manage to solve the problem of the surveillance cameras in the tunnel, I don't know if more than two people can fit into that submarine. It looked very small in the vision, almost like a child's toy."

"If it can seat two, it can seat four. We'll sit on each other's laps if we have to."

"It's not just about the space," he said. "What about air? Submarines have a limited oxygen supply that is calibrated for the number of people they are supposed to carry."

"I've been reading up on submarines," she said. "I found some novels in the library." When he grimaced, she lifted a finger to shush him. "I know they're just fiction, but they're based on real technology. We don't need to stay submerged for long. We don't need much. We just need to get away from the island and surface somewhere safe. It's a simple calculation. If we cut the maximum distance the sub can travel in half, the oxygen should be enough for double the occupants."

Eluheed was quiet for a long moment, and she could see him working through the logistics in his mind. "Even if we could fit four people, and even if the air lasted long enough, we still have the problem of the surveillance cameras in the tunnel."

"Tony might be able to help with that." The idea came to her suddenly, like a gift from the Fates. "Think about it. He knows a lot about technology in general. He might know how to disable cameras or loop the feed or whatever else. I don't know the technical terms, but there must be something he could do."

Eluheed was frowning, but there was calculation in his eyes. "He does know a lot about various things. He might act like a buffoon sometimes, but he's curious by nature and methodical when he wants to learn something." A smile lifted one corner of his mouth. "He might be useful."

Tamira felt hope blooming in her chest. "This feels right, Eluheed. Including Tula and Tony isn't just about being altruistic—it's strategic. Tony's knowledge could be the key to making the escape actually work."

"Don't get excited yet. There's still so much we don't know," Eluheed cautioned. "We don't know how to operate the submarine or how to navigate. Did the books you read have anything about that?"

"I don't think so, but I'll need to read those sections again. Maybe I'll find some clues." She lifted her hand and cupped his face. "We will succeed, Eluheed. The vision you shared with me, of Darien and me walking arm in arm in New York, that's proof that we make it out of here. I believe the Fates reward those who sacrifice for others, and including Tula and Tony in our escape is just the thing that can tip the scales. That's not the reason I want to do it, but I wouldn't mind a little supernatural help."

He arched a brow. "Since when do you believe in the Fates?"

"I have to believe in something," she said. "I believe that acts of selflessness are rewarded. Saving Tula from having her child stolen, giving that baby a chance at a real life, feels like what we're supposed to do."

Eluheed pulled her hand from his face but kept hold of it. "When I first thought about including some of the others, I resisted because it seemed impossible. Too many variables. But you're right about Tony. His knowledge could make all the difference. But how do we approach them? We can't just walk up and say, 'Hey, do you want to escape with us in a submarine that may or may not exist, to an unknown destination?'"

Despite the seriousness of the situation, Tamira laughed. "I'll talk to Tula. I just wanted to check with you first that you are okay with that."

"How can I say no?" He let out a breath. "This changes everything. It's not just our escape anymore. We're responsible for them, too."

"We were always responsible for each other," Tamira said. "That's what family does. And after five thousand years, they're all my family. I just wish I could save them all."

"You can't save everyone, Tamira."

"I know." The words tasted like ash. "But I can save Tula. I can save her child and its father. That has to be enough."

30

TULA

Tula followed Tony into the bathroom, the one place in her suite where she felt safe to talk freely.

"Do you want to join me in the shower?" he asked hopefully.

They hadn't been having much sex lately, and not just because of her hormones going haywire. She was angry at him for being obtuse, for not paying attention to her, for ignoring her moods instead of trying to soothe them.

"No. I'll wait here until you are done."

His grin widened. "You want to see me naked." He pulled his dirty shirt over his head and dumped it into the laundry basket.

She had to admit that he had a nice chest, muscular but not overly so, and her hands itched to touch his skin. But she couldn't allow herself to get distracted or let him seduce her.

"You are nice to look at." She sat on the edge of the tub. "I'll watch you shower."

Looking smug like a peacock, Tony removed the rest of his clothing and sauntered into the shower, putting on a show for her.

"Show off," she murmured.

"I heard that." He blew her an air kiss before turning the water on.

Showering, he used every opportunity to flex his muscles and look seductive, and in the end, Tula even managed to forget for a moment that she was mad at him and laughed at his shenanigans.

When he was finally done, he toweled himself dry and then draped the towel around his hips. He used another one to dry his hair.

"We need to talk," she said.

Tony lowered the towel he was using on his hair, and given the grimace on his face, he knew exactly what this was about.

The realization made her anger flare anew.

"You knew," she accused. "This whole time you were pretending to be dumb when you knew all along that I was pregnant."

He tossed the towel on the vanity. "I didn't know. I suspected."

"Suspected?" Her voice rose. "My breasts are swollen, my tummy is rounded like it has never been before, and I haven't been feeling well. I'm immortal, Tony, what could possibly be wrong with me other than pregnancy?"

He looked down at his bare feet. "I was afraid to ask."

The admission stopped her cold. "Afraid? Of what?"

Tony finally met her eyes. "Of your reaction. You have a temper, and I'm not good with confrontations. You know how much I hate it when you get riled up about something, and there is always something that makes you angry. I can't deal with that."

"So, you stayed quiet about something this monumentally important because you were afraid I'd yell at you?" The incredulity in her voice could have cut glass. "Are you seriously telling me you've been pretending not to notice that I'm carrying your child because you didn't want to deal with my temper?"

"That's not—" He stopped and ran his hands through his still-damp hair in frustration. "That's not the only reason."

"Then enlighten me, because from where I'm standing, you look like a coward who was more concerned about avoiding an uncomfortable conversation than supporting me through the most terrifying situation of my very long life." Her voice rose with every subsequent word, and she was yelling now, which was utterly stupid since the pregnancy needed to stay a secret.

"You're right. I am a coward," Tony said in a hushed voice. "But not just because I was afraid of your temper. I knew how much you dreaded this. That you didn't want this, didn't want this child. And I knew you'd blame me for it."

Tula opened her mouth to argue, then closed it. "Why would I blame you?"

He rolled his eyes. "Do I need to explain about the birds and the bees? Unless you were sleeping with others behind my back, it's my fault that you are pregnant."

Tula tried really hard to ignore the idiotic comment about her sleeping around. As if that had been an option. Tony was just being a moron.

"Did I ever put the responsibility of preventing my pregnancy on you?"

"No, but it still was my doing."

She shook her head. "I drank the contraceptive tea. It should have worked, but for some reason it didn't. Should I blame Elias for giving me the wrong herbs? Or the doctor before him?"

Tony let out a breath. "Maybe, but in the end, it was me. I caused this. I caused your anguish."

The fight drained out of her as suddenly as it had risen. "You didn't. You have enough to answer for without adding this to your guilt. Did you think that by staying silent and pretending not to notice, you were somehow protecting me?"

"No, I think I was protecting myself," he admitted. "From seeing the disappointment in your eyes. From confirming that I'd ruined everything for you. Every day I didn't acknowledge it was another day I could pretend that maybe I was wrong, that maybe you'd just gained some weight, and that maybe the wine was giving you heart-burn for other reasons."

"That's ridiculous—" She stopped herself, seeing the pain in his eyes. "I'm not blaming you, or even myself. I did everything right. I didn't forget or miss a dose. But the tea is not a hundred percent effective, especially on immortals. The Fates decided that it was my turn to suffer, that's all. But I could have used some care and attention, which I didn't get from you."

"I'm sorry." He sounded miserable.

"Nothing works forever," she said. "I knew that. I've always known that eventually my luck would run out."

Tony came to sit beside her on the edge of the tub. "I should have said something. Should have acknowledged it, supported you. Instead, I left you to carry this burden alone because I was too much of a coward to face my guilt."

"Your guilt," she repeated, finally understanding. "That's what this is really about. Not fear of my temper, but guilt."

He offered her a half smile. "Your temper is formidable. It was both. Can I make it up to you?"

She sighed. "We need to be there for each other. This child will either be taken away if it's a boy or condemned to mortality if it's a girl. Either way, I lose. But if it's a girl, at least you will get to see her grow up. You will probably die before her, like it's supposed to be for humans, so for you it won't be as heartbreaking as it will be for me."

"Thanks for the pep talk," he said sarcastically.

"It's the reality. You are human, and if we have a daughter, she will live and die a human." She turned to study his profile. "Do you want this child?"

The question seemed to surprise him. "Want? In another place, another life, yes. But here? God, no. How can I want that kind of fate for a child of mine?"

It was an honest answer, so she couldn't even get angry at him for not wanting the life growing inside of her. Yet she wished he'd answered differently.

Tony moved his hand tentatively to hover over her stomach, not quite touching. "May I?"

She took his hand and placed it on the slight swell of her belly. "It's your child as much as it is mine. For as long as we get to keep it, that is."

"I'm sorry for being such a coward."

"We're both cowards," she said. "I've been hiding it from everyone, also pretending it wasn't happening."

"What are we going to do?"

"Right now, we will go to dinner and pretend that everything is right in our world. By the way, I told the others."

He swallowed. "So, why keep up the pretense?"

"For the servants. For Navuh. The truth is that there is no point in hiding it because soon it will become impossible to hide, but I'm going with my gut, and it tells me not to make it official yet." She looked down at her belly. "I might miscarry. It happens in the first trimester."

That was one of the reasons she hadn't told anyone. On a subconscious level, she'd hoped for a miscarriage.

When, sometime later, they walked out of her suite and headed to the dining room, there was a new kind of silence between them. It wasn't the heavy, oppressive quiet of unspoken truths, but something a little lighter. The other ladies were already gathering, and Tamira caught Tula's eye with a questioning look. Tula gave a small nod. Yes, they'd talked. Yes, he knew. Yes, they were okay, or as okay as they could be under the circumstances.

Dinner passed in the usual manner, with conversations about the restoration work, the gardens, the weather, all the safe topics that filled their days. But Tula noticed Tamira and Elias exchanging glances, some form of silent communication passing between them.

As the meal was ending, Elias folded his napkin over his plate and leaned back. "I've overindulged and now I need to walk this meal off. Anyone interested in a walk in the gardens? The temperature has probably dropped to something bearable by now."

"That sounds lovely," Tamira said.

"Some fresh air would be good." Tony glanced at Tula. "Right?"

She nodded. "Sounds good to me. I ate a little too much as well."

That was a lie, but no one called her on it.

"Anyone else?" Elias asked.

"I have a book date waiting for me," Beulah said, and the others made similar excuses, some more convincing than others.

As the four of them emerged aboveground, the evening air was indeed cooler than the oppressive heat of the day, and Tula was glad of the suggestion. She and Tony walked behind Tamira and Elias, holding hands and feeling closer than they had in weeks, which was nice, but Tula had the sense that something was about to happen.

Something important.

31

ELUHEED

The guards stationed outside the double fence had given the four of them curious looks as they'd emerged from the pavilion and headed into the dark gardens, but no one had said anything.

It wasn't against the rules to venture outside the harem at night.

Immortals could see just fine in the dark, but Tony was human, and Eluheed was supposed to be human as well, so the guards must have wondered about it.

Other than the ladies, there were no immortals inside the harem, and it had been a deliberate choice by Navuh. Those guarding it from behind the fences were all immortals, though. It was evident in their unnatural stillness when they were stationary, and their fluid walk when they moved.

Eluheed wasn't like them, which had its advantages and disadvantages. The biggest advantage was that he could pass for a human because he didn't have any visible characteristics. Regrettably, the disadvantages outnumbered the one advantage. He couldn't provide Tamira with the pleasure of the venom bite, and he had a feeling that the other immortals were stronger and faster than he was.

Hopefully, he wouldn't have to face them during the escape because neither he nor Tony would prevail against one of them, especially since they wouldn't be armed.

The escape plan was a desperate move, and the chances of it succeeding were so pathetic that he wondered whether he should continue enabling this fiction and, on top of that, bring a pregnant female on board.

"It's indeed pleasant outside," Tula said.

"It's bearable." Tamira looked at Eluheed. "We should have brought water."

They should have, but they hadn't. They'd been in a rush to offer Tula hope, but now Eluheed was reconsidering the wisdom of that decision.

Was it too late to stop that wrecking ball?

Should he stop it?

The truth was that he was out of options, and the submarine was the only viable one. Bringing along Tula and Tony complicated things, but it also might make them more manageable.

As they entered the gazebo they sat on the cushioned benches, and for a moment, no one spoke. Eluheed looked at Tamira and lifted a brow, double-checking that she still wanted to go ahead and let the other two in on their secret.

She gave him a slight nod. It was time.

"We asked you both here because we have something important to share with you," Tamira said in a hushed tone. "But before I do, I want you both to swear on your lives that you won't tell anyone about what Elias and I are going to tell you."

Curiosity shining in Tula's eyes, she put her hand over her heart. "I vow never to reveal what I'm about to learn from you, and I secure my vow with my life."

Tony put his hand over his chest as well. "What she said."

Tamira shook her head. "Not good enough. You need to vow in your own words that you will never reveal to anyone what we are about to tell you."

"So serious." He rolled his eyes. "Fine. I swear to take this secret you are going to tell me to my grave. Now tell us what this is all about."

"It's about a possible way out of here," Eluheed said.

Tony straightened, his expression shifting from amused to focused. "A way off the island?"

Eluheed nodded. "It's a crazy plan, but it might work, and it's all we have."

"How?" Tony asked. "We can't even get out of the harem, let alone off the island. Are you thinking about sneaking into one of the ships delivering crews and building materials? I'm sure the port is heavily guarded, so even if you could figure a way out through those double fences and immortal patrols, it would be futile."

It seemed like Tony had given escape a lot of thought and had arrived at the same conclusions as Eluheed. There was no way out. But he didn't know about the submarine. No one did.

Well, Areana might know about it, but Eluheed wasn't sure of that.

"Navuh has a tiny submarine," Eluheed said, keeping his voice barely above a whisper. "It's hidden in a secret pen and accessible from a tunnel that connects the harem to Navuh's mansion."

Tony blinked. "How could you possibly know that?"

This was the tricky part. Eluheed had kept his abilities hidden from everyone except Tamira and Navuh. But if they were going to risk their lives together, Tony and Tula deserved the truth—or at least part of it.

"I have certain paranormal abilities," Eluheed said. "By touching a person, I can see events in their future or past. Lord Navuh uses my abilities frequently, and I accidentally accessed information he certainly didn't intend for me to see."

"Are you a seer?" Tula asked as if that hadn't been what he'd just said. "That's such a rare ability. No wonder Navuh has been giving you preferential treatment."

"I'm useful to him." Eluheed chuckled. "He hates it that he needs to let me touch him to get the visions. You should see his face every time he rolls up his sleeve and offers me his arm. He looks like he just stepped on manure."

That got a laugh out of Tula. "I know the expression you are describing."

Tony leaned forward. "So, you're saying that you can read people's minds when you touch them?"

He was obviously concerned about the many times their arms or thighs had brushed during their work in the gardens, but that wasn't how Eluheed's gift worked.

"Visions don't just pop into my head when I brush against someone. It needs to be intentional, and I have to concentrate and summon a vision. It helps if the person opens up to me, but it's not necessary."

Tony let out a breath. "That's a relief. So, what do you see when you summon a vision?"

"I get impressions, images, sometimes a chain of events, but it's not always clear or complete. Some visions are clearer than others, though, and the submarine was very vivid. Navuh keeps it as a last resort escape route for him and Areana. The craft is tiny, but I couldn't discern if it can seat two, three, or four people."

Tula glared at him. "So, why are you raising our hopes when you are not sure you even have space for us?"

"Because we will make room for you no matter what," Tamira said. "We'll cram into that vehicle. We don't need to get far from the island to surface and get comfortable. There are thousands of small islands in the Indian Ocean, so getting to land shouldn't take long."

Tony shook his head. "I still have a hard time believing Elias's seer story." He looked at Eluheed. "Can you prove it? Can you touch me and see something in my past or future that will convince me you can actually do it?"

This was dangerous territory. What if he saw their escape plan foiled? What if he saw them getting caught?

The probability of those scenarios was high, and if that was what he saw in Tony's future, they would have to bury their plan along with the hope that accompanied it.

"Give me your hand," he said, extending his.

Tony placed his hand in Eluheed's, but the connection didn't form right away. Tony wasn't a powerhouse like Navuh, and instead of the vision slamming into Eluheed's mind, like it usually did with Navuh or the enhanced soldiers, it started slow and hazy. Images flooded, but they weren't of the future. Tony looked much younger, more innocent, and in love with a girl who wasn't Tula.

She was young, seventeen or eighteen, with long blonde hair pulled back in a ponytail, and red-rimmed glasses perched on her upturned nose. Her figure was long and willowy, and she was leaning over a computer screen, explaining something to Tony, who looked at her with awestruck eyes.

Her name rose to the surface—Aya, no, it was Kaia. She

was too brilliant, too accomplished, too young, and not interested in Tony as a boyfriend.

Eluheed pulled his hand back, the connection severing. "I saw a tall, blonde girl with glasses. Seemed to me like she was a fellow bioinformatician. You were in love with her, but she was too young, a prodigy. Her name was Kaia."

Tony's face had gone pale. "That's not possible. I didn't tell anyone about her."

"Oh, who cares about Tony's old flame?" Tula snapped, her patience clearly wearing thin. "We have bigger problems than his former lovers."

"We were never lovers," Tony said defensively. "We were friends. Colleagues."

"It doesn't matter either way," Tula said. "What matters is whether this submarine actually exists, and since Elias proved that he can look into your mind, I believe that what he saw in Navuh's was real as well. How do we get to it?"

Tamira leaned forward. "The submarine is in a tunnel that connects Navuh's bedroom in the mansion to his quarters here in the harem, and I know how to get in, but there are surveillance cameras in the tunnel. The moment we enter, he'll know."

"What kind of cameras?" Tony asked. "How many? What's the setup?"

"We don't know," Eluheed admitted. "Do you know anything about surveillance?"

Tony was quiet for a moment. "Hassan has the architectural plans. They would show the electrical systems, and hopefully, include the surveillance network."

"Can you access them?" Tamira asked.

Eluheed nodded. "Hassan and I are on friendly terms." He turned to Tony. "We can go together, and one of us will distract him while the other will go over the plans."

"Or you can touch him," Tony suggested. "He doesn't need to know why you're doing that. You might invent some skin condition that you suspect he has."

Eluheed was impressed with Tony's improvisation. It would have never occurred to him to fake a skin condition to extract a vision, but then he'd been raised to live truthfully, so things of that nature weren't instinctual for him.

"I don't control what I see, so chances are that I won't get anything useful. The vision might be about Hassan's old flame, or his life outside the island. The only types of visions I routinely get are of betrayals. For some reason, the universe is generous in showing me those."

"You never know what you'll learn from touching him," Tony said. "And while you keep him busy pretending to ruminate over his skin condition, I will find the surveillance plans."

"That sounds like a good plan," Tula said. "Is there anything I can do?" She turned to Tamira. "By the way. How did you find the secret tunnel access in Areana's room?"

"I confronted her about it," Tamira said. "We all suspected that Navuh had a secret tunnel he was using to travel between the mansion and the harem, and since we never saw him enter or leave, we guessed that it was in his and Areana's quarters in the harem. I told her that all of us need to know where it is in case of an emergency, and she showed me."

"When was that?" Tula asked.

"Yesterday. She promised to show it to all the ladies, so you are probably next."

Tula shook her head. "After everything I sacrificed for her, she should have shown me that a long time ago."

Eluheed wondered what Tula had sacrificed for Areana, but he didn't dare to ask.

"The cameras are just one problem," he said, changing the subject back to what they should be talking about. "None of us know how to operate a submarine, so that also might prove a problem."

Tony waved a hand in dismissal. "That shouldn't be too difficult. I drove all kinds of vehicles when I was still free, and it's mostly intuitive. I just hope that Navuh left the keys inside."

"Keys?" Tamira asked.

"It's a figure of speech. The submarine is most likely locked, and a key is needed to enter, either an actual key or a code. We will need to figure out which one it is and disable or bypass it."

Tula let out a breath. "That's not the kind of information you can find in Hassan's office. How will you know?"

Tony shrugged. "No clue. We will tackle each problem when we get to it."

"That's not a plan. That's suicide," Tula nearly shrieked, but then slumped her shoulders. "We are all going to die. Navuh will find out and execute all of us."

"He won't," Eluheed said. "I had a vision about Tamira free and reunited with her son in New York. And if she survives, chances are that the rest of us will as well."

32

TAMIRA

Tamira pushed a piece of melon around her plate, the clink of her fork against porcelain joining the symphony of morning sounds—the soft conversations of her sisters, the gentle scrape of cutlery, the rustle of napkins.

"Are you eating that thing or painting with it?" Raviki said from across the table.

"I'm eating." Tamira speared the melon piece and brought it to her mouth.

The fruit was perfectly ripe, sweet with just a hint of tartness, but it might as well have been cardboard for all she tasted.

Two weeks had passed since that night in the gazebo when they'd laid out their insane escape plan. They'd been gathering information, with Tony and Eluheed visiting Hassan's office under various pretexts and poring over building plans.

And what had they learned?

That the surveillance system wasn't on any blueprint because it had been installed years after the original construction. They'd also learned that the island's infrastructure was held together by patch jobs, and after the devastation of the rebellion, so much of it needed replacement that it was almost like building it all from scratch.

Hassan was excited even though most of the work would be done outside the harem, and that was excellent for gathering information because he was eager to share the news with anyone willing to listen. That's how they knew that the main power generator was being replaced, but they didn't know precisely when.

Chances were that it would involve an island-wide outage, which would provide the guys a perfect opportunity to examine the surveillance in the tunnel while it wasn't active.

"The eggs are so good," Sarah said, though her own plate showed she'd barely touched them. "The kitchen must have gotten fresh ones. I wonder if those ships that bring building materials also bring groceries to the island."

Tamira's jaw tightened.

Just the other night, Tony had revisited the idea of sneaking aboard one of the vessels that arrived almost daily, bringing construction materials and work crews. But every angle they'd examined had led to the conclusion that it was impossible. They couldn't even figure out how to pass the double fence around the harem and evade the patrols, which were manned by Brotherhood soldiers, not mere humans like the harem guards. Then there was the issue of scrutiny at the docks. It would be suicide to attempt it.

"Tula dear, you should try to eat something," Beulah said gently. "Even if you're not feeling well."

Tula, who sat three chairs down, had been staring at her untouched toast with an expression of barely concealed revulsion. Her hand drifted to her stomach—a gesture that had become more frequent and more noticeable with each passing day.

"I'm not hungry," she said. "Just thirsty. Can someone pass me the orange juice, please?"

At least Tula had an excuse for her moods, her distraction, her occasional sharp responses. Tamira had to smile and engage in conversations, pretending that nothing was troubling her and that she wasn't mentally cataloging every item they'd managed to secrete away and what more she could pilfer.

So far they had two flashlights, stolen from the maintenance crew working on the pumps down in the bowels of the harem, a sharp knife from the kitchen that no one would miss, some rope from the garden shed outside, and a pair of wire cutters that Tony had claimed were broken and needed to be disposed of.

It was such a pathetic arsenal for such a monumental undertaking.

The men had departed earlier to check the supply room again to see if there was anything else they could add to their meager collection.

"You have to try the bread." Liliat passed the basket to Tamira. "It's really good."

Tamira accepted the basket, selected a roll she had no intention of eating, and passed it on.

"Is Areana joining us this morning?" Raviki asked, glancing at the empty chair at the head of the table.

"Later," Sarah said. "Lord Navuh hasn't left yet."

He was so unpredictable, sometimes leaving early in the morning before their breakfast even started, and sometimes staying late and keeping Areana busy until long after breakfast was done.

On those days, the goddess needed more time to recover, and Tamira wondered if Navuh was exhausting her with lovemaking or with his mere intense presence.

Not that it was any of Tamira's business, or that Areana ever shared with them what she and Navuh did in private. She was just glad that the goddess wasn't there. It was harder to pretend when those perceptive blue eyes were studying her, seeing through her façade with the wisdom of five thousand years of reading people. Tamira had a feeling that Areana knew something was going on, but so far, she hadn't confronted any of them about it.

When the dining room door opened and a man in uniform entered, Tamira's heart seized for a moment, terrified that Eluheed and Tony had been caught red-handed stealing from the supply room.

But if that was the case, it wouldn't be the engineer delivering the news. It would be one of the harem guards.

Letting out a breath, she forced a smile at Hassan that was the appropriate expression for his surprise visit.

"Good morning, ladies," the engineer said with a respectful bow. "I have an important announcement that I wanted to deliver in person. On Wednesday, there will be an island-wide power shutdown from eight in the morning until noon. The main transformer will be replaced, and we will be installing several new backup generators in the harem."

That was the news they had been waiting for, and Tamira regretted that Eluheed and Tony weren't there to hear it.

"Since the main power will be off and our own backup generators will be replaced, the pyramid will lose ventilation during this time," Hassan explained. "Everyone must evacuate to the surface by seven forty-five."

"Four hours without power?" Beulah asked.

Hassan nodded. "I'm afraid so. Once it is done, though, we should have no more of these annoying outages you were all complaining about."

The flickering lights and short outages had become so common that Tamira barely noticed them anymore, like background noise that only registered when it stopped.

"Thank you for letting us know," Liliat said graciously. "We'll make the proper arrangements." She glanced at Areana's vacant chair, probably thinking what the rest of them were thinking.

The first lady should have been there.

Hassan bowed again and departed, leaving a buzz of conversation in his wake.

"Four hours on the surface," Raviki mused. "It reminds me of the time we were working in the restoration tent. I wonder if they kept it along with the portable air conditioners. I would hate to spend that long in the sun."

"Maybe we can have another beach excursion?" Beulah suggested. "I don't mind spending four hours splashing in the waves."

"That could be lovely," Sarah said.

Tamira tuned them out.

It was better than they had expected. Four hours with no power meant four hours with no surveillance cameras and no alarms. It was almost too perfect, except for one massive problem—everyone would be on the surface. They'd have to find a way to either stay behind and hide until the evacuation was complete, or to sneak back in.

Unless...

She glanced at Tula, who had clearly arrived at the same conclusion. Their eyes met across the table, and Tula gave an almost imperceptible shake of her head.

Not here. Not now.

They would discuss it later, in private, in the safety of the gazebo or with the water running in one of their bathrooms.

The door opened again, and this time it was Areana, who entered looking composed despite what must have been an intense morning with Navuh. She moved with her usual grace to her chair, and servants immediately appeared to serve her breakfast even though she'd already eaten with her mate.

"Good morning, everyone," Areana said, her voice carrying that particular quality that always made Tamira think of silver bells. "I trust you've heard about Wednesday's power outage?"

"Hassan has just informed us," Beulah said.

Areana unfolded her napkin. "The entire island will be affected, but Lord Navuh assured me that security protocols will remain in place."

Of course they would. Tamira had no doubt that the patrols outside the harem would intensify. That didn't affect their plans, though. Immortal soldiers were not allowed in the harem proper, and new human guards would not materialize out of thin air.

"We should make an event of it," Areana said. "A grand picnic on the grounds. Instead of treating it as an inconvenience, we could make it a celebration. I need to check if they kept the restoration tent and if it can be erected in time for the blackout, so we will be comfortable. I can have the kitchen prepare cold foods the night before. Salads, fruits, cold meats, and cheeses. Things that won't require heating."

If everyone were in the tent, sneaking out would be easy. They could use a number of excuses, like bathroom visits or a walk in the gardens to enjoy a few private moments with their partners.

"That sounds lovely," Sarah said. "We could bring cushions, perhaps some games."

"Exactly," Areana said, and her gaze lingered on Tamira for just a moment too long. "We'll make the best of the situation."

There was something in those words, something in the way Areana said them that made Tamira wonder if she suspected more than she let on. But then Areana was turning to discuss menu options with Beulah, and the moment had passed.

33

ELUHEED

"Come in." Tamira ushered Tony and Tula into her room. "Can I offer you tea?"

"Yes, please." Tula sat on the couch with Tony. "The one you made for me the other time was wonderful. What was in it?"

"Ask Elias." Tamira turned to him. "I think there are coconut flakes in it, right?"

He nodded. "White tea, coconut flakes, safflower, and cornflowers. All are good for you."

Tula's hand rested on her belly, which was becoming more pronounced by the day.

"I need your advice," Tamira announced, her voice carrying the kind of brightness that meant she was performing for invisible watchers. "I've been thinking about adding some plants to the bathroom. I've been reading about how soothing it is to be surrounded by greenery, but we have only this one small plant in here, and nothing in the bathroom. I have no idea what to get and where to put it."

"I've become an expert thanks to Elias," Tony played along. "I know just what you need."

"Ferns would work well," Eluheed said, walking toward the bathroom. "I told Tamira that they thrive in humid environments, but she's not overly fond of them. Let me show you what we were thinking of doing."

They filed into the bathroom, and Tamira immediately turned on both taps, filling the space with the sound of rushing water. The noise would mask their conversation, though they would still need to keep their voices low.

For her and Eluheed, the careful choreography of conspiracy had become routine, but explaining two more people in their bathroom required a more inventive plot.

"You've all heard what's going to happen on Wednesday," Tamira said, dispensing with preamble. "That's our chance."

Tula leaned against the vanity. "Four hours without power. No cameras, no electronic locks, no alarms. That should be enough time to get to the submarine, figure out how to turn it on, and get out of here."

It wasn't as simple as that, and Eluheed was about to say so, but Tony cut in.

"Everyone will be on the surface." Tony sat on the edge of the tub. "How do we get to the tunnel without being noticed?"

"We hide," Tamira said. "During the evacuation chaos, we just remain in our rooms, and if anyone comes to check on us, we will say that we are on our way out and then duck under the beds. We need to put the flashlights and other supplies under the beds as well."

Tony shook his head. "I'm worried about Tula. There will be no ventilation in the entire harem, and the tunnel will be just as bad."

"Not necessarily," Eluheed said. "The underground complex is big, and without anyone breathing the air, it would take hours for it to become a problem. We'd have enough time to reach the tunnel, which gets fresh air from the cove, and get to the submarine."

"If it exists," Tony muttered.

Eluheed felt a flash of irritation. "Do you still doubt my foresight abilities?"

Tony had the grace to look uncomfortable. "No, I believe you can see things. But Navuh is devious. What if he planted that vision in your head? What if he wanted to test you? The guy is paranoid, and he suspects everyone of plotting against him."

Eluheed chuckled. "He's not paranoid. Everyone is, in fact, plotting against him because he's a ruthless despot. Some just want to get free, like we do, and others want what he has. But the truth is that I haven't considered that angle, and it's possible that he made up the submarine to trick me. We might not find a fork in the tunnel and a cove with a submarine."

"It's there," Tamira said. "That's the only way any of us can make it off the island, and since you've seen me in New York, we know that it will happen. We should all go together, and if there is no submarine or it's locked and we don't know how to access it, we will just return to the picnic. No one would be any the wiser."

"That's too risky," Tony said. "Elias and I should go first. We scout, confirm the submarine exists, and see if we can access it. And if it's viable, we disable the surveillance cameras on our way back."

"What about us?" Tula's voice carried an edge of hurt. "We just wait for you?"

"To provide cover," Tony said. "If we all go missing from the picnic, someone will notice. But if it's just the two of us, you can make excuses for us. Say we're checking on something in the gardens and that we'll be back soon. You can buy us time."

Tula shifted her weight on the counter. "What happens when the power comes back on and there's no feed from the cameras you've disabled?"

"Navuh is probably the only one monitoring that tunnel," Tamira said. "Only he gets to use it as it's his secret escape route. He wouldn't want security personnel knowing about it. And unless he has reason to check the feeds, he won't bother."

"It's risky," Eluheed said. "But everything about this plan is risky. We're gambling our lives on a vision, a submarine that is most likely locked, and our ability to operate a vessel none of us has ever even seen before."

The bathroom fell silent except for the sound of running water. Each of them was lost in their own calculations of risk versus reward, freedom versus death.

Eluheed's mind drifted to his sessions with the enhanced soldiers, the way their collective consciousness pulled at him, trying to pierce his mental shields. Each encounter left him more drained, his defenses harder to maintain. The curious presence that had been probing at his barriers was growing stronger, more insistent.

"There's something else I've learned today," he said quietly. "Lord Navuh told me that a new scientist is arriving soon to continue experimenting with the enhanced soldiers. A Russian he had extracted from an insane asylum."

Tony's eyebrows rose. "Navuh is trusting a psycho to continue the enhancement program?"

Eluheed smiled. "Brilliance and insanity often walk a thin line. Gorchenco, the warlord responsible for me being here, secured the scientist's release." Eluheed rubbed his temples, feeling the phantom pressure of the enhanced soldiers' minds. "He'll get here as soon as the new testing facility is completed."

"Why does that matter to us?" Tula asked.

"Because once the program resumes, Navuh will want me interacting with the test subjects regularly, and every session weakens my shields. Eventually, they'll break through and discover that I'm plotting escape."

Tony paled. "They could tell Navuh."

"Or worse." Eluheed joined Tula and leaned on the vanity counter. "They could use the information themselves. Thirty-nine minds working in concert, with knowledge of the submarine, the tunnel, and every other secret we've managed to gather."

Tula shifted again, her hand still on her belly. "Let's assume that you find the submarine and that you know how to operate it. What's your next move?"

"Once the cameras are disabled, it's a ticking clock," Eluheed said. "We should leave the next morning, right after Navuh leaves for the mansion."

"What if he doesn't spend the night in the harem?" Tula asked. "If there is a lot going on, he stays in the mansion."

"Then we wait another day. Our best window of opportunity is when he's traveling the tunnel."

Eluheed studied their somber faces. They were amateurs planning an impossible heist, but it was their only option, and the vision of Tamira in New York gave him hope that the impossible would become possible.

"We should get out of here," Tula said. "We've been in here for too long."

They filed out of the bathroom, Tamira turning off the taps. In the bedroom, they made a show of discussing plant varieties, with Tony even pulling out his notebook to sketch placement suggestions.

The conversation felt hollow after their real conversation, and Eluheed wondered if they were fooling anyone. To him, the performance seemed obviously fake, but then he knew it for what it was. To unsuspecting ears and eyes, it might seem genuine.

If they succeeded, they'd be free to find Tamira's son, free to search for Eluheed's sacred treasures, free to live as they pleased.

It was worth the risk, but it wasn't free of guilt.

They would be leaving the rest of the ladies and the entire population of the island to an uncertain future that didn't look good.

The Russian scientist would make everything worse. A madman working with mad soldiers, creating new abominations for Navuh's army. The thought of being forced to touch those new creatures, to open himself up to whatever twisted consciousness they might develop, made Eluheed's skin crawl.

34

TAMIRA

It was already hot at seven-thirty in the morning, the sun mercilessly beating down on the chaos of evacuation. Tamira stood near the pavilion entrance, watching servants hurry past with armloads of cushions, baskets of food, and folded blankets. Children darted between the adults, their excited voices rising above the general din. For them, this was an adventure—an unexpected holiday from the routine of chores and schooling.

"Mind the glassware!" a maid called as two young boys nearly collided with her. She was balancing a tray of cups, her face flushed more because of the heat than exertion. She was one among many, and they were all pitching in.

It always astonished Tamira how many servants worked to maintain the harem. She and the other ladies normally interacted only with the select few who served food in the dining room, cleaned their quarters, and took care of the laundry, but there were so many more.

The restoration tent stood ready on the lawn, its white canvas sides rolled up to allow what little breeze existed to flow through. Tables had been arranged beneath it, already laden with fruit, bread, cheeses, and cold meats prepared the night before. It looked festive, almost celebratory, and Tamira's stomach churned at the disconnect between appearances and reality.

Somewhere in the bowels of the harem, Eluheed and Tony were hidden in a utility closet on the fifth level. They'd slipped away during the evacuation confusion, when servants were busy gathering things for the outdoor picnic and guards were focused on clearing the floors. The plan was for them to wait until the building was empty, then make their way to Areana's quarters and the hidden tunnel entrance.

But what if the air ran out faster than they'd calculated? What if someone did a more thorough check and found them?

"Ladies, this way please!" A guard gestured toward the tent. "We need everyone accounted for before the power shutdown."

Tamira caught Tula's eye across the crowd. The other woman was helping a little girl carry a large pillow. She was dressed in a loose gown, but in the bright sunlight, Tula's condition seemed more obvious than ever.

"Where is Elias?" Beulah asked from behind her. "I haven't seen him or Tony this morning."

"They took the opportunity to explore deep in the gardens." The prepared lie flowed smoothly from Tamira's mouth. "Elias is searching for some rare medicinal plant that he's convinced must grow on this island. Tony went with him to help, and probably to escape the crowd."

Beulah frowned. "They should have waited for more pleasant weather to go exploring. They'll exhaust themselves in this heat."

"You know how Elias gets about his plants," Tamira said with what she hoped was an affectionate eye roll.

Two guards emerged from the pavilion, and Tamira's heart stuttered before she realized they weren't looking for anyone specific. They took positions at either side of the structure, each next to an entrance, their presence a clear message that no one was going back inside until the power was restored.

Having the men stay hidden rather than trying to sneak back in had been the right call.

"The last sweep is complete," one of them said into his communicator. "The building is empty."

Empty except for two men hidden in a closet. Tamira forced herself not to think about the lack of oxygen or let worry show on her face.

"Let's get in the shade," Sarah said, linking her arm through Tamira's. "The heat is already unbearable."

They walked toward the tent, joining the stream of people seeking relief from the sun. The children had already claimed the floor pillows in one corner, where someone had thought to bring board games, cards, and even a few balls for the braver souls willing to play in the heat.

"Tamira dear, where is Elias?" Areana asked as Tamira and Sarah joined her at the ladies' table.

"He and Tony are in the gardens," Tamira said, meeting the goddess's impossibly blue eyes that seemed to see through every pretense. "They are hunting for some exotic plant that Elias swears must be growing wild out there. You know how he gets when he's on a mission."

Areana's expression didn't change, but something flickered in her eyes—suspicion, perhaps, or simple curiosity. "It might take them all morning, and they will miss the picnic."

"That's what I said," Tamira agreed, allowing frustration to color her voice. "But Elias insisted that this was the perfect opportunity because he and Tony couldn't work in the inner courtyard today, and the herb garden didn't need any attention." She leaned closer to Areana and whispered conspiratorially, "I think that he just doesn't like crowds and looks for a good excuse to avoid mingling. He hates that people are still giving him the hero treatment because of what he did during the flooding."

"Hmm." Areana studied her for another moment, then smiled. "Well, I hope they find what they're looking for, and that they don't suffer heat stroke in the process."

She turned to talk with Beulah and Liliat, who were trying to convince her to try one of the board games.

Tamira released a breath.

"That was smooth," Tula murmured, sliding into a chair beside her. "You are scarily good at this, but she still knows something's off."

Tula knew Areana better than any of them, and Tamira had no doubt that she was right. "She always knows. The question is whether she will do anything about it."

"Probably not." Tula rose to her feet. "Let's go to the buffet. The servants won't start eating until we've filled our plates."

They made their way to the food tables, and Tamira was grateful for the excuse to load up plates. Four plates, two for them, and two for their supposedly plant-hunting partners.

"Hungry this morning?" Raviki asked with a raised eyebrow.

"We're taking the food to the gazebo," Tula said. "We are meeting Elias and Tony there when they're done with their treasure hunt."

"Why not have them come here?" Liliat asked.

"You know Elias," Tamira said. "He's not good with crowds. Besides, it's peaceful out there."

"Their loss," Liliat said. "They're missing out on all the fun."

The picnic was taking on a life of its own. Someone had brought out a guitar. One of the servants knew a few songs, and a small group had gathered to listen. In another corner, two kitchen maids were playing a card game with some of the older children.

These were her people. Even the servants felt like extended family.

"Are you okay?" Tula asked as she and Tamira walked away, each balancing two plates.

Tamira realized she'd been standing still, staring at a little girl who was braiding the hair of an even smaller girl. The child's concentration was absolute, her small fingers working with surprising dexterity.

"Yeah. I'm fine," Tamira said. "I'm just going to miss this."

"Don't say things like that," Tula murmured under her breath. "Not here."

"Sorry. I won't."

It was hard to shake the thoughts prompted by what they were doing. If they succeeded in escaping, what would happen to everyone here? Would Navuh rage at their disappearance? Would he take out his anger on those who remained?

Hopefully, he wouldn't.

He'd be coldly furious, but practical. The other ladies hadn't done anything wrong. The servants were valuable resources. He wouldn't waste them out of spite.

Probably.

"Are you coming?" Tula looked at her over her shoulder.

"Yeah."

They walked past the guards, who noted their departure but didn't comment.

The gazebo stood empty and welcoming, its vine-overgrown lattice providing blessed shade. They set the plates on the table and sat on the cushioned benches, finally able to drop their masks.

"How long has it been?" Tula asked.

Tamira checked her watch. "Twenty minutes since the building was declared empty."

"Is that enough time for them to reach the tunnel?"

"It should be." But Tamira wasn't certain.

They'd had to wait for the guards to finish their sweep, then navigate in complete darkness with only flashlights to guide them. The utility closet was on the fifth level, and Areana's quarters were on the first. They had to climb the stairs in the dark, then the careful process of stepping on the right spot, pulling and pushing the books in the correct sequence, and accessing the hidden door without triggering any alarms.

"You know what we haven't considered?" Tula asked suddenly.

"What?"

"That there might be more than one fork in the tunnel, and they won't know which one to take."

For a moment, Tamira allowed herself to panic, but then she remembered what Eluheed had said about his vision. "Elias saw Navuh and Areana running through the tunnel. He would have seen if there were more than one offshoot."

From their vantage point in the gazebo, they could see the top of the tent in the distance, and the colorful flag that someone had hung there. She could hear music drifting in the air and voices raised in song. It was surreal, this juxtaposition of ordinary life continuing while Eluheed and Tony attempted the impossible below.

"I keep thinking about what happens after," Tula said, her voice barely above a whisper. "If we make it out, we will have to find our way to Annani's clan."

Tamira lifted a brow. "What are you talking about? Annani is gone along with all the other gods."

"Right." Tula wiped sweat from her forehead with the back of her hand. "The heat is getting to me, and I'm hallucinating. Perhaps your son will help us. Maybe even Areana's son. They are fugitives just like we will be."

Tamira nodded. "We will be fugitives together, and—"

"Listen," Tula suddenly said.

The sounds of heavy footsteps preceded the appearance of two guards walking in the direction of the gazebo.

Tamira's pulse spiked before she noted their unhurried pace. They weren't coming to arrest anyone. They were probably just checking on them.

"Smile," she murmured to Tula. "We're having a lovely time waiting for our partners."

The guards stopped about twenty feet away, apparently satisfied that the ladies were where they'd said they'd be, then turned back and walked away without even a greeting.

"I hate this," Tula said once they were gone. "We are never left alone. There is always someone watching."

"Soon," Tamira said. "One way or another, soon it'll be over."

Somewhere beneath tons of rock and earth, Eluheed and Tony were either finding their salvation or walking into a trap. And all Tamira and Tula could do was sit in this beautiful gazebo and wait.

The watch on her wrist ticked steadily forward. Thirty minutes. Forty. An hour.

"They should be in the tunnel by now," Tula said.

"Yes."

Another pause. The sound of children's laughter carried from the tent, followed by applause. Some kind of performance, perhaps. Normal life continued its course, oblivious to the drama playing out in the shadows.

"I hate leaving them all," Tamira said.

Tula looked at her. "Our sisters?"

"Not just them. Everyone. They're all trapped here, too."

"We can't save everyone," Tula said softly. "We can barely save ourselves."

She was right, of course. But the guilt was there, regardless of the rationale, a weight she'd carry whether they succeeded or failed.

35

ELUHEED

The utility closet on the fifth level was too small for two adult males to squeeze in. Shelves lined three walls, stocked with cleaning supplies that gave off a chemical smell that made Eluheed's eyes water. He and Tony sat pressed against the wall, flashlights clutched in their hands but not turned on. In the darkness, every sound seemed amplified—their breathing, the distant voices of people evacuating the harem, footsteps on the nearby stairs.

"Seven forty-three," Tony whispered, the luminous dial of his watch the only visible light in the darkness.

Two more minutes until the final sweep, and then fifteen minutes until the power cut, and then a few more minutes to make sure that no one remained in the structure.

Heavy footsteps approached their door, paused, and Eluheed held his breath. The handle rattled, but they'd locked the closet from the inside.

The footsteps moved on.

"That was close," Tony whispered.

They waited in silence as the sounds of evacuation grew more distant.

"Fifth level clear!" A guard's voice echoed from the staircase.

More footsteps receded up the stairwell, then gradually, silence settled over the underground complex.

"Eight o'clock," Tony announced.

As if on cue, the faint hum that had been the background noise of their lives ceased. Ventilation, electrical systems, the pulse of the building itself, everything stilled, and the silence was absolute.

Eluheed clicked on his flashlight, the beam cutting through the darkness. "Let's go."

He unlocked the door, wincing at the click that seemed to echo in the stillness. The corridor beyond was pitch black, their flashlight beams creating dancing shadows on the walls.

They rushed on silent feet toward the stairwell, or as silent as Tony could manage, which left a lot to be desired, but then there was no one in the building, and even the surveillance cameras and microphones were off, so the stealth was more out of habit and fear than necessity.

Funny how the mind twisted things. The ventilation had been cut off only moments ago, and yet the air already felt heavier, even though they had hours before it became a real problem.

The stairwell was a concrete throat descending and ascending into darkness. Their footsteps echoed despite their efforts to move silently. Fourth level. Third. Second. Each landing looked identical in the flashlight beams, distinguished only by the numbers painted on the fireproof doors.

"Wait," Tony said suddenly on the second-level landing.

"What?"

"Listen."

Eluheed strained his ears but heard nothing. "I don't hear anything."

"Exactly. No dripping water, no settling sounds."

"That's a comforting thought," Eluheed muttered, continuing onward.

After the earthquake, the flooding, and the failure of essential systems on the island, it was good to know that the underground pyramid was structurally sound.

They opened the door on the first level and stepped out into the luxurious hallway.

"This way," Eluheed said. He'd been to Areana's domain before and knew his way around it, but everything looked different in the darkness.

The rich carpet muffled their footsteps, and their flashlights reflected off the cream-colored walls.

"In here." Eluheed opened the double doors to Areana's bedroom. "That's the bookcase," he said, finding it with his beam. "The pressure plate is under the third rose from the left in the carpet pattern, about thirty-three centimeters from the wall."

Tony crouched, studying the intricate floral design. "Found it." He pressed down, and there was a soft click.

"Now the books. Herodotus, Plato, Marcus Aurelius pulled out, then Ovid pushed in."

Eluheed found the correct spines and performed the sequence. For a moment, nothing happened. Then a click and a soft grinding sound. Part of the bookcase moved, but Eluheed had to push on it to open it all the way.

Beyond was darkness and the damp smell of earth.

They stepped through, and as Eluheed lifted his head to search for the surveillance cameras, he found them mounted at regular intervals along the concrete wall, connected with a wire that supplied their power. Cutting the cable would probably result in all the cameras in the tunnel going offline, which wasn't a good idea. They only needed to disable those that monitored the section up to the fork, and those leading to the submarine, if there were any in that section of the tunnel.

"Do you want to disable them now?" Tony studied them.

"Not yet. Let's find the submarine first. We don't want to leave evidence of sabotage if we are not going to escape this place. Eventually, it would be found."

"Right," Tony agreed.

The tunnel wasn't as wide as Eluheed had imagined, and a silly image popped into his head of Navuh riding a motorcycle back and forth between his mansion and the harem, his elaborate robes fanning out behind him like a knight's on horseback.

But that wasn't Navuh's style. The tunnel culminated in a wider area that was large enough for a compact vehicle to turn around. That wouldn't have been needed if Navuh were riding a motorcycle.

From where they stood, it sloped slightly downward, its walls carved from living rock and reinforced with concrete in some areas. The floor was all concrete. Their footsteps echoed as they made their way toward what Eluheed hoped was a fork. The slightly salty smell gave him hope that they would find it.

He didn't need to wait long. About twenty-five minutes into their walk, they found the fork in the tunnel, and this section was too narrow for a vehicle. Evidently, Navuh didn't plan to use one once he got to the fork.

They walked shoulder to shoulder through the narrow passage, and no more than ten minutes later the tunnel opened into a natural cave.

"Holy shit," Tony said. "It's real." His flashlight beam illuminated a wooden dock extending into black water and the vessel tied to it.

The submarine was sleek and modern. It resembled an elongated teardrop, maybe fifteen feet long, constructed from what looked like white composite material with a strip of dark glass running along its upper surface—a continuous canopy rather than portholes.

"That's a nice toy," Tony said, playing his flashlight over the smooth hull.

The craft sat partially submerged at a floating dock, its design indicating that it had been built for recreation or research rather than warfare. The transparent canopy would provide panoramic views underwater, and Eluheed could see four leather seats arranged in a row inside. The control panel looked more like a tablet than the console he'd expected.

It looked like a luxury sports car and was obviously a recent acquisition. Had Navuh replaced an older model with this one? Did he go off the island on his own without anyone knowing?

The craft bobbed gently in the black water, looking more like it belonged at a yacht club than hidden in a cave beneath a despot's island fortress.

"A rich guy's toy," Tony said. "I wonder how much a thing like this costs."

The entry hatch was integrated into the canopy—a section that would lift up on hydraulic struts. Beside it was what Eluheed assumed was a scanner, its small LED display dark.

The sub's high-tech seemed incongruent with the cave's rough walls.

"Look at this," Tony said, crouching beside the dock where a charging cable connected to the submarine's hull. "It's electric. Probably has lithium batteries."

"This makes sense." Eluheed peered inside the craft, looking at the console. "Navuh wouldn't want anything that required specialized training to operate. This is designed for civilians and probably has automated systems."

"GPS and tracking systems, too," Tony added. "We'll need to work out how to disable those, but first, we need to figure out how to get in and then how to turn it on."

"Here is the lock." Eluheed pointed at the scanner.

Tony scrambled up beside him. "Let me see." He trained his flashlight on the small panel beside the hatch handle. "It's a fingerprint reader."

"Are you sure? It could be a numeric pad."

"It's a scanner." Tony leaned over and touched the plate. The thing came alive, but there were no numbers on the display.

"Well, it doesn't look like a numeric code, but it might require an entire handprint."

Tony shook his head. "It's too small for that. The question is which finger is needed." He changed the angle of the flashlight's beam. "It's not the thumb, so I assume it's the pointer. Is Navuh right-handed or left-handed?"

"Right-handed," Eluheed said. "How do you suggest we get his fingerprint? Cut his finger off in his sleep?"

"Of course not." Tony chuckled. "It's possible to lift fingerprints from a smooth surface using tape and graphite powder, or even just tape if the print is fresh enough. I saw it done in a movie once. Then it's possible to transfer the fingerprint to whatever surface you want, and it works."

Eluheed stared at him. "Are you suggesting that we get Navuh's fingerprint from something he has touched?"

"It shouldn't be too difficult. All we need to do is intercept the maid who clears the dishes after Navuh and Areana's breakfast. We get the prints and transfer them to something we can use on the scanner."

"That's insane."

"Do you have a better idea?"

Eluheed didn't. "Would it actually work?"

"It should, in theory. The oils from skin leave a decent impression on smooth surfaces. With clear tape and maybe some powder from the kitchen, even flour might work, we could lift the print. Then it's just a matter of transferring it to something the scanner will read. Latex would be ideal, but even clear tape might work if we're careful. We can practice beforehand, so we don't mess it up with the real thing."

Eluheed rubbed the back of his neck. "That means we need more time and can't make our escape tomorrow."

"It's just a small delay. But we know the submarine exists, we know how many it seats, and we have a potential solution for accessing it." Tony swept his light around the cave. "This is a good spot, too. The cave opens to the sea. You can even see light from the entrance over there. Once we're in the water, we're free."

Eluheed looked across the water to where Tony indicated. There was indeed a lighter patch of darkness in the distance that suggested an opening to the outside.

"We need to disable the cameras," Eluheed said.

Tony considered that. "We shouldn't. Now that we know how close the sub is and how easy it is to get to it, we need to rethink our strategy. If we disconnect the cameras now and then have to wait one more day or two to get the fingerprints, the risk that Navuh would check the feed for some reason before we're ready to leave grows. Better to wait until we're actually escaping. One snip, and the power is cut to all of them. A few minutes of dead cameras won't matter if we're already gone."

It made sense, though it meant their next trip would be even more critical. Everything would have to work perfectly, from getting the fingerprint to accessing the submarine, and starting it without any idea how to operate it.

"There's something else," Tony said, crouching to examine the submarine's hull more closely. "Look at these."

Eluheed directed his light where Tony pointed. Small rectangular panels were set into the hull at regular intervals.

"Battery compartments," Tony said. "The question is whether they are charged and how long they can last."

Another unknown in an equation with too many variables already. But they were committed now. They'd found the submarine and confirmed it could hold all four of them. That was more than they'd had this morning.

"I'm sure Navuh would keep the submarine charged. It doesn't make much sense to have an escape vehicle that requires long refueling." He looked at his watch. "We should head back. We've been gone for well over an hour."

They made their way back through the tunnel, their lights creating shadows on the rough walls. The cameras watched blindly, waiting for power to return them to life.

At the bookshelf, Eluheed carefully reset the mechanism while Tony studied the books themselves.

"We need to know exactly which glass or plate Navuh uses," Tony said. "Can't risk getting the wrong prints."

"We'll get them all and use the bigger ones. Areana has dainty fingers."

"Good point," Tony agreed. "And the maid's fingers will be small as well."

36

TAMIRA

Tamira stared at the untouched food meant for Eluheed and Tony, the lie of their supposed meeting at the gazebo growing stale in the afternoon heat. They'd been gone for over an hour and a half now.

"We need to get rid of this," she told Tula, keeping her voice low. "It has occurred to me that they can't get out of the pavilion without our help. When they come out, they'll need us to distract the guards."

Tula nodded, casting nervous glances at the walkway leading to the gazebo. "We can dump the food in those bushes." She indicated a thick cluster of flowering shrubs. "With all the small animals living in the gardens, the evidence will be gone in minutes."

"Nevertheless, we should make an effort to hide it. Someone else might decide to seek solitude in the gazebo, and the smell alone will give the food away."

Tula crinkled her nose. "You are right. It has become pungent. But I have no intention of digging in the dirt with the fork to bury it."

"We'll just cover it well," Tamira said.

They scraped the food into the undergrowth, covered it as best they could with branches and loose leaves, and then stacked the empty plates as if the men had eaten and departed.

As they rushed back while trying to look like they were in no hurry, Tamira's mind cycled through all the possible disasters that could have befallen the men. What if they'd been trapped in the closet because someone locked it from the outside? What if the air had run out faster than calculated? What if someone had stayed behind and caught them? What if there was a battery-operated alarm at the entrance to the tunnel?

There hadn't been any commotion, and the guards were still standing at the two entrances to the pavilion, looking bored. Through the glass doors, she could see the darkened outlines of the interior.

"The interrogation committee is coming," Tula murmured in Tamira's ear.

Tamira's shoulders tensed before she forced them to relax.

"Ladies." Areana smiled. "I haven't seen you. Where have you been?"

"The gazebo," Tula said. "We got food for Elias and Tony."

"Aha." Areana moved to stand before them. "I was starting to wonder whether you decided to assist the men in their search for that exotic herb. Several people have asked about you."

"The men took a break and came to the gazebo to eat," Tula lied smoothly. "Wolfed down their food like starving animals and ran back to continue their hunt."

"In this heat." It wasn't quite a question.

"Men," Tula said with a shrug that made Areana's lips curl up in a smile.

"Indeed." Areana looked between them. "Are you waiting here for them to return?"

"We came to get water," Tamira said. "Elias forgets to hydrate when he's focused on something. We will take it to them."

That particular detail about Elias forgetting his thirst and hunger while working was true, and Areana would know it from the times he had worked in the indoor garden for hours without a break. The best lies were interwoven with truths.

"Yes, he does forget to take care of himself," Areana said. "But at least he's good at taking care of you." She smiled knowingly and walked away.

Tamira let out a breath. "Go watch the other door," she told Tula. "I trust you have a plan to distract the guard so the men can sneak by him?"

Tula grinned. "I'm the queen of distractions." She walked away with a sway of her hips that was more like her old self, before she discovered that she was pregnant and started to panic.

It was awkward to just stand near the pavilion and watch the door, and when the guard gave her a curious look, Tamira fanned herself with her hand. "The tent is too stifling. It's cooler here in the shade."

He dipped his head. "Of course, my lady. You can stand in the shade of the building, but you cannot enter."

"I know." She pouted prettily. "I can't wait for the power outage to end so we can all go back and enjoy air conditioning. I hate this heat."

He nodded with a smile, his posture relaxing.

Tamira was proud of herself. She still knew how to do that. How to disarm people and make them like her. She hadn't lost her touch.

A few moments later, a movement beyond the glass doors caught her eye. It was just a flicker, but it was unmistakable. Getting closer, she could see Eluheed through the glass, peeking through the stairwell door and motioning with his hand.

"The shade is shrinking," she excused her actions to the guard. "It's so hot." She fanned herself with her hand. "Is there any way you can leave your post for a few seconds and get me a bottle of water from the cooler in the tent? I'm starting to feel faint."

The guard looked torn. "I would have loved to, but I can't leave my post."

"Are you sure?" She wiped sweat from her forehead. "I'm so parched."

"I'm so sorry, my lady."

Behind him, she could see the stairwell door opening wider and Eluheed gesticulating to her.

The guard wasn't going to budge no matter what charms she employed. She should have asked Tula about her methods of distraction, but Tula was on the other side of the pavilion, watching the other door and probably flirting with the other guard.

Tamira's only option was thralling, which she hadn't attempted in centuries, and even then she hadn't been good at it. She'd never had use for the ability and hadn't practiced it.

Still, the guard was human and not very bright, and those types were the easiest to thrall because they didn't have any mental walls up.

She reached out with her mind, and her rarely used ability felt rusty and strange. As she'd suspected, the guard's consciousness was easy to access. *Your bladder is full. Painfully full. You need to pee so badly that you are about to embarrass yourself in front of the lady.* She pushed the thought, threading it into his mind like a needle through fabric.

For a long moment, his expression remained neutral, and she thought she'd failed, but then she saw his stance shift slightly.

She pushed harder, imagining the sensation herself and projecting it.

Urgent. Can't wait.

A muscle in his jaw twitched.

"I would really like a drink of water," she continued conversationally. "It will take you only seconds to run to the tent and get me a bottle. You can get one for yourself as well. You must be thirsty."

"I have to go." The words came out strained. "Can you please make sure no one enters? I'll be right back with your water."

"Of course." She gifted him with her brightest smile. "I'll stand guard until you return."

"Thank you, my lady." He dashed toward the nearest cluster of bushes.

Tamira stood with her back to the door, pushed it slightly open, and waved her hand. Eluheed and Tony ducked outside behind her and immediately beelined in the same direction the guard had gone.

Somehow, miraculously, no one had noticed, and as Tamira waited for the guard to return, her heartbeat eventually returned to normal.

The guy returned a few moments later, his face red with embarrassment and holding two bottles of water in his hands. "My apologies, my lady." He handed her a bottle.

"No need to apologize. Thank you for the water." She made a show of uncapping it and taking a long, grateful sip. "That was lifesaving." She rewarded him with another bright smile. "I feel revived."

She waved her hand and walked away, circling to where Tula was still watching the other door.

"We should return to the shade of the gazebo," she said. "It's much cooler out there."

Tula lifted a brow.

"Didn't you see them?" Tamira whispered. "They passed right by you."

"I didn't. I was busy charming the guard."

"Let's get more water and go find them. I bet they are thirsty."

They made their way to the refreshment station in the tent and picked more water bottles from the cooler while several people watched.

They found the men where they'd agreed to meet, both covered in fresh dirt, and their shirts soaked with sweat.

"That was quick," Tula said. "You're already in costume."

"Water," Eluheed said gratefully, taking the bottle she offered and draining half immediately.

"What did you find?" Tula demanded.

"The submarine exists," Tony said between gulps of water. "It has four seats, so we won't have to sit in each other's laps."

"It needs a fingerprint to open," Eluheed said. "We assume it's programmed to Navuh's."

Tamira's spirits took a nosedive. They couldn't get into the vessel without taking Navuh with them, and good luck with that.

"How are we going to get it?" Tula asked.

"We can collect his fingerprints from a glass he touched," Tony explained in a whisper. "I've seen it done in a movie, so I'm not a hundred percent sure it will work, but we can practice it before ambushing the maid after she collects the dirty dishes from Areana's apartment."

"When are we doing that?" Tula asked.

"Tonight, we practice," Eluheed said, "and if it works the way Tony says it does, he and I will wait for the maid in the service elevator and offer to take the tray of dirty dishes to the kitchen for her."

"I'll come with you," Tamira said. "She won't surrender the dishes just because you offer, and she might get suspicious. I can thrall her to give them up and forget she ever saw us."

Eluheed's brows shot nearly all the way to his hairline. "You can do that?"

She nodded. "I have just discovered that I can. I thralled the guard to leave his post. I made him think that he urgently needed to relieve himself." She chuckled. "I haven't done that in centuries and was afraid that it wouldn't work, but it did. I'm quite proud of myself."

"As you should be." Tula regarded her with open appreciation. "Females usually can't thrall."

"You know what they say about desperate times," Tamira said. "You do things you didn't think you could."

37

ELUHEED

The service corridor on the first level was just as nice as the rest of the floor, with plush carpets and cream-colored walls, but it was narrower, and no precious artwork hung on the walls or perched on top of pedestals.

Eluheed stood with Tamira and Tony near the service elevator, all three trying to look casual despite the hammering in their chests.

They shouldn't have been there. This area was restricted to staff, and the presence of a guard at the corridor entrance had been an unwelcome surprise.

"I didn't expect to see a guard in the servants' area," Tony whispered, shifting nervously. "You handled him brilliantly."

"Thank you." Tamira grinned. "I think so too. In fact, I'm getting better at it."

Eluheed had watched with admiration as she'd approached the guard with perfect confidence, her voice taking on that particular tone of authority that came from millennia of practice. "We need someone with exceptional hearing in the courtyard. There is a water leak somewhere, and we need to find it before it creates a problem. You are the perfect man for that, and Lady Areana will be very grateful if you help solve the mystery of that leak."

She'd later told them that she didn't need to speak the words. It was enough that she thought them and imagined herself pushing them into the guard's mind. She'd done that for them, so they would know what instructions she was giving him.

The guard hadn't hesitated. He'd practically run toward the staircase, leaving his post unmanned.

"How long do we have?" Tony asked again.

Tamira looked smug. "Since there is no leak, he will keep looking until I release him from the thrall. We don't need to worry about him anymore."

The service elevator dinged softly, and all three of them froze, but it was just a maid with folded linens. She gave them a curious look but said nothing and tried to hurry past them with her cart of freshly laundered towels and bedding.

"Wait," Tamira commanded.

The maid stopped and turned. "Yes, my lady?"

"You didn't see anyone standing out here." Tamira waved a hand. "Carry on with your duties."

The girl continued on her way in a less hurried way now that she was oblivious to anyone watching her.

"We should have done this last night after dinner," Tony muttered. "Less traffic."

Tamira shook her head. "The lord usually doesn't leave after dinner. I'd rather do it when he's not here."

"Right." Tony rubbed his chin. "I don't want him around either. Areana might show us mercy, but he won't."

"The maid with the dishes should be coming out soon," Tamira said. "I just hope that she comes out with plenty of glasses covered with his fingerprints."

Last night, they had practiced in Tony and Tula's bathroom, which they had turned into a makeshift laboratory, with tape, powder, and various glasses they'd borrowed from the trolley of dirty dishes from the dining room. It had taken several tries until they managed to lift a full fingerprint and not just a fragment, but Tony's technique had worked exactly as he'd described, lifting prints from glass using tape and transferring them. They'd practiced until they could do it quickly, cleanly, and without smudging.

The back door of Areana's suite opened, and the maid emerged backward, pulling a trolley laden with the remains of breakfast. There were several crystal glasses, which would do them no good with all that etching, but also regular glasses that were perfect for collecting fingerprints.

"Excuse me," Tamira said.

The maid started, her hand lifting to her chest. "My lady? How can I help you?"

"You can't, but I can help you. We will take some of these dishes for you and deliver them to the kitchen, you will forget that you saw us and that we took anything."

Tamira lifted her hand and brushed the girl's arm, just a light touch, but Eluheed saw the maid's eyelids drooping. "Rest a little bit. You look pale."

The girl nodded and leaned against the wall while they wrapped the glasses they needed in cloth, and the men stuffed them in their pockets.

"You can go now," Tamira told the maid.

The girl entered the service elevator with her trolley, sans just a few simple glasses that no one would miss, and pressed the button for the main kitchen on level seven.

As soon as the elevator door closed, the three of them rushed into the stairwell.

"Wait," Tony hissed as they reached the landing on the second level. "Someone's coming."

When the footsteps receded, Tamira opened the door and peered out into the second-level corridor. "All clear."

They stepped outside and rushed toward Tony and Tula's room. The ladies were hopefully still in the dining room, eating their breakfast and wondering where Tula, Tamira, and their partners were.

They made it to the room without incident, and as Tula opened the door, the four of them immediately continued to the bathroom.

"Finally! I was starting to think something had gone wrong."

"The maid took a long time to come out," Eluheed said. "But we need to leave everything here and go to breakfast, or the others will get suspicious. If anyone asks, you felt nauseous, and we didn't want to leave you alone."

Tula nodded, although she was just as eager as they were to get on with the fingerprint transfer. "Let's get this over with."

They made their way to the dining room, where the other ladies were already halfway through the meal, and several heads turned as they entered.

"There you are," Sarah said. "We were beginning to wonder what happened to you."

"I wasn't feeling well," Tula said, one hand on her stomach. "They stayed with me out of solidarity."

"You should eat something," Beulah suggested. "Even if it's just toast."

They took their seats, and servants immediately appeared with fresh plates. Eluheed forced himself to eat normally, though he couldn't taste anything. Tomorrow, at the same time, they would either be free or dead.

"Good morning, everyone." Areana entered with her usual flourish.

She took her seat at the head of the table and smiled at the other ladies before her gaze settled on Eluheed. "Good morning, Elias. Did you find what you were looking for in the gardens yesterday?"

The question caught him off guard for a moment before he remembered his alibi. He and Tony had supposedly been searching for a rare plant while everyone else was enjoying the picnic.

"I did not," he said. "But I'm not giving up. I know I will eventually find it." Maybe he would, but not on this island.

"Persistence often pays off," Areana said, and something in her tone made him wonder if she meant more than just plants.

"We should organize more picnics," Tamira said, changing the subject. "It was nice being outside together."

"When it's not that hot," Tula added. "Maybe in the evening next time."

"That's a lovely idea," Liliat agreed. "We could have lanterns to make it festive. The kids loved the morning picnic, and I'm sure they would love a nighttime picnic as well. We can even have bonfires and roast some potatoes."

The conversation continued, flowing around different topics that felt surreal in the context of their impending escape. They were discussing future picnics when they planned to be gone.

Every word felt like another lie added to the pile.

Raviki was describing a picnic they had all attended centuries ago in the old compound when Tula suddenly pushed back from the table.

"Excuse me," she said, her face pale. "I'm not feeling well again."

"I'll go with you," Tamira said immediately, rising to her feet.

Tony and Eluheed stood as well.

"I'll mix a herbal remedy for you that might ease your symptoms."

"Thank you." Tula smiled at him weakly.

"The poor dear," Beulah said sympathetically. "The heat isn't helping her condition."

They left the dining room quickly, with Tula playing up her nausea just enough to be believable. Once they were back in her bathroom, she straightened.

"That was awful," she said. "I hated sitting there and talking about future plans."

"It was necessary," Tamira said. "Now let's get to work, or no one will be leaving tomorrow."

Tony pulled on a pair of latex gloves. "The orange juice glass first," he said, unwrapping it carefully. "Multiple big prints here."

The fingerprints were visible even without powder, oil whirls, and ridges catching the light. Tony applied tape with the delicacy of a surgeon, pressing gently to capture every detail.

"That's perfect," Eluheed murmured, seeing the complete print transfer to the tape.

They worked methodically, lifting prints from each glass and creating multiple copies on the thin latex membranes. Each one had to be perfect.

They wouldn't get a second chance.

"Three good prints of the index finger on the right hand," Tony announced finally. "We also have several others that we will take with us just in case the index is not the right fingerprint."

Eluheed held one of the latex prints up to the light, seeing Navuh's identity captured in the swirls and ridges. Such a small thing to represent their freedom.

They cleaned everything meticulously, removing any trace of their work. The glasses would need to be returned to the kitchen somehow, but that could wait for later. For now, they had what they needed.

"We should keep to our normal routines," Tamira said. "We need to be visible." She looked at Tula. "You can stay here if you want. You have a good excuse."

Tula shook her head, and Eluheed caught a sheen of tears in her eyes. "I'm never going to see them again," she said. "I might as well spend the last day here with my sisters."

38

TAMIRA

When the bathroom door clicked shut behind Eluheed and Tony, who'd left to continue their work on the indoor garden, Tamira turned to find Tula gripping the edge of the vanity, her knuckles white against the marble.

"Tula? What's wrong? Are you really feeling nauseous?"

Tula shook her head, and then a sob escaped her. "I don't know how I'm going to do this." Her shoulders started shaking as tears streamed down her face. She pressed a hand to her mouth, trying to muffle the sounds, but they came anyway—raw, desperate gasps that seemed torn from somewhere deep inside.

"Oh, Tula." Tamira wrapped her arms around her.

"I'm never going to see them again," Tula choked out between sobs. "Areana, Sarah, Beulah, Liliat, Raviki. They're my family. How am I supposed to just leave them behind? Can we take them? I mean all but Areana. They can sit on our laps. He wouldn't miss any of us. He only cares about Areana."

The words hit Tamira like a punch to the gut, and suddenly her own eyes were burning. While she'd been focused on the escape, on the logistics and dangers, she'd managed to shove her feelings aside, but now they crashed over her, amplified by the tsunami of Tula's emotional turmoil.

"We can't take them," she whispered, her own tears falling now. "I hate to say it, but we can't trust them with this secret. They might complain, but they are content to be here. They are like birds who forgot how to fly and are afraid of the sky."

Tula nodded. "I know. I was like them until this." She put a hand over her belly. "The outside world terrified me, and I had much less reason than you to fear it. You are so brave."

Tamira shook her head. "I'm not brave. I'm desperate. I need to get Elias out of here and find my son."

They stood next to the vanity, holding each other as grief poured out of them. Grief for the family they were abandoning, for the relationships that had sustained them through millennia of captivity, for the familiar rhythms of their lives for the past five thousand years.

Something about what Tula had said didn't sit well with Tamira. What had she meant by having less reason to fear the outside world? But Tamira didn't have the energy to examine her words.

"I'm afraid that Navuh will take his anger out on them," Tula sniffled.

"He won't," Tamira said, though she wasn't sure of that. "They're too valuable to him. And they are innocent. They don't know about our escape plan, and they won't know where we've gone. Even we don't know where we are going."

"Areana suspects something." Tula moved to sit on the edge of the tub. "She gives me the look. The one that says she knows more than she lets on."

Tamira sat beside her, their shoulders touching. "If she knows, she's choosing to let us go."

They sat in silence for a moment, both lost in their own thoughts. Then Tula let out a shaky laugh. "Look at me, falling apart. It must be the pregnancy hormones. I'm usually more resilient than this."

"They are not making this any easier, that's for sure," Tamira said. "But we have no choice." She glanced at Tula's belly. "You know why you are doing this."

"I know." Tula closed her eyes for a moment. "I can't let them take my baby. If it's a boy, they'll turn him into another one of Navuh's monsters, raised to conquer and destroy. And if it's a girl..." She touched her stomach. "She'll grow up in this prison, age like a human while I stay young. I don't want to watch her wither and die while I remain unchanged."

"Darien isn't a monster," Tamira felt offended on her son's behalf. "Kalugal isn't a monster either. Some of them managed to retain their souls."

Tula's eyes widened as she realized that she'd hurt Tamira's feelings. "I'm sorry. I shouldn't have said that."

"It's okay. I understand what you're trying to say. This is so your child will have a life worth living. So he'll have freedom."

Tula nodded, taking a deep breath. "Thank you for giving me this chance. For including us. That was very brave and very generous of you."

Tamira smiled. "As it turned out, we're stronger together. Tony knows a lot about a lot of things."

"He deserves to be free too," Tula murmured. "He was stolen from his life, his dreams. Maybe he can even find that blonde bioinformatician he was in love with."

Tamira's eyebrows rose. "Do you want to get rid of him? Don't you love him?"

Tula shrugged, the gesture so casual it was jarring after her emotional breakdown. "Tony is okay. He's good company, decent in bed, and he cares about me. But he's human, Tamira. We both know there's no real future for us. I know that you have somehow reconciled yourself to Elias's mortality, but I can't do that."

"You are carrying Tony's child, and he deserves to be part of that child's life. Besides, who would you replace him with? There aren't exactly immortal males lining up for you out there." Tamira shifted on the narrow ledge. "Unless you want one of Navuh's soldiers, which I know you don't, even if they wouldn't report you."

"There are others," Tula said with such certainty that Tamira turned to stare at her. "Other immortals who are not part of the Brotherhood."

"What are you talking about? What do you know that I don't?"

Tula hesitated, biting her lower lip. "I can't tell you yet because we still might get caught. I'll tell you when we're safe. When we're off this island and far from here."

"Tula—"

"Don't. Just be patient."

Tamira studied her friend's face, seeing fear and determination there. Tula knew something that might endanger someone, and she wasn't going to budge.

"Fine," Tamira agreed. "When we're safe."

Looking relieved, Tula stood and walked over to the mirror to examine her tear-stained face. "I look awful."

"You look like a pregnant woman dealing with hormones." Tamira joined her at the mirror. "That's the perfect cover."

They both looked terrible, with red, puffy eyes and faces blotchy from crying, but they were immortal, and in moments all those signs of distress would disappear.

Tamira watched Tula carefully pat her face with a wet

washcloth, hands steady now despite the emotional storm that had just passed.

"Do you really not love Tony?" Tamira asked.

"I care about him." Tula put the washcloth down on the vanity. "He makes me laugh, and he's kind to me, but he's not the man of my dreams."

"Does he know?"

"He's not stupid despite acting like a buffoon sometimes." Tula turned from the mirror. "I never told him that I love him, so he can't claim that I led him on."

It was sad but honest.

Tula straightened her dress, checking her appearance one more time. "I'm not ending things with Tony, and I don't intend to keep him away from his child. But I can do all that without being in love with him, and if he wants to find happiness with someone else once we are free, I will not stop him."

"That's fair." Tamira smoothed a hand over her hair, which had gotten loose from the updo she'd crafted that morning.

"What should we do for the rest of the day?" Tula asked. "I can't just sit here thinking about tomorrow."

"We do what we always do." Tamira reached for Tula's hairbrush and ran it through her hair. "We can go to the library and help with the book restoration, or you can stay here and rest, watch a movie, or read a book, and I'll go alone and tell the others you are still not feeling well."

They'd already packed the few belongings they were taking with them, mostly jewelry they could sell and use to support themselves. Eluheed and Tony had talked about selling the submarine, but Tamira imagined it would be a much more difficult transaction than selling gold and precious stones.

"I need to be with them today," Tula said. "I can't squander my last day with my sisters."

"Can you manage to do that without crying?"

Tula nodded. "And if a few tears escape, I'll blame my hormones."

They left Tula's room together but parted in the corridor. Tamira headed toward the library while Tula went to the common room, where some of the ladies often gathered in the afternoon.

The library was quiet when Tamira entered, only Sarah and Liliat working among the damaged books. They looked up when she entered.

"Is Tula feeling better?" Sarah asked.

"She is," Tamira said, which was true enough. "The hormonal changes are making her emotional."

"Poor dear," Liliat said. "It's such a difficult time under the best of circumstances, and these are hardly those."

If only they knew how far from ideal the circumstances truly were.

Tamira took her place at one of the restoration tables, picking up where she'd left off the other day. The book in front of her was a history of somewhere she'd never been, but if their escape plan worked, she might visit the place one day and see with her own eyes what she'd only read about in books.

39

ELUHEED

The dining room felt suffocating despite the efficient air conditioning. Eluheed forced himself to take another bite of eggs, though they tasted like sawdust in his mouth. Across the table, Tamira was moving food around her plate with the same false attention to eating, while Tula sat pale and tense, holding Tony's hand under the table.

This was it. Their last breakfast in captivity—or their last breakfast alive.

"The indoor garden looks more beautiful every day," Beulah said, directing the comment toward Eluheed. "You and Tony have worked miracles."

"Thank you." Eluheed set down his fork. "But there is still a lot to be done, and we should get back to it." He rose to his feet.

Tony stood as well, wiping his mouth with his napkin. "Elias is a brutal task master."

Eluheed admired the guy's ability to joke under any circumstances. It was a gift.

"He's dedicated," Liliat said with a warm smile, which cut through Eluheed like a knife.

These women had been nothing but kind to him, welcoming him into their family, trusting him. And he was about to disappear without a word, leaving them to face whatever consequences might follow.

"We'll see you again at lunch, ladies," he said with a slight dip of his head, the lie smooth on his lips and guilt churning in his stomach.

As they walked toward the interior courtyard, Eluheed's heightened senses catalogued everything—the soft sound of their footsteps on carpet, the hum of ventilation, the distant murmur of servants busy with their daily routines. Would this be the last time he heard these sounds? Or would they become the soundtrack to his execution?

In the garden, they headed toward the large planter where they'd hidden their supplies yesterday, wrapped in waterproof material and buried beneath a transplanted fern.

The door to the garden opened, and Eluheed's heart stopped before he recognized one of the maids heading their way with two tall glasses filled with water.

"Lady Sarah asked me to bring these out to you," the maid said.

"Thank you." Eluheed took the glasses from her. "And

please thank Lady Sarah for her thoughtful consideration."

"I will." She dipped her head and turned on her heel.

Tony let out a breath. "I'm not even thirty yet, but my heart feels like it's going to quit on me."

Eluheed shook his head. "Just breathe deeply and imagine success. Tamira says that you need to believe in your goals for them to manifest."

"I'm trying." Tony watched him check the waterproof bundle that held everything they'd managed to gather. Four flashlights, a rope, wire cutters, a knife, the latex fingerprints, and some basic provisions in case they needed them. It wasn't much, but it was all they had. He and Tony weren't even taking a change of clothing. Space on the submarine was limited, and there were more important things to take.

They hefted the potted fern onto a wheeled cart and waited for the signal.

Eluheed's palms were sweating, and he wiped them on his pants. The moments stretched into infinity, every minute feeling like an hour.

Then he saw them, Tamira with her arm wrapped around Tula, who was hunched forward, one hand pressed to her stomach. They paused at the door, and Tamira caught his eye through the glass and nodded.

It was time.

Areana had arrived at the dining room, which meant that Navuh had left and was traveling through the tunnel.

They didn't have much time.

"Let's get moving," Eluheed said to Tony.

They maneuvered the cart through the corridor to the service elevator, where a guard stood, watching them approach.

"We are delivering this to Lady Areana's quarters," Eluheed said, keeping his voice casual. "She requested another plant for her quarters, bigger than the one I brought her before."

The guard's eyes narrowed slightly. "I wasn't informed."

"The lady must have forgotten," Tony said smoothly. "She made the request last night."

The guard studied them for another agonizing moment, then stepped aside and waved them through. "Don't take long."

The elevator ride up to the first level was short and yet felt interminable. Eluheed counted each second, and beside him, Tony was breathing too fast, on the edge of panic.

"Steady," Eluheed murmured. "Take a deep breath."

When the doors opened on the first level's service corridor, Tamira and Tula were already there, waiting for them, their small packs clutched in their hands.

Tula looked genuinely ill, her face pale and drawn.

"I'm going to handle the guard." Tamira handed him her pack and walked to where the guard was stationed near the entrance to Areana's quarters.

Eluheed watched as she approached the man with confidence and grace that came from millennia of practice.

"I need your exceptional hearing again," she said. "The leak in the garden has gotten worse. I need you to listen very carefully. It is okay if it takes you a long time to locate. This is more important than anything else."

The guard's eyes went slightly unfocused, then he nodded. "Of course, my lady. I'll find it for you."

When he walked away, Eluheed released a breath. There was nothing more between them and the tunnel except the hidden mechanism.

Tamira opened the double doors to Areana's bedroom, and he and Tony maneuvered the cart close to the bookshelf.

"Ready?" Tamira looked at him, her foot hovering over the third rose on the carpet.

He nodded. "Heroes Plot Military Overthrows," he murmured, reaching for the books a moment after the first click sounded. Herodotus, then Plato, then Marcus Aurelius, and then the final one—Ovid—pushed instead of pulled.

The soft click seemed impossibly loud in the quiet corridor.

Nothing happened.

For one heart-stopping moment, Eluheed thought they'd failed, that Areana had somehow changed the sequence or that Tamira had miscounted the roses.

Then the grinding sound began, and the bookshelf cracked open.

"We did it," Tony breathed.

Eluheed grabbed the pack from the planter and pulled out four flashlights, handing them to Tula, Tony, and Tamira. They had to move quickly now, before—

"That's quite impressive."

The voice froze them all in place.

Areana stood in the doorway to her bedroom, her expression unreadable. She wore a yellow silk gown, her pale hair pulled back, and she looked every inch the goddess she was—beautiful and utterly composed.

Eluheed's mind went blank with terror. They were caught. Everything was over. Navuh would kill them all, slowly, and probably make the others watch.

"Lady Areana," Tamira started, but the goddess raised one pale hand.

"Please, don't insult me with lies." She moved further into the room, her gaze sweeping over the open doorway, the loaded plant cart, and their guilty faces. "I've known something was happening for days. I've watched you whispering in corners, seen the looks you exchange. I feared—" She paused, and something like pain crossed her perfect features. "I feared you were planning to assassinate Lord Navuh."

Tula made a sound somewhere between a laugh and a sob. "Assassinate him? That's ludicrous. We'd never succeed. We just want to leave. I can't have my baby taken away from me."

Areana's impossibly blue eyes settled on her, and Eluheed saw understanding dawn in them. "You found the submarine."

"Elias saw it in a vision," Tula said, and her voice broke. She stepped forward, away from the others, placing herself between Areana and the rest of them. "This is my fault. All of it. They're doing this for me."

"Tula, no—" Tamira started.

"It's true!" Tula's hands went to her belly, cradling the small swell there. "I can't deliver my baby on this island. I can't let them take him away. I can't—" She dissolved into tears. "I have a feeling it's a boy. I'm always right about these things. And they'll steal him from me just like they stole all the others. They'll turn him into another warrior, another killer, and I'll be left with nothing but the memory of holding him for a few precious months."

She was crying openly now, tears streaming down her face as she sank to her knees before Areana.

"Please," Tula begged, her voice raw. "Please let me go. Let us go. I need a future for him. I need him to grow up free, to choose his own path, to be more than just another soldier in Navuh's army. Please."

Eluheed felt his own throat tighten. This was why they were risking everything—not for themselves, but for the unborn child who deserved better than what this island demanded, for Eluheed's charges that had to be returned home, and for Tamira, who'd never gotten to know her son.

Areana was silent for a long moment, studying Tula's tear-stained face. When she finally spoke, her voice was soft. "You won't be able to use the submarine." Areana's words fell like stones into water. "Even if you somehow manage to get inside."

"We have Navuh's fingerprints," Tony said quickly. "We lifted it from his breakfast glass. We can get in."

Areana's eyebrows rose slightly. "Clever. That will indeed get you past the biometric lock." She paused, and Eluheed saw something like regret in her eyes. "But the submarine won't start for you. It requires a code that only Navuh knows. It's never written down. He has it memorized."

The last embers of hope that had still smoldered in Eluheed's chest fizzled out. Of course, Navuh would have multiple layers of security. The fingerprint was just the first barrier.

They'd been focused on getting past it and had chosen to believe that they would find a way to make the submarine work.

Tula let out a sound of pure anguish, her body folding in on itself. "It's over then. All of this, all the planning, the risk, the hope, it's all for nothing."

She sobbed into her hands, her shoulders shaking. Tony moved to kneel beside her, wrapping his arms around her, but she was inconsolable. The sound of her grief filled the room, raw and terrible.

Eluheed felt his own despair rising.

They'd come so close. The tunnel was right there, open before them. The submarine waited in its hidden cove. But without the code, it was as inaccessible as if it were on another planet.

He thought of his charges, buried beneath Mount Ararat, awaiting his return that would never come. He thought of Tamira's vision of freedom in New York, walking with her son. Had that been real, or just wishful thinking translated into false prophecy?

Areana crossed the space to kneel beside Tula and took the sobbing woman into her arms, cradling her like a child.

Eluheed saw tears glistening in the goddess's eyes.

"Hush," Areana said softly, stroking Tula's hair. "Hush now. All hope isn't lost."

Tula raised her head, her face blotchy and tear-stained. "It isn't?"

"You know that there is another way," Areana said, sounding desolate and hopeful at the same time. "There is another way," she repeated. "I'll get you off this island." She turned to look at him, Tamira, and Tony. "All of you."

Eluheed felt the world shift beneath his feet.

Tula wiped her tears with the back of her hand. "Can they really do that? Rescue all four of us?"

Areana shrugged. "If they did it with one, they can do it with four." She swept her gaze over them again. "The four of you need to return to your duties and pretend that this never happened." She returned her gaze to Tula. "You should have trusted me."

Tula lowered her head. "Forgive me. I didn't think I was worthy."

"Oh, Tula." A single tear slid down Areana's cheek. "Don't you know that you are like a daughter to me? I love you, and I will be inconsolable when you leave, but I will always put your well-being and happiness before mine."

COMING UP NEXT
The Children of the Gods Book 101
Dark Island: Rescue

What fate awaits Tula and her child?

Will Tamira be reunited with the son taken away from her over a century ago?

Can Eluheed find a way to retrieve the sacred treasures buried beneath Mount Ararat?

What is Navuh hiding in the basement of his mansion?

Find the answers in the Dark Island trilogy, starting with Dark Island Rescue

To read a preview on the VIP Portal, Join the VIP Club

To find out what's included in your free membership, flip to the last page.

BONDS OF WINGS AND FURY
The Two-Faced God

READ THREE MORE CHAPTERS IN THE ENCLOSED
EXCERPT:

CHAPTER 1 WAS INCLUDED IN:
DARK SHAMAN: THE LOST TREASURE.

CHAPTERS 2 & 3 WERE INCLUDED IN:
DARK SHAMAN: LOVE FOUND.

IN A WORLD where dragons dominate the skies and colossal worms tunnel through mountains, three nations teeter on the brink of war.

Like every Elucian, Kailin must brave the perilous pilgrimage to Mount Hope's summit, where an ancient shaman will decide her fate. A select few are destined to bond with dragons, and for most, it's the ultimate prize. Not so for Kailin, who is hiding a paralyzing fear of heights and would rather sketch the magnificent beasts than ride them.

Alar appears to be a privileged Elurian seeking the glory and immortality of dragon riders. Yet beneath his aristocratic facade lies a secret agenda that could disrupt the delicate alliance between the reclusive Elucia and the cosmopolitan Elurian Federation.

When Kailin and Alar cross paths, sparks fly, and as they ascend the perilous mountain, hunted by shadowy assassins and tested by ancient rites, their unlikely bond deepens.

Defying a thousand years of tradition, an impossible selection puts the star-crossed lovers at the center of an ancient prophecy. But in a world where dragons have their own agendas and even the gods aren't what they seem, the greatest threat may yet come from within.

This new series takes place in the larger universe of the gods, and while it stands alone, the two series will converge.
The book is scheduled for release on January 17, 2026, but it may be released earlier.

Click HERE to read the enclosed excerpt chapters.

BONDS OF WINGS AND FURY

THE TWO-FACED GOD

CHAPTER 4: ALAR

"Wise words might avert unnecessary bloodshed, but when words fail, strike without mercy and aim to win."

—Commander Darius Hawke, Elite Forces' Vedona Academy

As Codric and I made our way toward the back of the line, I took stock of the scene around us. The central depot was a hive of activity, with Elucians from all walks of life waiting to board the cable car that would take us over the steep mountains to the nerve center of Elucia—Podana, the capital city.

My gaze shifted to the looming mountains above. The slopes were steep, ragged, untamed by time, and their peaks were so tall that they disappeared in the clouds. There was a menacing quality to the entire mountain range, but also a primal beauty.

Somewhere up there, dragons soared through aurora-painted skies.

"We are almost there," Codric murmured, his voice low enough so only I could hear him. "But I'll only start celebrating when we are seated in the cable car."

"I don't know if that's reason enough to celebrate," I said. "We managed to get here, but no amount of trickery and manipulation will help us become riders. We either have the gift or we don't."

Codric clapped a hand on my shoulder. "We have Elucian blood in our veins, cousin, even if it is heavily diluted."

I nodded. That part of the story hadn't been fabricated, but it was one of the reasons we had to hide our true identities. Our line was supposed to be purely Elurian, and discovering that we had an ancient Elucian foremother had been a pleasant surprise for me, but not for my father.

Stumbling upon that story must have been the hand of fate.

"Look what we've got here," someone drawled behind us. "Spoiled rich Elurian whelps who think they can be dragon riders."

A chorus of laughter and jeers followed.

I kept my face carefully neutral as I turned, though my muscles tensed instinctively. Four young men in grease-covered coveralls stood behind us in line, their stances threatening.

They looked to be in their late twenties or early thirties, so I knew that they weren't potential candidates for the Dragon Force, but they might still harbor resentment over not getting selected when it had been their turn on the summit of Mount Hope.

"We want to honor our Elucian ancestry by joining the pilgrimage," I said with as much calm as I could muster, pretending that nothing they had said offended me. "Of course, hearing our fates spoken by the famous Saphir Fatewever is the main attraction."

The largest of the four—a burly man with a shock of red hair—spat on the ground. "You hear that, men? These fancy lordlings think they have the same rights as us when their people abandoned the true ways of Elu."

Ah, so he was one of those. A religious purist who refused to accept the validity of the division of the Two-Faced God into two separate deities.

Codric shifted slightly beside me, moving into a better defensive position while maintaining his casual demeanor. "We're all children of Elu," he said, flashing his diplomatic smile. "Surely there's no need for—"

That had been the wrong thing to say, and the small crowd that had gathered around us seemed to second my assessment. There were far too many angry faces staring at us.

"Don't you dare invoke Elu," the short guy on the redhead's left snarled, stepping forward. "You Elurians wouldn't know true faith if it bit you in the—"

"Let's all calm down," I said, noting the two security guards who were watching from the sidelines but made no move to intervene. "We don't want any trouble."

Red-hair laughed harshly. "Too bad trouble wants you." He lunged forward, swinging a meaty fist at my head.

I'd been expecting it—his weight distribution telegraphing the move a split second before the attack. I stepped inside his reach, redirecting his momentum while sweeping out his legs. He hit the ground with a satisfying thud.

His friends didn't take kindly to that.

Two rushed Codric while the third came at me with a wild haymaker. My cousin handled his attackers with his usual grace, ducking under one punch while using his attacker's own force to send him stumbling into his companion.

My opponent was poorly trained but strong, his strikes fueled by anger and prejudice. I blocked his swing and countered with a quick jab to his solar plexus, driving the air from his lungs. As he doubled over, I hooked my foot behind his ankle and sent him tumbling down beside his red-haired friend.

"Stay down," I advised quietly. "This doesn't need to escalate any further."

Red-hair tried to surge up, but I placed my boot firmly on his chest. Not pressing, just reminding him of his position. Meanwhile, Codric had his two opponents effectively pinned, one in an arm lock and the other face down with a knee to his back.

Only then did the security guards finally move in.

"That's enough entertainment for one morning," the taller guard said, his tone almost amused. He gestured to his partner, who began hauling the workers to their feet. "You four are charged with disturbing the peace. You know the penalty for that."

"They shouldn't be allowed in here!" Red-hair protested, wincing as he was handed a ticket.

"That's not for you to decide," the guard said while his partner handed the others similar notes. "Off you go. When you get to the top, march yourselves to the security office and show your tickets to the supervisor."

I'd never seen a brawl being handled like that. He was letting them go and trusting them to report to the security office on the other side?

His partner turned to us. "If you gentlemen would come with me, we need to take your statements."

As we followed him to a dingy office tucked into the side of the building, my frustration mounted. Once inside, I couldn't hold back any longer. "Why did you wait so long to intervene? You were watching the whole time, and you saw that they were harassing us. And why did you just let them go?"

The guard's lips twitched into a knowing smirk. "I wanted to see how you, Elurian boys, would handle yourselves."

He shrugged. "Have to say, I'm impressed. That was some fancy fighting."

I clenched my jaw, stifling the impulse to demand to submit a formal complaint. In Eluria, the guards would have faced serious consequences. But we were visitors here, and if we made too much noise, we would be escorted out and not allowed to enter.

"That wasn't professional," Codric murmured.

The guard lifted a brow. "That depends on the objective." He pulled out a form and began filling it out. "You just proved what I had suspected."

I tensed. "And what's that?"

"That you're more than just a couple of soft merchants' sons dreaming of becoming dragon riders." He stamped the form and handed it to us. "This will get you access to the express line." He smiled. "For your trouble."

What the hells?

If he suspected us of not being who we seemed to be, why was he giving us access to the express line? Was this some kind of a joke, and we would get arrested when we got to the other side?

"Thank you." Codric reached for the form.

"Good luck," the guard said.

As we walked toward the shortest line, Codric bumped my shoulder. "Hey, at least we got to skip the queue."

"Don't you find the whole thing suspicious?"

He shrugged. "So, they wanted to test us. So what? We passed."

I shook my head. "The question is why they felt the need to do that. Something about us must have raised their suspicions, but then why did they still allow us to continue?"

"Elucians are strange people," Codric whispered. "We expected unconventional methods of interrogation, and we were right. I think they sent those guys to goad us on purpose to see how we would respond."

The whole episode made me uneasy, but I still couldn't figure out what the guards' objective had been.

The line continued to move, and soon we found ourselves at the front.

Stepping inside the car, I was caught up in Codric's enthusiasm and felt a thrill of anticipation.

This was it. We were in.

We entered along with a group of other passengers and took our seats. As the doors closed with a satisfying hiss, the car lurched, accelerated, and we began the ascent.

CHAPTER 5: KAILIN

Two dragons in one morning is more than I've ever seen around here before, but it isn't just fear I feel when their roars echo off the mountains. It's awe at their raw power, and I wonder if they sense something we don't or if they're watching us as well.

—From the journal of Kailin Strom

As I rushed into the classroom, my books tucked under my arm and a cup of caff clasped in my hand, Shovia regarded me with an amused expression on her face. "Gran keep you in the apothecary?" she asked when I took my seat next to her.

"I was late to work." I placed my books on the desk. "My feet hurt so badly after the trek this morning that I had to soak them before starting my shift. Normally, that wouldn't have been a problem, but with all the pilgrims arriving at Skywatcher's Point, the apothecary is busier than usual."

Shovia leaned back in her chair. "I thought you were done with training. You were supposed to stop a week before the pilgrimage to give your body a chance to rest and replenish its stores."

Since there would be no food during the climb and water would be rationed, it would have been best to take it easy, but my plans had to change after we'd been given our equipment for the pilgrimage.

"I would be done if not for the drakking boots. I'm still trying to break them in." I took a sip of my cold caff. "Why do they make us all wear the same stuff?"

"Humility and equality," Shovia quoted. "All pilgrims are assigned the same equipment. It is our tenacity that gets tested, not our ability to purchase the best equipment to help us on the trek."

"Yeah, yeah, I know." I rolled my eyes. "So no one has an unfair advantage, but that's the epitome of hypocrisy. The whole thing is about finding the few chosen ones who can communicate with dragons. There is nothing humble or equal about that."

For a moment, Shovia seemed lost for words, which didn't happen often. My best friend might not excel at academics, but she had a sharp tongue and life smarts to animate it.

"For the rest of us it is," she finally said. "The pilgrimage is a bonding experience, and it prepares us for our military service. It's not just about identifying a fresh crop of dragon riders."

She was right, of course.

Supposedly, the pilgrimage wasn't a competition. The goal was to make it to the summit, get one's destiny revealed by the shaman, and come down ready for service.

At least that was the official version. Rumors claimed that pilgrims were watched, and that their performance on the trek was taken into consideration when final assignments were determined.

I took a sip from my cold brew. "You should have joined me. You know that we will also be evaluated on our performance."

Between the two of us, Shovia was no doubt the better athlete. Her father was the coach at our old school, and he had made sure his daughter excelled at sports and aced all the fitness tests.

I, on the other hand, had done poorly on most of them, with rope climbing being my absolute worst.

Still, despite my failure to meet the qualifying minimum in this event, Coach Emil had given me a passing grade and allowed me to graduate, either because I had been an exceptional student in all the academic subjects or, what was more likely, because I was Shovia's best friend.

She chuckled. "Even with all your training, you'll still need me to drag you up the mountain to the summit."

"I'm much better now than I was four months ago, and I won't need your help."

Shovia was still smirking, which was annoying. "I love you, and I wish you the best of luck, but just in case you need help to finish the pilgrimage, I want you to know that I will not leave you behind for the medics to evacuate, even if I have to carry you on my back the rest of the way."

I knew that it wasn't an empty promise. Shovia wouldn't leave me behind even if she had to crawl to the finish line with me on her back. But I was a perfectly healthy twenty-one-year-old woman, and there was no reason for me not to make it to the summit on my own.

"I appreciate the sentiment," I said. "With all my heart. But don't worry. I will make it on my own two feet." I leaned over and kissed Shovia's cheek. "And I promise that I will not be the last to arrive. I won't be the first either. You, on the other hand, will probably be in the lead without even breaking a sweat."

Shovia regarded me with a serious expression on her face. "That's not how it works. We are divided into groups, and we can't overtake those ahead of us unless there is a good reason for it. The real enemy is the thin air and the hallucinations it induces, and how we deal with it will factor heavily into how we are judged. I'm pretty good with high altitudes, but I still have a zero chance of becoming a dragon rider. Not that I want to. You know which post I want."

I grimaced. "Spying's even more dangerous than dragon riding, and there is no guarantee the Spy Corps is the destiny that fate has in store for you."

Even though everyone had to serve, and women could theoretically be assigned to any arm of the force, Elu rarely chose combat assignments for women, probably because of the brutality and barbarism of our enemies. There were plenty of other jobs we could do that were no less important.

The two exceptions were dragon riders and spies, and the reasons for the exceptions were simple.

Dragon riders were rare, and good dragon riders were even rarer. If a woman could bond with a dragon, she was a rider. Besides, if she fell off a dragon or the dragon was hit and they both went down, there was no surviving that, and there would be nothing left of her for the monsters to violate.

As for spies, women made the best ones because Sitorians were dismissive of females, and they notoriously underestimated them.

"I know it's dangerous." Shovia assumed a dreamy expression. "But it's exciting, and I will get to see the world."

"What is there to see? Nothing is better than this." I waved my hand at the window. "We live in the most spectacular place in all of Aurorys."

Shovia turned to look at the view. "It's beautiful, but that's all I have seen since I was born. I want to see so much more."

Did she think it was a game?

"It's not safe for Elucians out there." I tried another angle.

I didn't want to lose my best friend, even if it was temporarily, when she was gallivanting around the world on assignments.

Shovia snorted. "As if riding a dragon over these cliffs and fighting off murderous hordes of monsters is safe."

"I'm not going to get selected, but speaking of dragons—" I intended to tell Shovia about my encounter with the two this morning, when our instructor flounced into the room with a whoosh of billowing skirts.

"Good afternoon, class," she chirped. "Are you looking forward to another fascinating lesson about the wonders of Aurorys?"

The woman was much too chirpy most days, and today her high-pitched voice exacerbated the slight headache I'd been nursing since the excitement with the dragons earlier.

I tuned her out.

I didn't need a comprehensive refresher to pass the last test before the pilgrimage. I still remembered everything I had learned about the physics of our planet, and I had my books to look up anything I was iffy on.

Instead, I turned to look out the window.

Skywatcher's modest academy building enjoyed one of the most spectacular views of Elucia. It was nestled on a narrow ledge carved into the side of a towering mountain, and the builders had incorporated large windows into the classrooms, saving the students from the boredom inside by providing them with a magnificent view of the rugged landscape outside.

Raw, untamed mountains jutted out of a vast ocean, while curtains of ethereal light danced across the sky, their colors shifting from deep greens to vibrant purples with streaks of red and blue weaving through the display.

Shadow and light played across the faces of the mountains, revealing and concealing their features in a constant, subtle flux.

In the distance, I could make out the faint silhouette of a dragon and rider gliding through the sky, a dark shape gracefully navigating the rivers of light. They moved in perfect harmony with the shifting magnetic currents—the ultimate conquerors of our world.

Was it one of the two I had encountered on the trail?

I had assumed that they had strayed from their training quadrants in the heat of battle, but seeing another dragon sailing through the sky over our area caused me to reassess that conclusion.

The Citadel and the aviary were not far from Skywatcher's Point, but it wasn't often that dragons flew over the town. Their training grounds were on the other side of the Citadel, and to see three of them in one morning was alarming.

As I considered possible reasons for their presence, dread pooled in the pit of my stomach.

Had worm tunnels been discovered nearby?

Were the dragons patrolling the area?

I shuddered as I imagined the vile demonic creatures pouring out of a tunnel dug out by one of their enormous worms. That was how they managed to sneak up on our villages unseen. The mountainous terrain of Elucia was impossible to infiltrate with a substantial ground force. There was only one port where people and merchandise were transported up from the valley, and it was extremely well guarded. No one we didn't want to let into Elucia could cross into our country through the official route.

The alternatives were either to fly over or to tunnel up.

Only Elucians could ride dragons, so that left the tunnels, which were dug out by the Sitorians' giant worms. They were as exclusive to them as dragons were to the Elucians, but unlike the dragons, the worms had no say in what they were forced to do. They were dumb creatures, enslaved and controlled by the Shedun.

I watched as the dragon twisted and dove through the air. As it got closer, I could see that it was black, but I wasn't sure it was the same one I had seen earlier. The rider leaned low, appearing as one with the beast's sinuous neck.

They plunged toward the ocean, pulling up at the very last instant. I recognized the maneuver. It was definitely the same one I had seen before.

The dragon twisted mid-air, jaws opening wide, and released a thunderous roar that echoed off the mountain's face and rattled the windows of the academy.

It wasn't a warning cry.

It was a victory roar.

I let out a shaky breath, my pulse slowly returning to normal as I watched the dragon glide away and disappear beyond the eastern peaks. Most likely, it had just been another practice run, but if there had been danger, it had been dealt with, and we were safe.

Still, three dragon sightings in one morning?

Danger must be close, even if we didn't realize it yet.

CHAPTER 6: ALAR

"The confidential information your allies keep from you may be the key to defeating your enemies. Pursue it and leverage it to your advantage."

—Commander Brusdick Gorlin, Elite Forces' Vedona Academy

Through the open window, I watched as the ground fell away beneath us, the enormous Elucian port of entry growing smaller and smaller until it was nothing more than a speck in the sprawling landscape below.

As we climbed higher, the world around us transformed. The vegetation changed, becoming sparse and hardy. And above us, the ribbons of light—green, purple, and blue—shimmered and swayed in a celestial ballet that now seemed almost close enough to touch.

"Would you look at that," Codric said, the awe in his voice reflecting my own. "The auroras are even more spectacular up close."

I couldn't look away. It was beautiful, alien, and unnerving.

Auroras could be seen from almost anywhere on Aurorys, but the sky seen from the flats of Eluria paled in comparison to this magnificence.

As the car swayed and climbed, the world below shrinking, I couldn't help but think about the structural integrity of the cable it was suspended from.

Next to me, Codric chuckled. "Stop worrying, Alar. We are not going to plummet to our deaths."

"Why would I worry?" I kept my sarcastic reply low for the sake of the other passengers. "We are only hanging from a cable thousands of feet above the ground."

"I knew it." He shook his head. "I saw you frowning at the cable before we boarded the car, checking out the bolts. You always pay attention to the smallest details and fret about their construction and how sound their maintenance is."

"Of course I do. Maintenance is done by humans, and if things don't get routinely inspected, people begin to slack off, and malfunctions happen. In the case of a cable car, a malfunction means death. We are trusting our lives to the work ethic of greasy fellows like the ones who attacked us."

He put his arm around my shoulders. "This is the only access to Elucia, save for on the back of a dragon or following a burrowing worm. Do you really think they would let it fall into disrepair?"

He had a point, but I wasn't ready to concede. "The Elucians are so focused on security that they might overlook maintenance and upkeep issues."

Travel in and out of Elucia was restricted, so the cable car rail was mostly used for bringing in merchandise and for transporting export goods. Shuttling passengers was secondary. Still, enough people sat in those cars every day for the rail to be a target for their enemies.

Dragon patrols were supposedly stationed along the way, guarding the rail, but I had seen none so far. In fact, I had never seen a dragon in person, only in films and photographs, and I couldn't wait for my first glimpse of one. Even if I didn't become a rider, seeing a dragon up close was almost worth the international scandal Codric and I were risking by sneaking into Elucia with fake identities.

Hells, a scandal was the least of my worries. It could get much worse.

After a while, I gave up on trying to spot dragons and turned my attention to the chatter around me. The lilting accents of the Elucians created a melodic backdrop to our ascent, and if I concentrated, I could catch snippets of conversations and glean more insight into the world I was entering.

"...the Shedun scum are relentless," said the guy sitting across the center aisle from us.

He was holding up an Elucian newspaper in front of his face, so all I could see was a portion of his profile.

"Any casualties?" the woman sitting next to him asked anxiously.

"Thank Elu, they were spotted in time." The guy folded his newspaper and put it on his lap. "They came through multiple tunnels simultaneously. Those drakking worms, burrowing up through our mountains like they were nothing but giant anthills. There was no way the defenders could reach the village in time."

The woman gasped. "Then how did they manage to avoid casualties?"

I leaned in, trying to appear casual as I listened more intently.

"The civilian patrols stopped them," the guy said. "They detected seismic activity and sounded the alarm. The civilians fought them off, holding the line until the riders arrived. The dragons roasted some of the vermin, but the rest managed to retreat into the tunnels and collapse them as they slid back down the shafts."

"Thank Elu it ended like that," the woman said. "It could have been another disaster."

"Indeed," he agreed, some of the tension leaving his shoulders.

"How much more of this can we endure?" she whispered. "When will it end?"

"I don't know," he said. "I don't know why Elu cursed us to live surrounded by those demon worshipers."

"Shush, Bendor." She put her fingers on his lips. "That's blasphemy. Some truths are known only to Elu."

Bendor didn't seem to agree, but he said nothing, probably choosing to avoid a theological argument with his companion.

A wise man.

"Hello." I turned to them. "I couldn't help but overhear your conversation. We've heard rumors about the Shedun in Eluria, but it seems to me that our media doesn't paint the full picture."

"No, it doesn't." The guy looked Codric and me over with suspicion in his eyes. "Pilgrims?"

I nodded. "My name is Alar, and this is my cousin Codric. We have a tiny bit of Elucian blood, so we decided to honor our distant Elucian ancestor and join the pilgrimage."

"I'm Bendor." He extended his hand. "And this is my sister Mira."

We all shook hands, and Codric flashed Mira one of his charming smiles.

"What else did your newspaper say about the raid?" Codric asked.

"Two nights ago, the civilian watch in one of the western villages, Marvaila, detected unusual seismic activity. Nothing too alarming at first—living in the mountains, you get used to the occasional tremor. But when the sensors detected activity at multiple points of origin, all converging on their village, they knew that something big was up."

This was far more detailed than what the Elurian media ever reported. Most Elurians didn't care about what was happening to the Elucians. After all, they had dragons on their side, so they could deal with the Shedun on their own.

Shockingly, some even sided with the monsters.

Irrational envy over the dragon pact and access to immortality for the select few was the breeding ground of hate.

"By the time the civilian watch realized what was happening, it was almost too late," Bendor continued. "The worms burst through at three locations, and the Shedun poured out like demons from the depths of hell."

"How can civilians manage to fight them off?" I asked.

I couldn't imagine Elurian civilians doing anything other than screaming and running for their lives, but by all accounts, the Elucians were made from hardier stuff.

"With everything they got," Mira said, her eyes flashing with anger. "Every Elucian is trained from childhood to defend our communities, and we all serve a minimum of four years in the Elucian Forces, with some of us serving much longer than that."

"We owe our existence to the dragons, Mira," Bendor said. "Without them, we would have perished already even if every Elucian fought to their last breath." He turned to us with a feral smile on his weathered face. "You should see the dragons at work. When they rain fire on the demons, the sky lights up brighter than the auroras, and the Shedun screech like the vermin they are as they try to outrun the inferno."

I shuddered, torn between awe at the power of the dragons and horror at the vivid description of destruction. Beside me, Codric's face had gone pale.

Mira sighed. "Despite our best efforts to preserve and nurture the dragon population, there are still not enough of them, and they can't be everywhere at once, but there is an endless supply of Shedun. Kill one horde, and two more pop up. We drive them back, and they return, over and over again."

Codric shook his head. "The reports we get barely scratch the surface."

What we thought we knew about the situation in Elucia seemed deficient, but that was one of the many reasons I was here.

As I'd suspected, the Shedun threat was far greater than what the Elurian council was led to believe, and the Elucians were fighting a constant battle for survival. My fear was that they wouldn't hold off the hordes forever, and once Elucia fell again, the Sitorians would turn on Eluria.

The Elurian council believed in the myth that the Shedun didn't represent Sitoria, and that they would never escalate their terror attacks into a full-on war again, but the truth was that they were fully supported by the majority of the Sitorians, who filled the Shedun ranks with a never-ending supply of young men eager to die for their god.

Others believed that if the Shedun were allowed to exterminate the dragons once and for all, they would stop their never-ending attacks on Elucia, but that was another fallacy perpetrated by the ignorant who didn't bother to actually educate themselves about the Sitorians and what their clearly stated end goal was—dominion over all of Aurorys.

The dragons were simply the largest hurdle in their way.

As a heavy silence fell over our group, I glanced out the window, and the auroras suddenly seemed cold and distant. How could the Elucians live that way?

Was this land's beauty really worth such horrors?

They could leave the dragons to fight the war against the Shedun and relocate to Eluria, where they could live in peace, but the ugly truth was that the Elurian leadership was happy to aid Elucians in their never-ending fight by supplying them with weapons, so they would keep the Shedun occupied and weakened.

The Elucians might have been nearly wiped out of existence during the two Extinction Wars, but they had fought ferociously, and even though the Sitorians won, their armies had been left in tatters and incapable of marching against Eluria. By the time they'd recovered and rebuilt, so had the Elucians, and the cycle had started anew.

As the cable car began to slow, the outlines of Podana, the Elucian capital, grew clearer.

Unlike the large Elurian metropolises, which housed millions in high-rise buildings made of metal and concrete, Podana was modest in both size and architecture. The capital sprawled across multiple levels of rugged mountainside, its older buildings made of local stone and the newer ones from a combination of stone and timber. The city seemed to grow organically from the rock face, with narrow, winding streets connecting the different levels.

Most buildings were low-rise, rarely exceeding three stories in height, and had steep, slanted roofs, indicative of the heavy snowfalls at these elevations. The walls were substantial, built to insulate against the cold mountain air, and many were whitewashed, reflecting what sunlight made it through the near-constant auroras. Others maintained the natural grays and browns of their building materials.

"In the pictures, Podana looked much grander than this." I waved a hand at the window. "I guess it was photographed from more flattering angles."

Codric nodded. "It looks like a village that grew into a city over time."

"That's exactly what happened," Bendor said. "Podana was one of the first communities the returning Elucians established, and we continued from there."

"Was there nothing left from before?" I asked.

He shook his head. "The predecessors of today's Shedun demolished every last building and fed the ruins to their worms to grind into dust. They wanted to ensure that our culture was erased from the face of Aurorys. There was nearly nothing left except for the ruined remains of the Citadel and Elu's temple." He leaned closer, his lips curving in a wry smile. "Thank Elu that our shamans managed to save some of the dragon eggs. They hid them so well that the demons couldn't find them even though they searched every cave and nook in these mountains for centuries."

Theirs was such a sad history, and it was a miracle that any of those long-ago Elucians managed to escape and find refuge in Eluria. The dragon eggs that had remained hidden and survived for over a millennium were an even bigger miracle.

Some believed that they had been obscured by magic, but that was superstitious nonsense that ignorant people with no understanding of science believed in. The problem was that there were enough of them to give the rumor wings.

The reality was that if not for the resourcefulness and sacrifice of the Elucian shamans, the magnificent creatures would have gone extinct. Most shamans hadn't survived, and the eggs they had hidden had either been destroyed or still remained in hiding. Only one shaman still lived, Saphir Fatewever, and the eggs he'd managed to shield and later hatch had been enough to revive dragonkind.

A miracle to some. A plague to others.

As we drew closer, I could make out more details. Small gardens were tucked into whatever spaces could be found, bursts of green amid the stone and wood. Waterfalls created by melting snow cascaded down the rock face, their spray catching the light and creating miniature rainbows. And everywhere, people went about their daily lives, tiny figures going about their business in this city in the sky.

"Look there," Codric pointed. "That's the famous Podana Academy."

I followed his gaze to a large structure near the heart of the city. While grander than the surrounding buildings, it was still built primarily of local stone and sprawled over several terraces.

"Indeed, it is," Mira confirmed. "The pride of Podana, where our brightest minds study and our scientists come up with wondrous new inventions in every imaginable field."

Her claim was a little boastful, but given how tiny the Elucian population was, their contribution to the sciences was impressive.

The Elucians revered learning, but the truth was that not many could afford to study in the academy, not because tuition was costly but because they needed to work to support themselves and their families. Most of the students depended on grants from the Elurian Federation, which financed a lot of the research in exchange for sharing the fruits of their labor.

In another life, perhaps I could have studied there, learning the secrets of Aurorys alongside the Elucian scholars. But that wasn't my path. I had a different mission, a different destiny to fulfill.

The cable car began to slow as we approached the central depot, which was a bustling hub of activity carved into the mountainside like the rest of the city.

Bendor stood, stretching his long limbs. "Good luck on your pilgrimage. May Elu guide your steps and lift your spirits."

After saying goodbye to Bendor and Mira, we disembarked and followed the throng of people into the depot. The cacophony of sounds and the press of bodies around us reminded me of the central transportation hubs back home, and the feeling of otherness that I'd been cultivating since our arrival at the foot of the mountains started to abate.

Elucians weren't all that different from Elurians when they were safe among their own and protected by walls and dragons.

"Come on," Codric said, tugging at my arm. "We need to find transportation to Skywatcher's Point."

Following the signs, we walked out to where a fleet of hover-cars was waiting for passengers and joined the line behind those who had arrived before us.

An attendant approached us with a friendly smile. "Where to, gentlemen?"

"We need to get to Skywatcher's Point," I said.

The attendant's smile broadened. "Pilgrims, eh? Well, you're in luck. Torvan here is your guy," he waved to a grizzled man leaning against one of the hover-cars. "The standard fee is a hundred lumen, and a tip is expected once you reach your destination."

"Who should we pay?" Codric asked. "You or the driver?"

"Either one is fine. You can pay Torvan directly, and he will forward the depot's fee later."

I had no doubt that he would. Elucians adhered strictly to the original principles of Truth laid down by Elu, and those left no room for cheating or even skimming a little from the top. Elurians followed the same Truths, but we were much less strict in the way we interpreted the original writings, which I was thankful for.

Without any wiggle room, Codric and I wouldn't be on our way to join the pilgrimage.

Torvan straightened, his weathered face breaking into a crooked grin. "So, you boys are here for the pilgrimage, eh? Hop in. I'll get you to Skywatcher's Point safe and sound and give you a tour of our beautiful countryside as a bonus, free of charge."

"Thank you." I pulled out my wallet, intending to pay him, but he stayed my hand.

"You pay when we get there. Not before." He opened the back door for us.

The interior of the hover-car was a little worn, but it was clean and smelled good, and two sealed water bottles rested in holders next to each seat.

"These are for you lads, and if you want to stop for a bite to eat, I can take you to a good eatery and wait until you are done."

"We are fine," I said despite Codric's hopeful expression. "We'll eat when we get to Skywatcher's Point."

"Very well." Torvan pulled out from the line of hover-cars. "The Pilgrims' Lodge has an eatery that is open at all times, but the selection is limited. You won't find any Elurian delicacies there."

"Are there any other eateries you can recommend?" Codric asked.

"Plenty." As the vehicle glided smoothly out of the depot, Torvan launched into a long sales pitch about every eatery in Skywatcher's Point. All five of them.

"So, what made you travel all the way to our remote country in the sky?" Torvan asked as we wound our way through the outskirts of Podana.

"Alar and I were always fascinated by dragons, and then we discovered that our great-great-grandmother was Elucian." Codric smiled at the driver who was watching us through the rear-view mirror. "After that, there was no stopping us. We had to join the pilgrimage."

Torvan nodded approvingly. "Good for you. Not many Elurians make the pilgrimage these days. Too scared of the Shedun attacking, I reckon."

Frankly, the Shedun hadn't even crossed our minds when we'd decided to go on this adventure. Not that knowing about the clear and present dangers these people faced would have changed our minds. We were determined to do whatever it took to become dragon riders.

"What's it like?" Codric asked. "Living here seems tough."

"You can say that again." Torvan laughed, a deep, rumbling sound. "It's not easy, but it makes us a family. We all care for one another because there is no one else who does."

I felt offended on behalf of every Elurian who had ever aided Elucians.

"That's not true," I said. "Elurians care. Your people found refuge among us, and when you decided to reclaim your ancestral lands, the Elurian Federation helped."

Without us, the Shedun would have probably wiped them out of existence the moment they returned to these mountains. Eluria armed the returning Elucians and provided backup.

"Truth," Torvan said. "Elucia owes Eluria a debt of gratitude, but now we are on our own and take care of each other. We deal with our enemies." He turned to look at us. "We keep the Shedun busy so they don't turn their attention to you."

I nodded because he was right, and I would not offend an Elucian by parroting the half-truths printed in Elurian newspapers. There were advantages and disadvantages to our loosened adherence to the truth and our more moderate interpretation of Elurion's dictates. That being said, according to Elucian scholars, abandoning the path of absolute truth would eventually lead to Eluria's downfall, but it hadn't happened yet, and our society was successful and prosperous, so I didn't expect it to fall apart anytime soon.

Then again, abandoning the path of truth was part of turning a blind eye to what was happening with the Sitorian Union and their global domination ambitions.

As we left the city behind, the landscape became more rugged with jagged peaks stretching as far as the eye could see, their snow-capped summits disappearing into banks of clouds. Forests of hardy pines clung to the lower slopes, giving way to bare rock and ice higher up.

"Do you see that one over there?" Torvan pointed to a distant peak. "That's Mount Fury. That's where the first riders made their pact with the dragons."

The thought of those first riders forging a bond that would shape the destiny of an entire nation filled me with awe and a bit of longing.

Those riders were legendary, their names forever etched into the fabric of Aurorys's history.

ORDER YOUR COPY TODAY!

NOTE

Dear reader,

I hope my stories have added a little joy to your day. If you have a moment to add some to mine, you can help spread the word about the Children Of The Gods series by telling your friends and penning a review. Your recommendations are the most powerful way to inspire new readers to explore the series.

Thank you,

Isabell

Also by I. T. Lucas

BONDS OF WINGS AND FURY

1: Bonds of Wings and Fury: The Two-Faced God

THE CHILDREN OF THE GODS ORIGINS

1: Goddess's Choice

2: Goddess's Hope

THE CHILDREN OF THE GODS

Dark Stranger

1: Dark Stranger The Dream

2: Dark Stranger Revealed

3: Dark Stranger Immortal

Dark Enemy

4: Dark Enemy Taken

5: Dark Enemy Captive

6: Dark Enemy Redeemed

Kri & Michael's Story

6.5: My Dark Amazon

Dark Warrior

7: Dark Warrior Mine

8: Dark Warrior's Promise

9: Dark Warrior's Destiny

10: Dark Warrior's Legacy

Dark Guardian

11: Dark Guardian Found
12: Dark Guardian Craved
13: Dark Guardian's Mate

Dark Angel

14: Dark Angel's Obsession
15: Dark Angel's Seduction
16: Dark Angel's Surrender

Dark Operative

17: Dark Operative: A Shadow of Death
18: Dark Operative: A Glimmer of Hope
19: Dark Operative: The Dawn of Love

Dark Survivor

20: Dark Survivor Awakened
21: Dark Survivor Echoes of Love
22: Dark Survivor Reunited

Dark Widow

23: Dark Widow's Secret
24: Dark Widow's Curse
25: Dark Widow's Blessing

Dark Dream

26: Dark Dream's Temptation
27: Dark Dream's Unraveling
28: Dark Dream's Trap

Dark Prince

29: Dark Prince's Enigma

Dark Queen

Dark Spy

Dark Overlord

Dark Choices

Dark Secrets

Dark Haven

86: Dark Awakening: New World
87: Dark Awakening Hidden Currents
88: Dark Awakening Echoes of Destiny

Dark Princess

89: Dark Princess: Shadows
90: Dark Princess Emerging
91: Dark Princess Ascending

Dark Rebel

92: Dark Rebel's Mystery
93: Dark Rebel's Reckoning
94: Dark Rebel's Fortune

Dark Rover

95: Dark Rover's Luck
96: Dark Rover's Gift
97: Dark Rover's Shire

Dark Shaman

98: Dark Shaman: The Lost Treasure
99: Dark Shaman: Love Found
100: Dark Shaman: Eternal Love

Dark Island

101: Dark Island: Rescue

PERFECT MATCH

Vampire's Consort
King's Chosen
Captain's Conquest

THE THIEF WHO LOVED ME

MY MERMAN PRINCE

THE DRAGON KING

MY WEREWOLF ROMEO

THE CHANNELER'S COMPANION

THE VALKYRIE & THE WITCH

ADINA AND THE MAGIC LAMP

THE CHILDREN OF THE GODS SERIES SETS

DARK STRANGER TRILOGY

INCLUDES A BONUS SHORT STORY:

THE FATES TAKE A VACATION

DARK ENEMY TRILOGY

INCLUDES A BONUS SHORT STORY:

THE FATES' POST-WEDDING CELEBRATION

DARK WARRIOR TETRALOGY

DARK GUARDIAN TRILOGY

DARK ANGEL TRILOGY

DARK OPERATIVE TRILOGY

DARK SURVIVOR TRILOGY

DARK WIDOW TRILOGY

DARK DREAM TRILOGY

DARK PRINCE TRILOGY

DARK QUEEN TRILOGY

DARK SPY TRILOGY

DARK OVERLORD TRILOGY

Dark Choices Trilogy
Dark Secrets Trilogy
Dark Haven Trilogy
Dark Power Trilogy
Dark Memories Trilogy
Dark Hunter Trilogy
Dark God Trilogy
Dark Whispers Trilogy
Dark Gambit Trilogy
Dark Alliance Trilogy
Dark Healing Trilogy
Dark Encounters Trilogy
Dark Voyage Trilogy
Dark Horizon Trilogy
Dark Witch Trilogy
Dark Awakening Trilogy
Dark Princess Trilogy

MEGA SETS

The Children of the Gods: Books 1-6
Includes bonus 2 short stories & a companion guide for books 1-6
The Children of the Gods: Books 6.5-10
Includes a bonus companion guide for books 6.5-10

The Children of the Gods books 11-16
Includes a bonus companion guide for books 11-16

Perfect Match Bundle 1

CHECK OUT THE SPECIALS ON
ITLUCAS.COM
(https://itlucas.com/specials)

FOR EXCLUSIVE PEEKS AT UPCOMING RELEASES &
A FREE I. T. LUCAS COMPANION BOOK

JOIN MY *VIP CLUB* AND GAIN ACCESS TO THE VIP PORTAL AT ITLUCAS.COM

TO JOIN, GO TO:
http://eepurl.com/blMTpD

Find out more details about what's included with your free membership on the book's last page.

TRY THE CHILDREN OF THE GODS SERIES ON AUDIBLE
2 FREE audiobooks with your new Audible subscription!

FOR EXCLUSIVE PEEKS AT UPCOMING RELEASES & A FREE I. T. LUCAS COMPANION BOOK

JOIN MY *VIP CLUB* AND GAIN ACCESS TO THE VIP PORTAL AT ITLUCAS.COM

TO JOIN, GO TO:

http://eepurl.com/blMTpD

INCLUDED IN YOUR FREE MEMBERSHIP:

YOUR VIP PORTAL

- READ PREVIEW CHAPTERS OF UPCOMING RELEASES.
- LISTEN TO GODDESS'S CHOICE NARRATION BY CHARLES LAWRENCE
- EXCLUSIVE CONTENT OFFERED ONLY TO MY VIPS.

FREE I.T. LUCAS COMPANION INCLUDES:

- GODDESS'S CHOICE PART 1
- PERFECT MATCH: VAMPIRE'S CONSORT (A STANDALONE NOVELLA)
- INTERVIEW Q & A
- COMPANION GUIDES FOR BOOKS 1-16

IF YOU'RE ALREADY A SUBSCRIBER AND YOU ARE NOT GETTING MY EMAILS, YOUR PROVIDER IS SENDING THEM TO YOUR JUNK FOLDER, AND YOU ARE MISSING OUT ON IMPOR-

TANT UPDATES. TO FIX THAT, ADD isabell@itlucas.com TO YOUR EMAIL CONTACTS OR YOUR EMAIL VIP LIST.

Check out the specials at
https://www.itlucas.com/specials

Printed in Dunstable, United Kingdom